AN AMBITIOUS ENGAGEMENT

KYLIE GILMORE

Happy reading!

Kylie

This book is a work of fiction. Names, characters, places, brands, media, and incidents are the product of the author's imagination or are used fictitiously. The author acknowledges the trademarked status and trademark owners of various products referenced in this work of fiction, which have been used without permission. The publication/use of these trademarks are not authorized, associated with, or sponsored by the trademark owners. Any resemblance to actual events, locales, or persons, living or dead, is purely coincidental.

First Edition: December 2015
Cover design by The Killion Group
Published by: Extra Fancy Books

ISBN-10: 1942238134
ISBN-13: 978-1-942238-13-3

To my own personal cheering squad. Mwah!...

CHAPTER ONE

Luke Reynolds downshifted his Porsche 911 Carrera on the winding country road leading to the Majestic River golf course and grumbled to himself, "Friggin' ass crack of dawn."

He accelerated and flew over a dip in the road, shaking up the car and making him take a deep breath. He wasn't a morning person to begin with, but to be up this early on a Monday for a seven a.m. tee time in Connecticut, a good hour's drive from his Upper West Side Manhattan apartment, was ridiculous. The only reason he'd agreed to the ungodly hour was because his prospective client, Bentley Williams, had told him Ken Ward, Luke's competitor for the account, had already agreed to the time.

Grr...he had no idea who this upstart Ken was. He'd never heard of him before and could find literally nothing on him. He scratched his light brown beard, considering his competitor. *Must be some kind of stealth sabotage from a rival wealth management company trying to take advantage of the newly made billionaire.*

Bentley had unexpectedly inherited the Williams Oil fortune after his older brother died of a heart attack. He'd heard rumors that Bentley was a little eccentric and that his family had put him in charge of *non-oil*-related activities. In other words, parties. That was just fine with Luke. He enjoyed a good party, especially if big spenders were there who needed some guidance in their future investments. Luke wanted this client so badly he could taste it. His firm, Campbell Financial Group, had a rare opening on the small team focused on the top tier of wealthy clients. If he could land Bentley, that promotion was his. Not to mention job security. His boss had recently confided, in a not-so-subtle attempt to light a fire under him, that the firm planned on downsizing every team except their top tier.

If anyone needed a financial planner, it was Bentley. He was both frivolous and generous, a terrible combination for a billionaire. The man owned a minor league hockey team that had never won a season and poured money into a charity, Dress the Kids, that donated used designer clothes to poor kids. Unfortunately, the only people that seemed to be benefiting from that charity were the employees hawking the donations on eBay.

A cherry red Mustang started tailgating him. He hit the brakes, annoyed, and the car got right up on his bumper. He powered down the window and hollered, "Back off, asshole!"

He glanced in the rearview mirror to see a blond woman gesturing to him to speed up.

He slowed even more. It was a no-passing zone—a narrow road with no center line and plenty of blind curves.

The Mustang gunned the engine and passed him with a roar. "It's a thirty-mile-per-hour zone, Grandpa!" the woman yelled as she passed, nearly clipping his car and forcing him off the road. He slammed on the brakes, stopping a heart-stopping inch from a giant oak tree.

He smacked the dashboard. *Grandpa?* He was thirty-two years old! In his fucking prime! He hit the accelerator and veered back on the road, quickly catching up to her. He rode the tail of the Mustang, who sped up, dangerously fast for this stretch of dimly lit road. The sun was still partially hidden by the trees. He slowed. *Fuck it. Let that idiot end up wrapped around a tree. Not him.*

He blew out a breath and told himself to calm down. He mentally reviewed what his firm could offer Bentley through their connections and collective experience. What he personally could offer with his

track record of successful investments, his prior years
of experience on Wall Street, trading stocks and
managing portfolios, and twenty-four-seven access to
him through his personal cell number. He was more
than ready for the big time as a financial planner to the
rich.

By the time he arrived in the lobby of the Majestic
River country club, his golf bag thrown over one
shoulder, he was completely composed. Bentley, his
thirty-year-old potential client, greeted him with a
boyish grin. He was a good head shorter than Luke's
six feet, and his messy brown hair falling into his blue
eyes only added to his boyish look. He wore a
blindingly yellow polo shirt with pink and green plaid
Bermuda shorts. Two beautiful blondes stood on
either side of him; one of them towered over him.
Hell, maybe when you were a billionaire, you could
have two blondes at all times. Luke had a couple
million stashed away, partly earned, partly inherited
from his asshole biological father, which never hurt in
the woman department, though he'd never had a
threesome. He didn't like to share.

The tall blonde smiled at him, but his world
stopped when the short blonde met his eyes with a
fiery glare. The contrast of all that fire combined with
her petite, almost angelic beauty had him soaking her
in longer than was polite. Her blond hair was pulled

back in a small ponytail that accentuated her delicate cheekbones and jaw. Smooth, creamy skin, pink lips, and a sexy athletic body trim and toned with perky breasts, in a simple white polo shirt and white shorts. His hands actually tingled with the need to touch, until he reached her fiery blue eyes again and suddenly realized *why* all that fire was focused on him. This was the woman who'd run him off the road! She'd better not turn Bentley against him for his part in their little game of chicken. He pulled his wayward thoughts back on track and reached out to shake Bentley's hand.

"Nice to meet you, Bentley, I'm Luke Reynolds."

Bentley shook his hand vigorously, which made his messy brown hair fall even further into his eyes. He tossed his hair back with a shake of his head. "Great to meet you too! Hope it's not too early for you. I'm an early bird by nature."

"No problem at all," Luke said smoothly. "Had a coffee on the drive in."

"Good, good," Bentley said, all early-bird smiles. "This is my wife, Candy." The tall blonde beamed. With her high-heeled sandals, she matched Luke's height.

Luke shook her hand and gave her his full-on charming smile that always worked on women. "So nice to meet you, Candy."

"You too," Candy chirped. "I'm just here to watch.

Bennie likes me to meet all of his business associates."

Bentley pulled Candy close, one arm wrapped around her waist. "I just can't bear to be separated from my Candy. I love being married."

"Me too, sugar bear," Candy said.

They rubbed noses and cooed at each other.

"Everyone should be married," Bentley said with a goofy smile. Considering Bentley had only been married six months, Luke was sure the shine would rub off soon. Though two of Luke's five brothers had married, with one soon-to-be married, Luke still found the whole love thing to be more of a random event. Like getting struck by lightning. His own parents' marriage and bitter divorce had made an impression. But their story wasn't so different from half the country. With a fifty percent divorce rate, it was a wonder anyone ever felt optimistic enough to tie the knot. His brothers were on the good side of that statistic, he hoped, but only time would tell.

He turned away from the lovebirds and met the baby blues of the horrible driver. Her expression was grim.

Luke decided to be the bigger person. "Sorry about earlier. I'm not much of a morning person."

She crossed to him. "I noticed," she said with an unexpected smile that made him instantly wary.

"So you two know each other?" Bentley asked.

Luke started to shake his head when the short blonde said, "Yes."

And then she went up on tiptoe and kissed him. Her warm lips brushed over his and a jolt of raw lust gripped him. Her flowery scent washed over him as she whispered in his ear, "I'm Ken." He stiffened. She pulled back, and her lips curved into a sweet smile. "Love you."

Luke was rendered mute—a strange, foreign experience for him. He prided himself on being a smooth talker. Love? Ken was a woman? She *kissed* him. He wasn't sure which of those things was more of a mind fuck. Actually the kiss was pretty—

"Honey, don't be shy," Ken said, smiling up at him from her five feet and change of devious woman height. "You can tell Bentley."

Luke slowly blinked. "Tell him what?"

She looped her arm through his. "That we're engaged." She beamed. "The jeweler is resizing my ring. That's why I'm not wearing it right now."

His brain finally kicked into gear, and he sucked in a breath to correct that hideous lie, but something went down the wrong pipe, and he ended up choking like crazy while Ken helpfully pounded his back.

"Wonderful!" Bentley exclaimed with a huge smile. "I hadn't heard. Luke, I know you work in the city and, Ken, you're in Connecticut. How'd you meet?"

Luke hesitated just long enough for Ken to reply quite convincingly, "Through mutual friends."

Bentley beamed. "Now our little competition will have a happy ending no matter what."

"What competition?" Ken asked.

"Best score today gets my business." Bentley beamed like his announcement was the best part of everyone's day. "But now it will all stay in the family. Awesomesauce, as Candy says!"

Candy smiled. "I do say that."

Wait, he had to win the game? He was okay at golf, not great. He glanced at Ken. She smirked.

"You can't be serious," Luke managed.

"I look forward to it," Ken said.

Bentley beamed. "Don't worry, Luke. Once you're married, you share the money. Right, Candy?"

"That's right!" Candy sang.

"Thank you," Ken said graciously. "You won't be disappointed. I've been studying your company and your current investments, and have so many—"

"Let's not talk business now," Bentley said with a dismissive wave. "Let's go hit the course."

He and Candy led the way outside. Luke grabbed Ken's arm and pulled her back out of earshot. He got in her face and spoke in a harsh whisper. "What the hell do you think you're doing?"

"I'm making sure he likes us," she said, matching

his harsh whisper.

"By lying?"

"You saw him with Candy," she hissed. "He loves being married."

"Couldn't you just pretend to be engaged to someone other than me?"

She slowly shook her head. "That probably would've been better. I blame your sexy smolder."

He stepped back. "My what?"

"You were smoldering at me, like maybe you liked what you saw." She shrugged. "Too late now."

"I was not..." He trailed off as he realized he must've been too obvious in his once-over. Dammit! He jabbed a hand in his hair. He had to nail down this business, and losing it in front of Bentley wasn't going to help. Still, this was crazy. Where the hell did she get off? Running him off the road, calling him Grandpa, announcing they were getting married, for crying out loud!

He glared at her, and she glared right back. He couldn't afford to damage his reputation. In the wealth-management business, results and an honest reputation were critical. And the wealthy elite were a small circle where word got around fast. They'd be lucky to have a job at all if Bentley thought they were screwing with him.

He kept his voice low. "And what happens when

Bentley finds out the truth?"

Her chin lifted. "I plan on breaking off the engagement next week."

He stared at her defiant little chin, which was a mistake because his gaze caught on her slender throat exposed by the lifted chin. A very unwanted desire pissed him off even more.

"You're a horrible driver," he snapped. "You ran me off the road."

"I did not. I passed you."

"And nearly clipped my car."

She tsked. "Please. I'm an excellent driver."

He gritted his teeth. "Ken is a man's name."

"It's short for Kennedy."

"I'm sure you get that all the time. Why do you abbreviate it? You should go by Kennedy if you don't want any confusion."

Her blue eyes flashed, and he ignored the jolt it gave him. "I should go by what I want people to call me."

"Try tailgater."

"You were the one driving like an old man."

"I was tired."

She smirked. "So are old men."

He straightened to his full six feet. "It wasn't fully light! That road had dangerous curves—" He clamped his mouth shut when he realized he'd gotten loud.

"So do I!" Candy piped up, which made Bentley throw back his head and laugh. The happy couple were by the door, waiting for him and Ken to catch up.

"You're a riot, honey!" Bentley said. He turned to Luke and Ken. "Isn't she?"

"You're a lucky man," Luke said.

"Mmm-hmm," Ken said.

Bentley beamed again. "I'm thrilled you're getting married! I've talked to a number of financial planners, but none of them had that special something I was looking for on a personal level. So I narrowed it down to you two. Luke because of his reputation and Ken because of her incredible record. But I just couldn't decide, so—" he lifted his palms "—I'm letting the game decide."

Luke's brows shot up in surprise. Ken's record? She couldn't be past twenty-five. How much experience could she possibly have?

They followed Bentley outside to the golf course that had another party of four on it. Luke had thought for sure they'd be the only ones crazy enough to take on a Monday morning seven a.m. tee time. Luke puzzled over the fact that Bentley had already narrowed it down to him and Ken as Bentley took a few practice shots on the putting green. Clearly Luke had more experience, so that should automatically give him the advantage. He took a few practice shots and stepped back to let Ken take a turn. She had a flawless, controlled swing. *Dammit.*

"Ready to go?" Bentley asked when they'd finished warming up.

"Ready," Luke and Ken said in unison.

Bentley signaled for a couple of caddies to join them. The young men checked out Candy surreptitiously, who preened under the attention. Bentley remained oblivious.

"Ladies first," Candy said, gesturing for Ken to take the first shot. "I'm just going to watch."

"I'll go last," Bentley announced.

Ken lined up with the ball, her hips wiggling as she adjusted her stance. Luke tried valiantly not to notice her heart-shaped ass in those snug white shorts and gave one of the leering caddies a good glare for doing the same. The ball arced beautifully in the air with an impressive drive, landing with what would surely be an easy approach to the green. Luke broke out in a sweat over the game that he had a sinking feeling he was not going to win. Why would Bentley put his financial future in the hands of a game? Was he really as crazy as people said?

Bentley and Candy started sucking face.

Ken raised a brow at him. He bristled and lined up his shot, closing his eyes for a moment as he tried to visualize the end result.

"Don't fall asleep," Ken teased.

His eyes flew open. He swung hard in a drive that

hooked left, landing in the small sand trap just off the green.

"Too bad, Grandpa," Ken whispered as she brushed by, her flowery scent temporarily distracting him.

"Why are you here?" he whispered, snagging her by the elbow. "You look like you just graduated college."

She leaned into him and smiled, probably for Bentley's benefit, though Bentley was still busy stuffing his tongue down Candy's throat. Not an easy task given that Bentley was a good five inches shorter. "I graduated two years ago. I'm the hungriest at the firm, and my boss knows it. I'll do anything to nail this account."

"Even me?" he asked in a husky voice meant to scare her off.

She lifted her chin defiantly, and he stared at the pulse point in her throat beating rapidly. "Whatever it takes," she whispered.

He stroked one finger over the wildly thumping pulse of her throat and felt himself go hard. Fuck. This could not be happening. He was getting sucked in by her intriguing vulnerability coupled with the ballsiness. She didn't flinch at his touch or pull away; instead she held his gaze steadily. He had the strangest Neanderthal urge to toss her over his shoulder and bring her back to his place. This was insanity. He was not a Neanderthal kind of guy. He was smooth, sophisticated, cultured. He'd worked damn hard to be.

"Don't play with me," he warned.

"I play to win," she growled.

Yes, growled. He'd never been so turned on. What was wrong with him?

"My turn, lovebirds!" Bentley called before teeing off with a gorgeous swing that had his ball even closer to the hole than Ken's.

Ken leaned against his side, one arm wrapped around his waist, and the way she fit perfectly made him actually imagine for one bizarre moment that they were a couple.

"When I win," she said out of the corner of her mouth in a low voice meant only for his ears, "we'll both be happy about the shared business. And then you'll quietly walk away."

"Like hell."

"Thanks, sweetheart!" She pulled away and gestured toward the green. "Your turn." She smirked. "Furthest away goes next."

It hit him as he stalked toward the rough that Ken was exactly like him—fiercely ambitious, calculating, and driven.

He mentally rubbed his hands together. Let the games begin.

CHAPTER TWO

As they approached the ninth hole, Ken gave herself a little pep talk that she could pull this off. She'd gone rogue on this deal. Her boss had no idea she was here. She was, in fact, a lowly assistant. When she'd heard of Bentley's recent inheritance, she'd seized the opportunity to pull in a big client. Everyone at work was buzzing about the possibility of bringing Bentley's business to the firm. Her boss had made no headway with snagging Bentley's attention despite numerous calls, invitations to lunch, dinner, and drinks, and even sending a huge fruit basket. Ken had suggested an invitation to golf, which her boss ignored because his bum knee made it difficult to play. She'd tried to invite herself along for golf, suggesting her boss ride in a golf cart, but she'd ended up irritating him with her persistence and was shooed out of his office.

But she couldn't let a client like Bentley slip away. Newly made billionaires didn't come along every day.

So she sent Bentley an invitation to play golf on her own. If she pulled in this business, not only would she get promoted to a job that actually met her qualifications as a college graduate with a degree in economics, she'd get the pay raise she needed for her father's medical bills. Spinal surgery, rehab, and ongoing physical therapy weren't cheap, even with insurance. Not to mention the serious debt her family had fallen into, her sister's looming college tuition bill (she was in her first semester), and her three younger siblings still living at home in their crowded two-bedroom apartment. Her mom's part-time bookkeeping work barely covered the rent. Then there were still utility bills and groceries to pay for. Her brothers, both teenagers, could eat, especially seventeen-year-old Alex. She felt the familiar tightening in her chest when she thought of Alex and forced a deep breath in and out.

She caught Luke's irritated glare.

She never should've said they were engaged. Desperation made her blurt that out. And now she couldn't take it back or she'd look like a lying fool. She was shocked that Luke hadn't called her on it in front of Bentley, which would've immediately sent her home in defeat. Maybe he didn't mind playing along because she'd assured him it was just for a week. Or maybe it was because of the way he looked at her like he wanted to devour her. She could never feel comfortable with him. Luke's slickly handsome look with the designer label clothes, expensive haircut with blond highlights, and neatly trimmed beard didn't fool her for one minute. It was a thin veneer over a natural aggression and raw sexuality that simmered just below the surface. She liked bookish men that didn't try to take over. Before his accident, her dad had ruled their little household—a benign dictator. She loved the man dearly for all he'd done for her, but the truth was, he'd taken care of them so well that when he couldn't anymore, due to his injury, everything fell apart. Never depend on a man was her mantra. Especially never get involved with a domineering man.

In any case, she was kicking Luke's ass in golf and that was the important thing. She had to make sure Bentley still felt good about his game, though, so she held back a bit. Golf was her sport and a good thing too because it paid off big time in the boys' club of high finance. Her dad, a gym teacher before the accident, had taught her and her four younger siblings every sport invented from the time they could walk, searching for the one sport they could excel at. Golf was hers.

She took her turn and watched as the ball soared and landed exactly where she wanted it on the green, merely inches from the hole.

"Amazing!" Bentley exclaimed. "Have you thought about going pro?"

Luke cast her a sideways glance beneath hooded eyes. His lashes were long and thick, framing dark blue eyes. Seemed like a waste for a man to have those kind of lashes. Hers were skimpy. Without mascara, you could barely see them.

She smiled at Bentley. "I'm much more interested in helping my clients make investments with a solid return." Golf had never been her passion, definitely not enough to make her want to live and breathe it the way the pros did. It was just something she enjoyed for fun and was exceptionally good at. She'd set a record on the collegiate women's golf circuit in her freshman year. And then broke that record her senior year.

Bentley nodded with enthusiasm. "We'll definitely be playing more golf together. Hey, maybe you could give Luke a few pointers."

She turned to a scowling Luke. "Maybe this weekend?" she asked politely. Engaged people presumably saw each other on the weekend. How much longer would they have to keep up the charade? Hopefully Bentley would choose her as soon as the game ended, Luke would vanish from the picture, and she'd be free from the sticky lie.

Luke squared his shoulders and sent her a look that clearly said *it will be a cold day in hell before you give me golf pointers.*

"Ooh, honey!" Candy exclaimed, bouncing in place. Her breasts didn't move. "Let's invite them to the cottage for the holiday weekend."

Ken swallowed hard. This weekend was Labor Day—a three-day weekend.

Bentley and Candy turned to her. "Would you like that?" Bentley asked. "We were all set for a romantic weekend—"

"We definitely wouldn't want to interrupt that," Luke asserted.

Bentley grinned. "No interruption at all. We hired some staff to make it a spa weekend. We can all enjoy it. Do a little sailing. And I'm having a dinner party on Saturday night. Maybe some new clients for both of you. What do you say?"

"We'd love to!" Ken exclaimed. The more new clients, the better.

Candy clapped. "Wonderful! I'll text you the address. Arrive on Saturday at seven a.m. sharp. Bennie likes to start the party early. You'll love it! It's in Greenport, right where the river meets the Sound! Gorgeous!" Greenport was a wealthy enclave along the Long Island Sound. His "cottage" was most likely a mansion with some cutesy cottage touches.

"Thank you," Luke said with a forced smile. "We look forward to it."

Candy started talking excitedly to Bentley. Ken immediately crossed to where Luke was standing, silently smoldering. His scent was intoxicating—crisp, fresh, with a hint of musk—probably some uber-expensive cologne. She grabbed Luke's hand and squeezed. He returned the squeeze firmly, which for some reason relaxed her.

"Spa weekend?" he asked quietly.

"It's what they do," she whispered. "They" being the rich.

Luke wrapped an arm around her shoulders and pulled her close. She worked to control the blush she felt creeping up her neck. "There's two ways this weekend could go," he said in a low voice.

She lost the battle of the blush as her cheeks and neck burned. "I know."

He met her eyes. "You know?"

She nodded. A disaster if they were found out. Or a disaster if they weren't. And then they'd be stuck together for as long as it took Bentley to make a decision. Or they could pretend to break up, and then there'd be this awkward *pretending to be friendly after being engaged while courting the client* act that made her head hurt just thinking about it. She really needed Bentley to make a quick decision.

Luke dropped his arm from her shoulders and took his shot. It fell short of the green by several feet.

Bentley turned to Ken. "I hope you like massage. I hired an excellent masseuse. Two, actually, for couples massage." He stroked Candy's arm. "Though Candy is the best masseuse—"

"That's how we met," Candy put in.

"But I wanted her to have a break." He kissed the tip of Candy's nose. "It's your turn to be massaged, lovey."

"Sounds wonderful!" Ken chirped. The two of them were nauseatingly lovey-dovey. Ken had had her share of boyfriends, no one serious, but just shoot her now if she ever came off that disgustingly sweet. Seriously. Love didn't have to be all kisses and sweet words. Her parents had never been that way.

Luke eyed her speculatively. She ignored him.

By the time they finished the game, she and Bentley were both under par. She slightly more. And Luke was five strokes over par.

Luke stopped abruptly in front of Bentley as the caddies put the clubs away. "Does this mean you're going with Ken's firm?"

Ken held her breath.

"Let's not talk business," Bentley said. "Let's just have some fun together. Time enough for all that later."

Candy bit Bentley's earlobe. He smiled serenely.

Ken and Luke exchanged a look. She was

beginning to suspect Bentley never wanted to talk business. She needed a signed letter of intent for her firm sooner rather than later. Before her family was forced to declare bankruptcy. Collectors were already calling and sending dire notices. Her sister Frank was going to have to leave her first semester of college if that tuition bill wasn't paid in thirty days.

"When would be a good time?" Ken asked with a bright smile.

Bentley turned to Candy. "When do I like to talk business, Can?"

She giggled. "Never."

"The Flaming Penguins are bleeding you dry," Luke said. That was Bentley's minor league hockey team. She had no idea why he'd bought it. They'd never had a winning season.

Ken jumped in with her own financial advice. "Dress the Kids has some red flags with their leadership." Dress the Kids was a charity that donated used designer clothes to kids that could never afford them. Unfortunately, many of those clothes ended up on eBay by the people who worked at the nonprofit. They probably kept some of the clothes for themselves too. "A better alternative would be to start a foundation—"

"Who wants ice cream?" Bentley asked.

"I love ice cream," Ken said with a smile. *Sure, it's*

barely eleven a.m., but the client is always right.

Luke's arm dropped over her shoulders. "Me too." A flash of heat went through her. For some strange reason, the more Luke touched her, the more difficult it became to act casual about it. She felt extremely overheated and uncomfortable.

"There's a place about ten minutes from here," Bentley said. "Follow me."

He and Candy led the way back through the country club.

"I'll drive," Luke said to her as he held the door of the club open for her.

"I'll drive, honey," Ken said, smiling sweetly up at him. He gave her a dark look in return.

Bentley and Candy slipped into (what else?) a white Bentley convertible.

She and Luke stopped in the parking lot between their two cars in opposite rows and had a stare down. She refused to let his size and arrogant stance intimidate her. So what if she was a petite five feet two to his six-foot muscular frame? She was strong on the inside, where it really counted. She needed to be in control. In the driver's seat, literally and figuratively.

"It'll look bad if we drive separately," she told him before getting into her car.

He heaved a sigh and slid into the passenger side. She bit back a smile and turned on the car, blasting the air-conditioning in the hopes of blocking out his delicious cologne that made her want to lean in and breathe deep.

"No need to gloat," he said.

"I didn't say anything!" She stared straight ahead, waiting for Bentley to pull out, and tried not to smile some more. Though it was very, very difficult. She felt a gloat coming on.

He pressed a warm thumb into her cheek. "Your dimple is showing."

She frowned because his touch felt too good, firm and warm. He wouldn't be like her fumbling, unsure boyfriends of the past. This was a man with confidence who'd take charge.

"I know a good place you can stick your thumb," she said.

He dropped his hand. "How did you even get here?" he barked. "What boss in their right mind would send a rookie to bag Bentley?"

She met his eyes and said in as steady a voice as she could muster on the thin ice she knew she was skating, "Everyone else at the firm struck out. He wouldn't meet with them." That much was true. She left out the part about her initiative in extending the golf invitation.

"It still doesn't make sense how you got here." A beat passed, and she could practically hear his brain cranking, piecing it all together. She turned away. "Wait. It's the golf, isn't it?" He laughed. "Bentley just wanted a good golf partner."

"No." Bentley had asked what her handicap was, though. Maybe he'd heard about her college records too. A quick Google search would've pulled up that much.

"Yeah. Damn, Kennedy, you're not going to win this thing. What experience do you have?"

She stared straight ahead. "Don't call me Kennedy."

"That's your name."

"Everyone calls me Ken." What was taking Bentley so long? He appeared to be chatting with Candy while he played with her hair. *Let's move it, people!*

"I'm not calling you a man's name when you're clearly the fairer sex."

She heated just hearing the word *sex* roll out of that deep voice. "I'm not—shut up! I've been working my ass off the last couple of years learning everything I can from Simon."

"Simon Barrett? *You're* a direct report to Simon Barrett?"

"Yes and yes."

"Bullshit. What are you, his secretary?"

She flushed because that was a little too close to the truth.

"Holy crap. The balls on you."

"I'm not his secretary!"

He whistled under his breath. "Don't tell me you're the intern."

She met his eyes. "I'm not."

He pulled his cell out. "I'm calling him. He probably doesn't even know you're here representing the Barrett Group."

"No!"

"Tell me exactly how you got here."

She hesitated.

"Tell me," he ordered.

Bentley finally backed out of his parking spot. "I invited Bentley to play golf and told him what I could do for him."

He punched in a number on his cell. "I'm dialing."

She broke out in a sweat and turned to him. "I'm Simon's assistant, okay? Golf was the only 'in' I had and I need the promotion."

Luke shook his head. "I'd laugh, but I'm afraid Bentley is just crazy enough to go with an unproven commodity because he likes the cut of your jib."

"I need the promotion for a very important reason," she said.

"Which is?" he drawled.

"My family needs the money."

His eyes widened. "You have kids?"

"No—"

"Look—" he fixed her with a hard glare "—I'm only going along with this long enough to convince Bentley that I'm the better choice."

"Whatever."

Luke snorted. "I give you credit for initiative, but you are in way over your head. This client is mine."

She kept an eye on Bentley slowly making his way toward the lot's exit near where she was parked, and turned on the radio to her favorite station, drumming her fingers on the steering wheel in time to the rap. The edgy, aggressive lyrics and beat always amped her up. She needed to be aggressive at work. Rap helped.

Bentley pulled out of the lot, and she followed him.

Luke turned the volume down. "So my fiancée likes rap."

She raised a brow. "Lemme guess. Easy listening?" She turned the volume back up a little so she could hear it and still hear him.

"How old do you think I am?" he asked in a seriously offended voice.

She waited at a red light behind Bentley and turned to take him in. Light brown hair with blond highlights, dark blue eyes with some laugh lines, light brown beard and mustache with no gray in it. "Thirty?"

He cocked his head. "And that's old to you?"

"Guys my age can't afford expensive cologne."

His brows scrunched together. "What are you talking about?"

She waved a hand airily and checked on Bentley. Still stopped at the light, waiting on a left turn. "Your cologne. It must be expensive to smell that good."

"You think I smell good?"

She glanced over to find him grinning. She sucked in a breath and faced front. That smile was killer. Could bring a woman to her knees with the full-on charm. Lucky for her, they were enemies, so there was no chance of succumbing.

She shrugged in response. He didn't need any more flattery for that puffed-up ego. The light turned and she followed Bentley onto the main road.

"I'm thirty-two," Luke said, "which, by the way, is not old."

"Doesn't matter to me how old you are," Ken replied. "You're the one hung up on age. You think just because I'm twenty-three—"

"You're twenty-three!" he exclaimed.

She glanced over at his shocked expression. "Yes."

"How are you two years out of college, then?"

"I turn twenty-four next week. Geez, get over the age thing. Just because I'm young doesn't mean I can't do the job. I can, and I will." She gripped the steering wheel tighter. She knew she didn't have a lot of experience, but she'd studied hard, read everything she could get her hands on in finance, and kept up with everything her boss, Simon, worked on.

Luke was quiet. She took a deep breath in and out. Damn, he smelled good. She switched to breathing through her mouth. Several minutes passed to the sound of rap. Ken snapped the radio off when the song turned a little too sexy for present company. She stared at the tail of Bentley's car as she drove and tried to figure out the fastest way to close this deal before she had to either go through with a spa weekend or come clean to Bentley and Candy.

Bentley waved out the window, gesturing to a roadside ice-cream stand with a giant wooden ice-cream cone sporting a smiling face.

Luke piped up. "What'll you give me to spend a weekend playing your fake fiancé?"

She stiffened, not liking the sound of this. "What do you want?"

His voice became husky. "What do you have to offer?"

She flushed. He couldn't be asking what she thought he was asking. That was low. And entirely demeaning. So why was she getting turned on? It was that damn expensive cologne. And the deep, husky voice. She followed Bentley into the parking lot.

"Golf lessons?" she asked in what she hoped sounded like a normal, casual voice.

"Try again."

"I don't do sexual favors!" she blurted.

He barked out a laugh. "You think I want you?"

She felt like falling into a hole. "Shut up," she muttered.

That set him off, laughing like a damn hyena.

"Go to hell," she said.

He kept right on laughing. Jerk. She felt like slapping him just to shut him up. She parked a few spaces away from Bentley. Candy and Bentley started kissing as soon as they parked, so she took the opportunity to give Luke a good glare.

He wiped his eyes, still chuckling. "Good one, Kennedy."

"It's Ken," she said through her teeth. She got out of the car and slammed the door.

He appeared at her side a moment later and laced his fingers with hers. "You're cute when you're angry," he said in a low voice.

Bentley and Candy kept right on kissing inside their car.

She pressed a foot on top of Luke's, intending to bear down on it with her heel, but he grabbed her and lifted her so both her feet were on top of his, her back to his front. His arms wrapped around her waist from behind, the heat and strength of him shocking her long enough to give him a chance to move with her, walking in tandem toward the ice-cream stand. She was stuck, carried along like part of a cutesy couple, and that was how Bentley and Candy saw them when they finally emerged from their car. She'd never been so embarrassed in her life.

"There's the happy couple!" Bentley exclaimed.

"Look how cute they walk together!" Candy exclaimed.

"Kennedy loves it," Luke proclaimed. Grr.

Bentley and Candy walked alongside them now, holding hands. "Try the banana split," Bentley said. "We love it."

"Sounds good!" Ken said brightly, trying to act like she always did cutesy couple things.

"I'll feed it to you, sweetheart," Luke whispered in her ear.

She suppressed a shiver. What had she unleashed?

CHAPTER THREE

Luke watched from across the picnic table as Bentley and Candy fed each other spoonfuls of banana split. What was an engaged man to do? He eyed Kennedy sitting next to him, picking at their shared banana split. He refused to think of her as Ken, she was much too feminine for that name. And she'd felt shockingly good in his arms earlier. She was light as a feather, but her petite frame was merely a smokescreen to what she really was—a fighter. She wouldn't break or bend. And damn if he wasn't already having fun sparring with her. She kept surprising him too—the soft blushing looks, the fiery temper, the rap. His life had become a predictable routine, even the parties he went to in the city had the same kind of people all the time— polished, rich, self-involved. The women he met were jaded and, outside of the bedroom, bored him to tears. Sex had always been a game to him, particularly fun if he found a woman who liked to be dominated, but even so, lately he'd felt like he was in a rut.

He was actually considering spending the weekend at Bentley's cottage with her. Only because he knew once he won the business, she'd want nothing to do with him, which made it a natural end to their time together. He'd feel the same way in her shoes. No point in moving forward once you'd been shown up. It was perfect. Besides, he wasn't looking for anything long term and especially not with a deviously ambitious woman like her.

"Open," he said, holding a spoonful of vanilla with hot fudge out to her.

Her blue eyes sparked fire, but she opened. He smiled and fed her the spoonful.

She jabbed her spoon in the ice cream, taking half the scoop and a big glob of hot fudge. She held the dripping spoonful up. "Your turn."

He leaned back. "That's too much. It's going to drip down my—"

She jabbed the spoon in his direction, so he quickly grabbed her wrist and swallowed the ice cream. Then he looked in her blue eyes while he licked the spoon. She shivered.

"Cold?" he asked, biting back a smile. He still held her petite wrist and stroked his thumb over the pulse point, which was, satisfyingly, beating rapidly. The attraction definitely went both ways.

"No." She blushed and her lashes fluttered down as she looked at the table. She pulled her wrist from his grasp.

He glanced over to Bentley and Candy again. Candy giggled as Bentley dabbed her mouth with a napkin and then kissed her. Sickeningly sweet. But at least Luke knew how to fit in. Sweet, lovey-dovey gestures would make Bentley believe he was with more of his kind of people.

"Do I need a napkin?" he asked Kennedy, hoping she'd take the hint to mimic Bentley and Candy. *Dab and kiss, baby.*

"No. Well, there's a little…" She pointed with one pink polished finger to his left cheek. "Right there."

He purposely wiped the wrong spot. "Did I get it?"

She shook her head.

He dabbed his chin. She shook her head again, and he handed her the napkin. Their eyes met, hers were fiery again. He forced a straight face.

When she just kept glaring, he raised a brow. She threw the napkin in his face. He couldn't help it, he laughed.

"It's so nice to meet another couple as happy as we are," Bentley said. He twirled a long lock of Candy's wavy blond hair around his finger, brought it up to his nose, and breathed deep.

"How long have you been together?" Candy asked

with a smile.

Luke wiped the ice cream off his face. "How long's it been, baby? Feels like forever."

"Aw," Candy said, leaning into Bentley.

Kennedy looked to the sky and for a brief moment Luke thought she'd cry uncle. "Four months, three days, and eleven hours."

"Omigod, they count to the hour!" Candy exclaimed. "How many hours have we been together, Bennie?"

"Feels like just yesterday!" Bentley exclaimed.

"Aww, sugar bear," Candy cooed. "I love you."

"I love you more," Bentley replied.

They rubbed noses before throwing their arms around each other and kissing again, ice cream forgotten. *Let the lovefest continue.* He glanced at Kennedy, who was staring at their rapidly melting ice cream. He fought the urge to push her face first into it. Just playing around. Maybe a good food fight. That was as far from professional as you could get. Something about Kennedy's straight-laced tension made him want to loosen her up. She was too young to be so serious.

Luke leaned close to her ear. "Would you like me to feed you the banana?"

She stared at the extremely phallic-looking banana and then elbowed him in the gut.

"Oof," he moaned for her benefit. She hadn't really hurt him.

She stood. He stood too, waiting to see what she'd do next.

Bentley and Candy were back to feeding each other ice cream, gazing deep into each other's loving eyes.

Kennedy headed back to the ice-cream stand, muttering to herself. He quickly followed. She grabbed a handful of napkins.

"Care to share?" he asked. They were a good distance from Bentley and Candy, but he kept his voice low just in case.

She glared, her gaze dropped to his groin, and he took a careful step back as he realized maybe he'd crossed the line. "No low blows," he said.

"You'd probably enjoy it," she spat. But then her face crumpled and she turned away.

"Hey, hey, hey." He moved around to where she was staring in the distance, blinking rapidly. "I'm sorry. I crossed the line."

"I really need this," she said in a choked voice. "And I don't appreciate all your…" She waved a hand in the air. "You know."

He knew better. He never crossed that line in the business world. "Hey, I'm sorry. I was joking around. It won't happen again."

"I made my bed—" she met his eyes with a sour expression and blue eyes shiny with unshed tears "—now I have to lie in it."

The shiny eyes were killing him. He hadn't meant to make her feel bad. He wanted to stroke her cheek, to wrap his arms around her.

He shoved his hands in his pockets. "From here on out, I'm going to treat you like any business competitor."

She brightened. "Yeah?"

He deflated, all hopes of a fun weekend fling gone. "Absolutely."

She nodded once. "So, um, how's Friday night for a meeting? You know, to go over the basic facts on each other for the weekend."

His eyes snapped to hers. There was no fucking way he could keep things professional on a weekend getaway with her. She was asking the impossible.

He moved in close, wanting both to remind her of the attraction between them and to look like a couple in case Bentley and Candy were watching. He spoke in a whisper near her ear; the delicate shell flushed pink. "Here's the deal. As long as you want to pretend we're engaged, I can't promise to keep it professional. I'm sorry I just can't."

"I thought you didn't want me," she said in a small voice.

He met her eyes. "I lied."

"But you laughed like a hyena!" she exclaimed, hands on her hips.

"I never said I was a prince," he said with a devilish grin.

She shoved his chest, and he grabbed her wrists and held them there. "You in or out, Kennedy? You started this game. Do you have the guts to finish it?" His gaze dropped to her mouth. He suddenly really wanted to kiss her.

"I-I—" she stuttered.

He released her hands. "Spit it out."

Her eyes flashed at him. "Yes. I'm in."

He couldn't help but smile. "Perfect. Where do you live?"

"Clover Park, but—"

"Really? I grew up in Clover Park too." He cocked his head. "I don't remember you."

She leaned close, up on tiptoe to whisper in his ear, and her scent like flowers, soft and delicate, washed over him, making him want to get this weekend fling started right away. "Shh. We're supposed to know each other already."

He fought his natural instinct to make a move and put his hands behind his back.

"Garner's for drinks at eight?" she asked in a soft voice.

"You got it." He looked over to where Bentley and Candy were smiling and finishing up the last of their banana split. He figured his and Kennedy's banana split was a melted mess. He turned to her. "Want any more ice cream?"

"Blech. It's too early to eat ice cream. It's not even lunchtime."

He felt the same way. He headed back to the picnic table and Kennedy kept up with him. He snagged the bowl and tossed it in the garbage can on the far side of the parking lot. When he headed back, he took one look at Kennedy smiling and chatting with Bentley and Candy, and picked up the pace because, while it was one thing to want Kennedy, it was an entirely different thing to lose a client to her.

She gave him a tight smile. "Candy was just telling me about the aromatherapy body scrub they have planned for the weekend."

"Don't forget the couples massage," Bentley put in.

Body scrub? "Sounds very relaxing," Luke said.

"You two should go first," Candy said. "We like to treat our guests special."

"Oh, that's not necessary," Kennedy said at the same time Luke said, "Wouldn't hear of it."

Bentley and Candy exchanged a look and burst out laughing.

Kennedy frowned and shot him a look. Were Candy and Bentley onto them?

"What's so funny?" Luke asked.

Bentley shook his head. "I told Candy men don't like body scrubs." He wrinkled his nose. "You end up smelling like flowers."

"And then we women want to lick every inch of you," Candy purred. She looked to Kennedy. "Right?"

Kennedy blushed all the way to the roots of her hair. Even her neck was flushed pink. His fingers tingled again, aching to touch.

"That's right," Kennedy said. "Not that I ever had a body scrub, but I'm sure—"

"You never had one!" Candy exclaimed, brown eyes wide. Like it was a shocking thing that someone had never had a spa treatment. "Then you're definitely first. Bennie, let's call in someone to do mani-pedis too. The full treatment."

"You got it, sweetcakes," Bentley said.

"We can't wait," Kennedy said with a forced smile.

"Us too!" Candy exclaimed.

Luke gave up the fight to keep his hands off Kennedy. He wrapped an arm around her slim shoulders and pulled her against his side. "This will be an experience."

She wrapped an arm around his waist. "I can't wait for you to smell like flowers," she purred.

"Me too," he said in a husky voice. "For one hot reason." If Kennedy was going to play the game, he was all in.

She turned, wrapped her arms around his neck, and kissed him softly, more of a brush across his lips. She pulled back, dropping her arms, and looked up at him with a little smirk on her face. So she liked being in control, did she? Didn't like when he came on strong, but it was okay for her? Sorry. Luke didn't play that way.

He was vaguely aware of Bentley and Candy heading back to their car and knew he didn't have to put on a show, but he wanted more.

He slid his hand around the nape of Kennedy's neck and pulled her in for a hard kiss. He felt her sudden intake of breath, felt the moment she yielded, her lips softening, opening for him as her hand clutched his shirt. The thrill of victory ran through him, and he thrust his tongue inside the heat of her mouth, deepening the kiss.

"Let's go, you lovebirds," Bentley called cheerfully from a distance away.

Luke broke the kiss and pulled back, on edge with a sharp need for more. Kennedy's eyes gazing back at him were dark with desire.

In that moment he knew with a certainty that should've scared the hell out of him, that should've

told him to run for the hills, but instead excited him—
There was no turning back.

CHAPTER FOUR

Kennedy sat on a bar stool at Garner's Sports Bar & Grill on Friday night and did a quick calculation of what she could afford tonight. She'd purposely asked Luke to meet her after dinner. She didn't have a corporate account to charge a meal to and there was no way she was letting Luke pay for anything. That would make their meeting too much like a date. She fully intended to go through with this weekend with him, but that didn't mean they'd be hooking up. She had five dollars to spare. The rest of her take-home pay had gone toward rent and groceries for her brothers and sister. She was losing weight from skipping meals, but it was the only way to stretch their measly dollars and her brothers, Alex and Quinn, were in the middle of a teenaged growth spurt. Jamie, at thirteen and a girl, was pickier in what she ate, but Kennedy still made sure her sister wasn't shortchanged on nutrition. Her stomach grumbled and she snagged a pretzel from the bowl on the bar. She'd only had crackers with peanut butter for dinner and that was hours ago.

The cheapest thing on the menu was soda. That was the best she could do. Though she really wanted a fruity cocktail. It'd been so long since she'd treated herself to something that wasn't absolutely necessary. She scanned the menu a second time. She could probably swing the light beer on tap. She'd wait for Luke to arrive before ordering.

She set the paper she'd prepared on the bar top along with a small notebook and pen. She'd created a short fact sheet on herself of the things Luke should know. Her age, her middle name, where she went to school, names and ages of siblings, taste in music, books, movies, and hobbies. No pets, so that was easy. The apartment complex didn't allow them. She couldn't imagine what else he'd need to know. This was surely enough to pass as a couple. Ooh, maybe she should add how they met. She pulled the cap off her pen and started writing in her notebook, inspired with the little bit of romantic fiction.

A masculine voice rumbled in her ear, and she jumped. "What're we writing?"

She glanced over her shoulder to find Luke grinning at her. Her pulse skittered. That smile was…wow. And she'd spent a little too much time this week thinking of that body that reminded her of her favorite ball player on the Yankees. It wasn't just the muscles, it was an almost graceful quality to the way he moved, comfortable in his own skin, strong and confident.

He slid onto the barstool next to her, and she breathed in his delicious cologne and pure manly Luke. She set her pen down. "I was writing the story of how we met."

He signaled to the bartender, Josh. "Ah, yes. Through our mutual friends. So exactly how did it go down?"

"It was a Tuesday in April."

"A Tuesday, huh? So it must've been after work."

"Yes. We were shopping—" She stopped because his hand was on her arm. "What?"

"We did *not* meet shopping."

"Yes. We were both shopping for a Mother's Day present with our mutual friends."

"In April? And do you really think guys shop with their friends?"

She bristled. "Mother's Day was only weeks away."

"No guy shops weeks ahead of time." He turned to Josh, a thirty-something guy with short brown hair, who'd just arrived. "Hey, Josh, could you get me a Sam Adams?" He turned to her. "What do you want? Something fruity?"

"I'll take a Coors Light."

Josh nodded and started pouring.

"Beer drinker, huh?" Luke asked. "I would've pegged you for a margarita kind of girl."

Margaritas *were* delicious and expensive. She lifted one shoulder up and down and returned to her notebook, crossing out shopping for silk scarves for their mothers. She'd imagined they'd reach at the same time and during that one electric touch, they just knew. It sounded good anyway.

"Change hers to a frozen strawberry margarita," Luke called to Josh.

She turned in shock. "Don't order for me. A beer is fine."

"My treat," he said.

She shook her head. "You don't—"

He leaned close. "I saw the way you lit up when I mentioned the margarita. Let me get this one. You get the next one. Okay?"

She couldn't afford what he'd ordered. God, this was so embarrassing. She bit her lip and stared at the notebook. Maybe she should just go. Maybe she shouldn't show up at Bentley's cottage tomorrow at all. Who was she kidding? She was way out of her league. Luke was going to take over and win the business. She was just a lowly assistant. She closed the notebook and stood.

"You're leaving?" Luke asked.

She nodded, the lump in her throat preventing speech. She turned to go.

"Get back here," he said, snagging her by the belt loop of her jeans and giving her a tug.

"Luke!"

His lips curved into a slow, sexy smile. "Sit down there. I want a decent story in that notebook. Not some frilly shopping trip."

She huffed. He tapped the notebook. "Start right here with Luke Reynolds was the dreamiest man I ever clapped eyes on. Every story should start like that."

"You're so arrogant," she muttered. But she settled back on the bar stool. Her frozen margarita arrived, the glass lined with salt on the rim, looking all smooth and strawberry-licious.

"Drink up," he said, lifting his glass to her and watching her over the rim.

"Stop telling me what to do," she said before grabbing the glass and taking a long, delicious sip. She let out a blissful sigh.

"Good, eh?" he asked. He snagged her fact sheet off the bar. "Birthday next Tuesday. Tuesdays must be your lucky day."

She didn't reply, and he kept reading the fact sheet about her. She went back to her story of how they met. What was a manly way to meet someone on a Tuesday night? She had no clue. She hardly went out at all.

Usually she was working. Occasionally she met up with some friends in town, hanging out at their apartments. Lack of funds sort of put a crimp in her social life. Ooh, maybe they met at Garner's during Ladies' Night. She'd been to a few of those with her friends, Julia and Hailey. Couldn't beat two-dollar beer night.

"We met at Ladies' Night," she informed him, madly scribbling the scene with her and Julia and Hailey hanging out at the bar. Maybe Luke came over with two friends and they all started talking. Then she and Luke found they had something in common, maybe they both liked some great book like *The Wind in the Willows*. She'd read the story at least fifty times to her younger brothers and sisters. She'd always been more like a mom/babysitter to them since she was six years old before her parents felt ready to have more kids. Everyone commented on how she didn't look like her siblings. She was the only blond-haired blue-eyed person in her dark-haired family. Some people even went so far as to ask if she was adopted, which stung because it was half true. Her mom had explained at a young age that the man Kennedy thought of as dad had adopted her after her mom had her. Her parents had only been nineteen at the time. She'd never met her biological dad. Her half brothers and sisters were the ones who truly belonged to both parents. Kennedy had done her damnedest to make it not matter. And to make sure her stepdad never regretted taking in another man's child. She never wanted him to think of her as a burden, though she knew raising a kid at nineteen while working and going to classes had been hard on her parents.

She bit her lip. Where was she in her love-at-first-sight story again? Ooh! They talked all night and knew it was love. Yes, that could work.

She felt a hot breath by her ear and realized Luke was reading over her shoulder. "When did we hook up?" he asked in a low voice that hummed through her.

Her cheeks flushed. "I don't know. Maybe, um, two months later?"

He chuckled. "If I picked up a woman in a bar, we sure as hell wouldn't be *talking* all night."

"You'd hook up the first night you met?"

"Sure."

She met his eyes and took in his serious, jaded expression. This was a man who'd never been in love. "That's not romantic."

"Sure it is." He took a long swallow of beer. "Men like action. That's what we call romantic."

She considered that. No, that couldn't possibly be true. She hadn't slept with any of her boyfriends that quickly. She glanced over to find his lips curved in a small smile, which was extremely irritating. He was entirely too smug and confident. A regular know-it-all.

"You know nothing about love," she said before taking a healthy swallow of margarita. So smooth, so sweet, the tequila was already going to her head. Everything around her took on a soft, fuzzy feel.

"You know nothing about the real world," he said, raising a brow in challenge.

She scowled and drank more margarita.

"Slow down there," he said, "you look like a lightweight."

She drank some more to spite him. God, that was good. She rested her head in her hand and smiled dreamily to herself. What was better than a bar hookup? She turned to him. "How about a blind date?"

"With who?"

"With me, silly!" She laughed because it was so obvious. They were both from Clover Park. Some mutual friend set them up to meet for dinner here at Garner's. Then they talked. Maybe they kissed goodnight and that was so passionate that they knew right away it was true love. She sighed happily and wrote that down.

He leaned over her shoulder again to read. "Meh. Fine. Not as good as the hookup, but fine. We could do a passionate kiss. Was there tongue?"

She considered that quite seriously. Luke chuckled. "You're teasing me!" she said. "Bentley isn't going to ask us that."

Luke grinned. "He'll assume everyone kisses like he does." He stuck out his tongue and waggled it around. She burst out laughing. That was exactly how Bentley looked making out with Candy. "You should smile more. You look like the weight of the world is on your shoulders half the time."

"That was probably because of you!" She wiggled her shoulders, which felt extremely light for the first time in a long time. Good old strawberry margarita.

She shoved the fact sheet in his hand. "Here, memorize my stuff. Then tell me yours."

He started reading aloud. "Twenty-three, a lightweight—"

"It doesn't say that!"

He continued. "Two brothers, Alex and Quinn; two sisters, Frank and Jamie...what's with all the unisex names?"

"My mom didn't want us girls to be held back in the business world with feminine names. She had high hopes for us, I guess."

"Ken, Frank, and Jamie." He made a face. "Francesca?"

"Yup!" She drained the margarita and beamed. Then she pulled five one-dollar bills out of her purse and dumped all of the change on the bar top with a clatter. "Five dollars and twenty-seven cents," she announced.

He snagged the bills and shoved them back in her hand. "Put that away. I got it."

"I pay my own way." She put the bills back on the bar.

He shoved them in the back pocket of his jeans. "To be returned to you later."

She reached for them, and he snagged her hand and held it against his ass. She tried to pull her hand away, but his grip was just firm enough to hold. She blew out a breath and accepted the hold. It was kind of nice, him holding her hand, her holding his ass. She had to get used to him touching her anyway if they were going to make it through this weekend.

He dropped her hand and went back to the fact sheet. "Middle name is Iris? Do you all have flower middle names?"

"Yes. Well, us girls do. Those were the names my mom liked best, actually, but after she got pregnant with me..." She trailed off. She'd never told anyone about that.

"What?" he asked, turning and meeting her eyes with his stunning dark blues. They were nearly, what was that color called? Like the dark blue of Monet's starry, starry sky. No, *The Starry Night*. She sighed dreamily as she gazed into their fathomless depths.

He leaned back and considered her speculatively. "Are you drunk?"

"No." She wiggled her fingers in front of her face. "Silly."

"Yeah, okay." He shook his head and went back to the fact sheet. She went back to her notebook and wrote Mrs. Kennedy Reynolds. Then she added swirls around the Ys and the Ss. Too bad there wasn't an I or she could dot it with a heart.

"All right," he said. "I get the picture. And, by the way, your taste in books, movies, and music is bizarre."

She stopped her pen in midair, disrupting another fancy cursive Mrs. Kennedy Reynolds in her notebook. "What do you mean?"

"I mean none of this goes together." He tapped the paper. "Rap, *The Wind in the Willows* and other fantasy novels, and your favorite movie is *Good Fellas*? It's like you can't decide if you're a dreamy hippy or a tough gangster."

"I'm both. I like rock too." She waved a hand airily. "Who doesn't?"

"Who's your favorite band?"

"Griffin Huntley."

"Oh yeah? Me too. I caught him at Madison Square Garden last month. His solo stuff is even better than when he was with Twisted Star."

"True." She pursed her lips, a little jealous he got to go to the concert. "Lucky duck."

He took a pull on his beer. "Still, most of your stuff doesn't go together. I think you're confused."

She jabbed a finger in his face. "Tell me *your* facts. Maybe *you're* the one who's confused."

He grabbed her finger. "You left out the most important stuff on your fact sheet."

"Like what?" she asked, scanning the paper. She was pretty sure she'd covered the important stuff.

He took her finger and made it point at a blank space at the bottom. "Like your boyfriend history."

She hadn't thought of that. She turned to him. "What do you want to know?"

He released her finger, probably so she could write. "Length, duration…"

Her brows scrunched down as she tried to remember. "I never measured. Gosh, I dunno, six inches? And duration…ten minutes."

Luke burst out laughing. Her cheeks burned. She smacked his arm as she realized he'd been teasing her again.

"I meant length of time you were with them," he said once he could stop laughing. "Duration of relationship." That set him off again.

She glared at him. "You purposely made it sound like—" she lowered her voice "—sex."

He shook his head, still grinning. "Oh no. Don't put this on me. That was your dirty mind."

"That was yours!"

He got serious as he stared at her notebook. She followed his gaze to where it said Mrs. Kennedy Reynolds a bunch of times.

"That was just practice for this weekend," she reassured him with a pat on the shoulder. *My, my, my.* She kept patting his shoulder, sort of petting it because it was so nicely formed and so warm.

Luke cleared his throat. "Okay, here we go, facts on Luke. Now write this down 'cuz there's a quiz at the end."

She picked up her pen. "I'm an excellent test taker."

"I bet you are. I bet you loved school."

"I did!"

He shook his head. "If you weren't so cute, I'd be pretty pissed at you for dragging me through all this, *Mrs. Kennedy Reynolds.*"

She giggled. "Luke..." She leaned in close and looked deep in his dark blue starry eyes. "We should have professional boundaries when we're not with Bentley."

"Fine, you're not cute."

She pouted.

He held her chin and turned her back to the

notebook. "Birthday is March fifteenth. I'm thirty-two, remember that. Not a grandpa."

She wrote that down and turned to him. "When I first met you I thought you were older than thirty-two. I was just being nice when I guessed thirty."

He huffed. "What is it? The beard?" He scratched his beard.

She shrugged. "I don't know. I never saw you without it."

He scowled. "That's it. I'm shaving this beard."

"You'll still always be ancient to me," she sang.

He scowled some more. "You're really enjoying this, aren't you?"

She nodded and slurped her margarita. This was more fun than she'd had in a long time. Must be the delicious frozen margarita. When she was rich, she'd have margaritas every day.

"You want another margarita?" he asked, eying her empty glass.

She licked her lips. She'd love one, but her cash was in his back pocket and that definitely wouldn't cover two margaritas. "That's okay."

"Just tell me if you want one." He signaled to the bartender. "I'm getting another beer."

"But your cash is in my pocket," she said.

He looked back at her. "What?"

"I mean my cash is in your pocket."

He held up a hand. "I got it."

"Lu-u-uke, I can't repay you."

"Don't worry about it. I remember what it was like to be your age, living paycheck to paycheck." He stopped himself and closed his eyes. "God, I feel old." He jabbed a finger at her. "You better stop calling me Grandpa."

She grinned cheekily. "Or what?"

"Or I'll be forced to prove my virility."

She giggled. As if he had to. He was by far the sexiest man she'd ever met. Maybe the sexiest man in America. She beamed, silently thanking him for the beautiful scenery.

He tapped the end of her nose. "You want something to eat? I'm afraid you're swimming in tequila."

She shook her head and tipped to the side. Luke grabbed her arm and held her steady. "How's nachos sound?" he asked.

"Delicious," she admitted.

He nodded once, ordered the food and drinks, and turned back to her. "Ready for more facts?"

She lifted her pen. "Ready."

"Five brothers. In age order: Gabe, Vince, Nico, same age as me, Jared, and Angel. I'm closest with Nico."

"I should meet Nico."

He snorted. "No, you shouldn't."

"Why not?"

He leaned closer, and she breathed deep. They should bottle this Luke scent. Oh, wait, they already had. It was cologne. She smiled to herself at her little joke.

Luke tugged on a lock of her hair. "He's the best looking of the bunch. Women fawn all over him. No way am I losing my fiancée to my brother."

Her head muddled for a moment. Should she insist on meeting his brother? No, no, no. They weren't really engaged.

"Don't think so hard," he said. "Smoke's coming out of your ears."

She turned to him. "You like messing with me."

He bit back a smile and tapped the bar. "I do."

"I like messing with you more," she said, leaning against him.

He grinned down at her. "I sincerely doubt that."

Her second margarita and his beer arrived, and they both took a sip. "Tell me your favorite things," she said.

"Hot women who can't hold their liquor," he responded immediately.

She stiffened. Was he talking about her?

"Write it down," he insisted.

She dutifully wrote it down, flushed, and took a

long, refreshing sip of margarita. He chuckled.

She threw the pen at him, but he ducked. Then he held up a finger, snagged the pen off the floor, and handed it back to her. "You dropped this."

"Be serious!" she exclaimed. "I'm supposed to know you. I need real facts. Do you want to screw this up?"

He stopped smiling. "I do not."

"Okay, then. Tell me your favorite things for real."

"Money, money, money."

She felt the truth in those words and didn't need to write it down. She knew that burning ambition, that drive to build something from nothing. Money gave you options, plain and simple.

"Favorite book?" she asked.

He shook his head. "Nah."

"Favorite music?"

"Rock."

She wrote that one down. "Favorite movie?"

"*Good Fellas.*"

She set her pen down and gave him an exasperated look. That was *her* favorite movie. "Stop teasing."

"I'm not."

They stared at each other for a long moment. "I'm funny how?" they said at the same time, quoting the movie.

"Do I amuse you?" Kennedy asked.

"Like I'm a fucking clown?" Luke asked.

"Not fucking clown," she said with a laugh. "Just clown."

Luke shook his head. "Damn, Kennedy. It won't be so tough to play your lover."

She sputtered. "You mean my fiancé."

He met her eyes with a smoldering gaze, and her pulse raced. "Same thing, though, isn't it?"

Her mouth was suddenly dry. She took a healthy swallow of margarita, earning a brain freeze. "Ah." She pressed her fingertips to her forehead.

"Press your tongue to the roof of your mouth," Luke said. "It warms it up and makes the brain freeze go away."

She did while he watched. After a few moments it passed. "You're a genius," she said.

He inclined his head. "My brother Jared's a doctor. Clues us in to little gems like that. You get the headache when the cold stuff touches your upper palate."

She rested her chin on her hand. "Fascinating."

He smirked. "Now you're teasing me." He took a sip of his beer. "Anything else you want to know?"

"Sleeping arrangements?" she asked. She never would've brought it up sober, but it was a concern. Bentley and Candy would surely give them the same room.

"I suppose you want me to do the gentlemanly thing and take the floor."

She let out a breath of relief. "That would be great. Thank you!"

"I'm not a gentleman."

She scowled. "I'm not sleeping with you."

"Then you can take the floor. This was your idea."

She gave him a good glare and then just looked her fill. Took in his light brown hair with blond highlights, which must've cost a fortune, dark blue eyes, straight nose, sensual lips curved into a small smile. The sexy trimmed beard. It was all too much. "You're too good looking," she said.

He raised a brow. "Never heard that one. Any other complaints?"

"Yeah." She looked him up and down. "You're too sexy too. With that expensive cologne. The muscular shoulders. The ropey forearms." She jabbed his bicep and met hard muscle. "What, are you a gym rat?"

He flashed a perfect white-toothed smile. "I work out."

She pointed at his mouth. "That perfect smile. Augh!"

The nachos arrived, and she dug in. Some hot cheese burned the roof of her mouth, which she quickly soothed with frozen margarita.

Luke shook his head sadly. "My sins are never-ending. Anything else?"

She lifted a finger. "Yes. Arrogant, overly confident, know-it-all, money-grubbing, unprofessional—"

"Whoa, whoa, whoa. I am *not* unprofessional. Yes to the other things, but not that. I apologized when I stepped over the line. Once." He leaned close. "And correct me if I'm wrong, but I've done nothing but return *your* advances since then."

"What!"

He raised his brows. "You kissed me first *and* you felt up my ass."

"I did not!" She flushed. "You made me grab your ass!"

"When you tried to steal my money."

Her hands formed fists. "That's my money in your back pocket!"

"Kennedy," he said in a calm, low tone.

Her breath was coming hard. "What?"

"Can you sit down? People are staring. You're kinda loud."

She hadn't realized she was standing. She glanced sheepishly around at the curious people at the bar. She slunk back onto the bar stool and took a nacho.

After she chewed, she said, "You shouldn't have let me embarrass myself."

"You're tough to control."

She could hear the smile in his voice and glanced over. He winked. She was torn between slapping him and kissing him. That margarita really went to her head. Never have a margarita on an empty stomach. She ate some more nachos.

"I've got a few complaints too," he drawled.

She scowled. "Like what?" He was probably going to ream her out for bringing him into this stupid fiancé charade in the first place. But these were desperate times—

"Your beauty is much too delicate and feminine for your name."

She jabbed a chip in some guacamole. "I can't help my name." She met his dark blue eyes. "Wait, what?"

"Not only that. You're too, um, hmmm..." He pressed a finger to his lips. "How can I say this without getting in trouble? There's kind of a double standard here."

"What double standard?"

"You can say I'm sexy—" he leaned close, and her breath caught "—which is *awful*, but if I say it back, I come off looking unprofessional."

He raised his brows, waiting for her answer. She stared at his mouth, which was not smiling, but somehow drawing her in. She found herself leaning forward—

And fell right off the bar stool.

CHAPTER FIVE

Luke caught Kennedy before she could hit the ground. Then, shockingly, she wrapped her arms around his waist and buried her head against his chest. He held her for a moment, unsure what to do. Was this a signal? Or was this a friendly hug? His body was urging him to move things forward. To kiss and taste and touch. To bring her back to his place and bury himself deep inside her.

She lifted her head and met his eyes. "I'm sorry," she said softly.

The soft voice triggered a primal instinct to protect. To claim her for himself and keep everyone else away. "For what?"

"For getting you into this mess. I understand if you don't want to go through with it."

He was actually looking forward to it. Not that he wanted spa treatments. But he'd already been fantasizing about Kennedy in nothing but a towel for a massage, and a teeny bikini while they went sailing. Sharing a room would definitely lead to more. That much was crystal clear the more time he spent with her. When he'd sparred with her on the golf course, he'd still been reeling in shock that she was his competitor. But after their kiss he'd seen her a lot differently, not just as a competitor, but as a beautiful, complex, sexy woman.

He faked a grimace. "Oh, I'm going through with it, all right."

"You must hate me," she said miserably, which made him feel guilty.

"Hey, you know—"

"But I have good reasons! My family needs me. They're in debt. Three of my siblings still live at home, the college tuition bill is due for Frank, the rehab center sent the unpaid bills onto a collection agency—"

"Hey, I don't mind." He lifted her by the waist and set her back on the bar stool. He really couldn't hold her much longer without kissing her. Some part of him just wanted to take away all those worries and let her be the carefree twenty-three-year-old she should be. "Let's just enjoy this weekend. No business unless Bentley brings it up. We'll play the couple in love and pretend this is our life. We'll be Bentley and Candy for one fabulous weekend. I think we've earned a weekend of fun."

She was silent.

"What do you say?" he asked, elbowing her. "Can I be the doting boyfriend? Can I say sweet words and hold your hand and—" he let out a mock gasp "—kiss you on the lips?"

She giggled and glanced sideways at him. "Have you ever been the doting boyfriend?"

He hesitated. His longest relationship was three months, and if he was honest, he'd never made much of an effort for any of his relationships. It just wasn't a priority in his life.

"If I say no, will you still let me try?" he asked.

She nodded. He stole a nacho and ate it. She started eating again.

"Sweetcakes," he said, trying it out.

She smiled.

"Honey...pie," he added. "Bentley was a great example." He picked up a nacho loaded with toppings. "Now let's see you do Candy."

She widened her blue eyes. "I wuv you, sugar bear." She leaned in and rubbed noses with him. He froze. Their eyes met and an electric attraction hummed between them. They broke apart.

"Pretty convincing," he said before shoving the nacho in his mouth.

"You too," she said, draining the last of the margarita.

"So, uh…" For only the second time in his life, he was at a loss for words. It was the "wuv" that threw him. The first time had been when Kennedy announced they were engaged.

"Eat," she said, shoving the nacho platter toward him. "I can't finish this whole plate by myself."

They ate for a few moments in silence.

"How come I don't remember you from town?" he asked.

"My dad taught at a private school about an hour from here, so me and my brothers and sisters went to work with him every day. We all went tuition-free. We left really early, like six thirty, and didn't get back until six or seven. He coached after-school sports and we were all required to do them. Plus you were eight years ahead of me in school."

He took a sip of beer. "Yeah, but what about the summer? What about the weekends?"

She shot him a look. "Why do you care so much? I'm sure you wouldn't have given me the time of day. When you were going to prom, I was nine years old."

He dropped his head in his hands and groaned.

She patted his back. "Age is just a number. Don't worry. They make pills for that now."

He shot straight up in his seat. "I don't need a pill to get it up!"

"Dude!" a beefy tattooed guy down the other end

of the bar hollered with a raised fist. "You tell her."

His cheeks burned. He glared at the people staring and tittering around the bar. Kennedy was grinning.

He tugged a lock of her hair and then lingered, stroking her soft hair over her shoulder. "Enjoying yourself?"

She met his eyes with a huge smile. "Yes, I am, actually."

She was getting used to him, getting comfortable, which would've made it easy to go in for the kill and rip this client right out of her grasping fingers, but instead he felt himself softening toward her. He liked her way too much for someone he was competing against.

His voice came out hoarse. "What am I going to do with you?"

"You're going to marry me," she said with a grin.

The truth of those words hit him like an electric shock. "You're right."

She turned back to the nachos, her face flushed pink. "Not for real. For show." She waved a hand in the air. "You know what I mean."

"Yeah." He shook his head. What was wrong with him? Buying into the fantasy. This was pretend. He had to keep his eye on the prize. His gaze caught on Kennedy's delicate jawline, and he turned away. The real prize, he told himself. Not her.

Definitely not her. She was a temporary reward on the way to the prize.

"Come on," he said. "I'll take you home."

"I don't want to go home," she said. "It's early."

"We've got an early gig tomorrow."

She shot him an irritated look and wiped her mouth with a napkin.

He had to get her safely home and away from him. Because the more time he spent with her, the more he wanted her. So badly that he couldn't even take the time for his usual smooth talk and found himself blurting, "You want to go back to my place?"

"To sleep with you?"

"Just to hang out," he said in a last minute attempt at playing it cool. Then he came up with a brilliantly persuasive reason. "We could drive in together to Bentley's place in the morning. More convincing that we're a happily engaged couple that way."

"I guess."

"So you'll come with me?" His voice rose in excitement. *Cool it.*

"I don't think so."

Disappointment made him drop the charming act. "Why not?"

She met his eyes dead-on. "I don't trust you."

"You can trust—"

"You'd probably tie me up in the closet and go to

Bentley's by yourself."

"Tying you up never crossed my mind." But now that he thought about it...

She lifted a finger. Then she wrote down an address on a page in her notebook, ripped it out, and handed it to him. "Pick me up in the morning. I'm on the way to Greenport anyway."

He tried to contain his disappointment. He'd be with her all weekend. What was the rush? He shouldn't sleep with her anyway, right? She could have some devious plan cooking up in that brain of hers. Just look at how she concocted a devious plan for him. As quickly as he thought about the risk of sleeping with her, he shut that worry down. He would given the chance. He didn't live his life by what he should or shouldn't do, only what he could do.

He pulled out his cell. "Number?"

She rattled it off, and he programmed it in. Then she programmed his number and snickered.

"What's so funny?" he asked, pulling her cell toward him. She'd put his name in as Devil.

He held up his cell where he'd entered her name as Honey. His was much more complimentary. It occurred to him that, despite their obvious chemistry, she really did see him just as the enemy. That thought stung more than he'd thought possible.

He stood. "I'll bring you to hell if that's what you

want." He knew how to play hardball. He could get down and dirty with the best of them.

She stood and beamed up at him. "And I'll show you a taste of heaven."

"Fuck," he muttered before he cupped the back of her head, hauling her close and settling his mouth over hers. He didn't care that they were in a crowded bar. The need overwhelmed everything else. She sagged against him as he kissed her long and deep. She tasted like strawberries and spice, her lips soft and warm. His other arm wrapped around her waist, pressing her close. He couldn't stop. The more he kissed her, the more he wanted. *More.* He slid his hand over her ass. *Oh, God, more.*

A few catcalls rang out from around the bar.

He pulled away reluctantly. She stared at him, two fingers over her lips. He was throbbing, painfully hard, and still wanted her with a fierceness that wouldn't easily subside. He had to push her away before he acted on his lustful impulses.

He chucked her under the chin. "You shouldn't have tangled with the devil."

She pulled up her cell and rapidly typed. "There," she said, holding it up to him. "Now you're Grandpa."

He fought back a grin, knowing she was pushing his buttons for the same reason he was pushing hers. To put some space between them. He pulled up his cell and changed her name too. He showed it to her without comment. One word that made her gasp and made him smile.

Mine.

~ ~ ~

Kennedy speedwalked to the bar's exit in as close to a straight line as her still-tipsy body could manage. She desperately needed a breath of fresh air and to get well clear of Luke. Unfortunately, Luke snagged her elbow and walked with her.

"Just mine for the weekend," he said. "No need to freak out."

She shook him off and kept walking. "I'm not freaking out." She knocked into the hostess stand and a pile of menus toppled to the floor. "Sorry!" she said to no one. The hostess had already left after the dinner rush. She squatted down to pick them up, lost her balance, and landed on her ass.

Luke tsked. She glared up at him where he was shaking his head. And not helping her. He definitely wasn't a gentleman. She scrambled up to her knees, gathered all the menus, and put them back on the hostess stand.

Luke looped his arm through hers and walked her out the door.

"Oh, *now* you play the gentleman," she snapped.

"I don't want you falling on your ass again." He stopped on the front sidewalk. "Now I don't want you to get the wrong idea, but I honestly don't think you should drive. Will you come back to my place? You can sleep this off and be ready to go in the morning."

"Ha!" She put her hands on her hips. "Ha-ha-ha! You think I just fell off the turnip truck."

He chuckled. "Yes. It's clear to me you did fall off the turnip truck and into a vat of tequila."

"I'm not going home with you."

He let out a long-suffering sigh. She mimicked him with her own long-suffering sigh.

He smiled, which made her want to smack him. "At least let me drive you home."

"Why was that my second option? Hmmm?" She rose up on tiptoe and got in his face. "Why didn't you say that one first?"

He grinned unrepentantly. "Because I'm a devious non-gentleman."

She backed away. "That's right."

"I'm right here," he said, pointing to his dark blue Porsche just a few feet away. "Where'd you park?"

"In the back lot."

"Then why'd you come out the front?"

"I was in a hurry to get away from you!"

He cocked his head to the side. "Well, that worked out great. You want a ride?"

"Probably a good idea," she admitted. "The streetlights are too bright, and you're practically glowing with a golden aura." She gestured broadly from his shoulders to knees, indicating the aura around his body.

He raised a brow. "Sure, okay. Get in." He unlocked the car and opened the door for her. Once she got in, he got in the other side and handed back her five dollars. She stuffed the money in her purse without comment. "Your car will be fine in the back lot for a few days. This is Clover Park."

She let out a sigh. "I know."

"Where do you live?"

"In the apartments on the edge of town. You know, Clover Ridge."

"Got it."

It suddenly occurred to her as they pulled out on Main Street that maybe Luke shouldn't be driving either. "Maybe we should've gotten a cab."

"Why?"

She studied his hands, which seemed steady on the wheel. "Are you sure it's safe for you to drive?"

"Pfft. I had one beer. I barely got a sip of the second one because I was too busy finding out all about the length and duration of your sexy times." He chuckled.

She crossed her arms and stared out the window.

But then curiosity got the better of her. "What about yours?"

"Nothing special."

He glanced over at her, and her gaze caught on his mouth, remembering the way it had felt against hers, firm and just right, the rough feel of his beard. She sighed.

One corner of his mouth lifted. "You okay over there?"

"Yes." She straightened up and forced her gaze back to his eyes, but he was looking at the road. She admired his profile for a long moment—stop it. She had on margarita goggles. As soon as she sobered up, she'd remember how horrible he was. He was her biggest threat, her competitor. *The enemy.*

She ran her fingers through the soft hair at the nape of his neck. He was quiet, so she kept doing it.

"What was your longest relationship?" she asked. "Have you ever been in love?"

"Three months and no."

She ran her fingers through her own hair. Somehow his was softer. She played with his hair again. "That's good."

"Why is that good?"

"Because love makes you do stupid things. Least that's what my mom always says, and considering how things worked out for her and my dad, I'd have to say she's right."

"How did things work out for them?"

"Lots of love, not a lot of money."

"That doesn't sound so bad."

She dropped her hand. "It sucks to be poor!"

"I can't believe I'm saying this, but are they happy?"

She rolled down the window and stuck her head out in the breeze.

"Kennedy?"

"Would you please stop calling me that? You make it sound like a pretty name and it's not. It's plain."

"You are anything but plain."

She turned back to him. "They were happy until the money dried up. So obviously love can only take you so far."

"You've never been in love either," he said.

"How can you tell?"

"Because you're so cynical about it. I get it. But I gotta tell you, I've seen it in action. My brother Nico fell hard. And, honestly, after his first marriage, I never thought he'd marry again. I've never seen him so happy. He's getting married next month."

"Well, goody for him."

He snorted. "Yeah. Goody for him. So hurry up and fill me in on you. Any allergies? What do you do when you're not pretending to be engaged or drinking too much or bagging rich clients?"

She put both hands to her head. "One question at a time. Geez. My head is spinning."

"What do you like to do?"

"Not much. I work, I help out with my younger brothers and sisters."

"Help out how?"

"I make sure they get their homework done, their clothes are clean, their lunches packed, and dinner made."

"Your parents don't do any of that?"

"My dad can't. He's disabled. My mom is doing some of that, in between working and driving my dad to doctor appointments. I'm just picking up the slack. It's easy for a kid to get lost in the shuffle."

He stopped at a stop sign. There wasn't much traffic in Clover Park. "You still live at home?"

"Yeah. It's just easier that way. I can help out. Save on rent."

"Wow. More power to you. I love my family, but I couldn't wait to have my own place. King of my own domain, ya know?"

She couldn't imagine living alone. "Don't you ever get lonely?"

He hit the accelerator and didn't answer right away. Finally, he said, "Nah. How could I with such a big family? I just pop back home for Sunday night dinner and the whole gang's there. Some sister-in-laws now too and a baby nephew, Miles."

She shuddered. "I'm in no hurry to have kids. I've spent most of my life helping raise the younger ones. Oldest girl is a built-in babysitter."

"Huh."

"What's that mean?"

"Nothing."

"It must mean something."

He lifted one shoulder up and down. "Nothing. Just maybe one day you'll meet a man and you'll want to have his babies." He shook his head with a smile. "Listen to me, I sound like my sister-in-law Zoe. She's rubbing off on all of us with her dream of seeing me and all of my brothers married with babies."

"I'd only have kids if my husband helped *a lot*. Better yet, he could stay home with them while I go to work."

"I'm sure anyone you marry would be willing to do their part. You'd settle for nothing less."

She yawned. "Damn right." Unlike her dad. Her parents' marriage was very traditional with her dad making the money and ordering everyone around while her mom stayed home and took care of the house and kids. It had worked great until her dad couldn't do his role anymore. She wasn't sure her parents would ever adjust to a new way of doing things. One that required her mom to take on the leadership role while her dad stayed in the background.

Luke tugged a lock of her hair. "Look who's getting sleepy at such an early time on a Friday night. Now who's acting like a senior citizen?"

"Shut up," she muttered. Next thing she knew Luke was nudging her shoulder.

"We're here," he said.

She must've drifted off for a few minutes. "I'm awake."

"See you bright and early tomorrow. Six fifteen."

She gazed at him. He gazed back. She couldn't help but feel drawn to his confident, altogether appealing demeanor. She reached out and stroked his soft beard. "This tickled me when you kissed me. I've never been kissed by a man with a beard."

"Anything else you'd like to try with a man with a beard?" He waggled his brows. "I could think of a few things."

Heat pooled between her legs as she imagined one of those things vividly. "Nothing!" she blurted, her cheeks burning. "I can't think of a single thing!"

He barked out a laugh. She shook her head and hurried out of the car and over to her first-floor apartment. Luke waited for her to get inside, which was kind of sweet. She wiggled her fingers at him. It wasn't so bad having a fake fiancé.

CHAPTER SIX

Having a fake fiancé was the worst thing that had ever happened to her. First of all, Luke shaved his beard. She really wished he hadn't done that. Because now he didn't look too old for her. He looked young, could pass for twenties, and he was breathtakingly beautiful—cheekbones women would kill for, a strong jaw, and sensuous lips that seemed to be permanently curved into a small smile that drove her crazy. Like he knew the effect he was having on her. Without the beard, his dark blue eyes were all she could focus on, drawing her in, again and again. Well, except for his body, which filled out a white T-shirt just tight enough to show off his broad shoulders and defined biceps. She was sure he'd chosen that color and fit to flaunt his golden tan and muscles. To her dismay, he was in full-on doting-boyfriend mode. And he was good at it.

She seriously wanted to kill him.

He was messing with her head just so he could get the advantage with Bentley. He had to be. There was no way he suddenly fell in love with her overnight.

Though it really felt like it. The minute they arrived at Bentley's "cottage," aka a huge mansion, Luke was super affectionate. He walked around the front of his Porsche and let her out of the car. Then he carried her duffel bag for her, riding along on top of his Porsche wheeled suitcase (yes, Porsche like his car), and entwined his fingers with hers as they walked to greet their hosts. Bentley and Candy waved enthusiastically from where they stood on the other end of the circular driveway by the front door.

She took in the mansion—a sprawling arts and crafts two-story home with attached five-car garage. Solar panels on the garage roof surprised her. It had a huge front porch the length of the house, with rocking chairs where she'd love to sit and not worry about her family or her job or her fake fiancé.

"Welcome to the cottage!" Candy exclaimed when they reached them. She hugged each of them in turn.

Bentley kissed her on the cheek and shook Luke's hand. "Welcome! Right this way to start your relaxing weekend! Staff is ready for you." He signaled to a young man waiting by the garage, who hurried over. "Joe will park your car for you."

Luke slowly handed over his keys. "Easy on the

clutch."

Joe nodded quickly. "Of course, sir."

She felt frozen in place. They had staff at their beck and call. She could never fit in here.

"Let's go, sweetheart," Luke said, giving her a little tug.

She followed him into a large two-story foyer done entirely in honey golden wood—hardwood floors, wood-paneled walls, and a long wood staircase. Above her hung a chandelier of artistically twisted wood.

A middle-aged woman with dark brown hair fashioned into a neat chignon approached. Her white pants suit had crisp creases in the pants. She stopped in front of her and Luke and greeted them with a nod. "Hello, Mr. Reynolds, Ms. Ward, I'm Elizabeth, and I will see to whatever you need this weekend."

"Nice to meet you," Kennedy said, feeling sure she could never ask the woman for anything. She was used to doing whatever needed doing herself.

"Let us know if we get out of hand," Luke said with a wink.

The woman blushed and smiled. "Rascal," she said. Then she seemed to remember herself and got serious. "Your room is upstairs, third on the right. Change into the robes and come back here. I'll show you to the spa for your body scrub."

Kennedy swallowed hard. She'd brought a bikini,

hoping she could get away with wearing that for the couples spa treatments. She wasn't quite ready for couples naked time in front of Luke and spa people she'd never met. Suddenly even the bikini felt risky with the affectionate, young, and ready-to-prove-his-virility Luke around. She really wished she could put his beard back on him. It was much easier to see him as too old for her then.

"Thank you," Luke said. He led the way upstairs, and she followed behind.

Their room was huge, done in masculine shades of deep red and taupe with a mission-style king-size bed and way more furniture than they'd ever need. Two dressers, an armoire, nightstands, a bench at the end of the bed, a sitting area with two high-back chairs and matching footstools. Paintings of beach scenes decorated the walls.

"Nice," Luke said. He pointed to the bench at the end of the bed. "There's your bunk."

"Ha-ha."

His lips curved into a knowing smile that made her want to smack it right off. He was enjoying this entirely too much at her expense.

He set down the luggage by the bench and wandered into the en suite bathroom. "Kennedy," he called, "you've got to see this shower."

She peeked into a huge glass stall. "Holy crap!

That's bigger than my bathroom at home."

He went up close to it. She joined him and looked around. "Do they have enough spray going on?" she asked. It was a double tiled stall with a long bench running along the back wall. There were two rainshower spouts from the ceiling, two regular showerheads, and two shower hoses. "I imagine it would be tough to miss a spot."

He grinned. "It has steam too." He pointed out the dial for steam. "This is going to be fun."

She took a step back. Then another. "I'm not showering with you."

"Steam?" he asked. "With towel?"

She eyed the long bench in the stall, imagining the luxury of just sitting there, letting the steam melt her cares away. She turned back to him. "Maybe."

He grinned. "You know you want to. Look, I know you don't know me that well, but I promise I'm not going to suddenly turn animal on you. So relax. This'll be a fun weekend. We'll make a good impression on Bentley and not worry about business until the day we leave. That's three days of fun. You with me?" He held out a hand to her, palm up.

She stared at his hand. He wiggled his fingers, gesturing her over. The invitation promised fun, and she found herself drawing closer before finally putting her hand in his. He pulled her in close so they were toe-to-toe. She looked up at those dark blue eyes twinkling with mischief, and immediately had second thoughts.

"You know we can't really get involved, right?" she asked. "I just want to be sure you know that. The last thing I need is to get involved with a business associate."

He dropped her hand. "I'm not your associate. I'm your competitor."

"Exactly."

"So we won't get involved."

"Oh." She felt silly. "Good."

"Good." He regarded her seriously, his dark blue eyes searching hers. "How old do I look without the beard?"

She looked away because he was way too good looking without it. "I don't know."

"Come on. Throw me a bone. Tell me I don't look like a grandpa."

Her lips twitched. "You don't look like a grandpa."

"Uncle?"

She met his eyes and grinned. "Brother."

He gave her ponytail a tug. "Let's find those robes and get scrubbed down." He made a funny, snarly face. "You ever get scrubbed before?"

She wrinkled her nose. "No."

"A first for both of us." He crossed back to the

bedroom. He returned to the bathroom a moment later with two thick white robes. "Are we supposed to be naked under these? I never did a day at the spa before."

"I won't be."

"What're you wearing?"

"My swimsuit."

"Okay, I will too." He pulled off his T-shirt and she took in the most beautiful man chest she'd ever seen with a smattering of chest hair leading to a happy trail and a bulging...she jerked her gaze back to his. He grinned and turned to go back to the bedroom. His back was all golden skin and muscular. "I feel you looking," he called over his shoulder.

"I was not looking!" She slammed the bathroom door. Then she remembered her swimsuit was out there in her duffel bag. She waited a few minutes before finally calling, "Are you decent?"

"Sometimes," he called back.

She blew out a breath of aggravation. "I mean are you dressed?"

"No."

"Tell me when you're dressed. I left my swimsuit out there."

A beat passed. "Okay, I'm dressed."

She stepped out to find him standing there in blue and green swim trunks, looking all relaxed and casual.

She hurried past him, pulled out her black bikini from her duffel bag, and rushed back toward the bathroom.

"Slow down," Luke said in a teasing tone. "You're going to break something running around like a scared deer."

She stopped dead in her tracks. "I am *not* a scared deer."

"I told you, just relax. It's going to be a fun weekend. Loosen up."

She glared at him, mostly because he seemed so casual, and she was very close to freaking out. "I can't relax just because you told me to," she huffed. "I have to get comfortable. These things take time." She shook her bikini at him. "Don't you know anything about women?"

He tilted his head. "Apparently not."

"Well, stop telling me to relax." She shook her bikini at him again. "Stop leering at me." Another shake. "And stop flirting."

"Is that a bikini?" he asked. "It looks nice and skimpy."

She barely resisted stamping her foot. "Did you hear anything I said?"

"And what would you like me to do instead?" He crossed his arms, making his biceps bulge. "Educate the Neanderthal man you're engaged to."

She waved the bikini in the air. "Just act normal."

"I am acting normal."

"Then act like me. Friendly, but not too friendly."

He pointed at her. "You got it."

She walked at a leisurely pace into the bathroom, not wanting Luke to think she was acting like a scared deer. Okay, she was nervous. She could admit it. She'd never done the full spa treatment and certainly never with a man she barely knew. A flirtatious, entirely too good-looking, sexy man, who clearly wasn't too old for her. If she'd met him at a bar, she would've—

She took a deep breath in and out before stripping down and slipping into the black bikini. It was a simple top that tied in the back with a decorative silver ring between her breasts and matching rings by each hip. She wasn't big on top, or bottom, actually. She had an athletic, almost boyish build, with small breasts and narrow hips. She sighed. Put her next to the busty Candy and she knew where all the attention would be. Which was just fine. She pulled on the robe and finally relaxed as the warmth and thickness of it enveloped her. It hung all the way down to her ankles. She stepped out of the bathroom.

Luke immediately hurried to the other side of the room. "Don't look at me," he called in a falsetto. "I need my robe."

She grabbed his robe where he'd left it on the bed and handed it to him. He took it and then took a big step back from her, eyes wide. Then he quickly turned his back to her and slid the robe on like he had something to hide.

"Okay, I get it," she said. "Dork."

He turned and grinned. "Comfortable now?"

She shook her head, an unwilling smile tugging at her lips.

He crossed to her, dropped an arm over her shoulders and pulled her close, placing a kiss on top of her head. "Let's go get scrubbed."

They walked downstairs, barefoot, where Elizabeth waited exactly where they'd left her. "Follow me," she said briskly.

They walked past a huge family room filled with more mission-style furniture, a billiards room, and a library to get to a long hallway that led to a private spa. She and Luke exchanged a look. The spa section was hidden from the front of the house. They stepped inside a dimly lit room with two massage tables already draped with crisp white sheets. Classical music played through speakers in the ceiling, accompanied by the soothing sound of rushing water from a waterfall display in the corner. A young blond woman stepped into the room from another door and greeted them warmly.

"So nice to meet friends of Bentley's," she said. "I'm Pam. And you must be the happily engaged couple Luke and Ken."

"That's us," Luke said.

"Bentley told us all about you," Pam said with a bright smile.

"He did?" Kennedy asked.

"Sure, we had a staff meeting via video conference call yesterday. You can remove your robes and lie down on your stomachs. First we'll exfoliate with the body scrub, followed by hot towels and a massage. Then it's on to the outdoor waterfall shower. Sound good?"

"Yes," Kennedy said stiffly. She waited for Luke to take off his robe first.

"Here, let me help you with that, honey," Luke said, untying the belt on her robe.

She couldn't push him away and the devilish look in his eye said he knew that very well. This was part of the charade. The last thing she needed was Pam reporting back to Bentley that they weren't what they seemed.

He made short work of it and pushed the robe off her shoulders, taking her in as he slipped it off her arms and away from her. He swallowed visibly, no hint of mischief in his eyes, only heat. She quickly climbed up on the table and lay face down. She turned her head toward Luke. He disrobed and climbed up on the other table.

He made a small kissy noise at her. She felt herself flush and turned her head the other way.

"What kind of scrub would you like?" Pam asked. "We have apricot, blueberry, or coconut."

"We'll both take coconut," Luke said.

Kennedy turned her head back to face him. "We will?"

"We don't want to clash. We should smell the same, right?"

"And what's wrong with apricot?"

He raised his brows. "You have to ask? I don't want to smell like fruit. I want to smell like a tropical beach."

"Very good choice," Pam said.

Pam got to work on Luke's back. He winked at Kennedy. She turned her head the other way.

The door opened again and a large blond man walked in. "There you are, David," Pam said. "She's ready for you."

Kennedy stiffened. How could she possibly relax with a large man she never met putting his hands all over her?

"Nope," Luke said. "No man's hands touch my future wife except mine. Pam, you just mosey right over there to Kennedy."

She turned her head back to Luke and he nodded almost imperceptibly. She fell in serious like with him for understanding her concern.

Pam chuckled. "Young love."

Luke eyed David. "I'll wait for Pam."

"But then it's not a couples massage and treatment," David complained. "I'm very skilled. This is why I'm here."

Kennedy quickly changed gears. Luke wasn't comfortable with a guy massaging him. She didn't want to make things difficult when Bentley had gone to all this trouble on their behalf. "It's fine. David can do my treatment."

Pam and David worked efficiently, exfoliating them with the coconut body scrub, working over their backs and then their fronts. She quickly got used to David's hands and found herself relaxing with his firm, strong touch.

"David will be back in a minute with the hot towels," Pam said. "Go ahead and lie on your stomachs again." She busied herself putting things away.

"I feel very fresh," Luke whispered.

She suppressed a giggle. "You look very fresh," she whispered back.

David returned with a stack of steaming hot towels that he and Pam layered over them. It felt heavenly. She relaxed with a soft *aah*.

After several minutes with the hot towels, Pam and

David brought over some massage oil. "Would you mind if I untied your top?" David asked Kennedy. "It'll be easier without the strings in the way."

"Uh, sure." He untied it.

"Nothing I haven't seen before, right, honey?" Luke asked.

Everyone laughed except her. She was not turning over without everything securely in place.

"You really should take off the bottoms too," Pam said. "I'll put a towel over you for privacy. You too, Luke."

Luke peeled off his trunks without hesitation. Kennedy quickly looked away, but not before catching a glimpse of tight butt. Geez. Now what? Should she tell Luke to close his eyes?

And then without her saying a word, he did. Just closed his eyes on his own. She pulled a towel over her and quickly slipped her bottoms off.

Then they started the massage, each masseuse working on them from neck to shoulders to back, over the butt, and down their legs. Twenty minutes in, she felt like a limp noodle. She'd never had a massage in her life. She had to save up and get more of these.

"You can roll over now," Pam said to Luke.

She couldn't help it. She peeked. Sweet glory, the man was hung. And then he was covered again.

"You too," David said to her.

"Uh, can I get my top back?" Kennedy asked.

"Of course." David helped her put it back on, tying it in the back. She carefully rolled over, making sure the towel covered her.

David started on her scalp, and she relaxed again. Thirty minutes later, they finished. She and Luke sat up. She smiled at him goofily. He grinned.

"Onto the rinse," David said. "Right this way."

They followed him outside to an eight-foot waterfall shower. David stuck his hand in, testing the water. "Nice and warm. Just rinse, and when you're done, follow the stone path around to the side door for your soak."

David left. She and Luke dropped their towels on a nearby bench, still wearing their swimsuits. She added her hair band too. Luke grabbed her hand and pulled her under the spray. She felt like she was under a real waterfall. The water pressure was amazing. Luke soaked his hair and pushed it back. The water ran over him in rivulets, making him look like one of those cologne ads where the guy just stepped out of the water, dripping muscles and sex.

She closed her eyes and tipped her head back in the spray. "We reek of coconut, don't we?"

"Yeah. But nothing a waterfall and a soak can't cure. I like your bikini."

She opened her eyes. Yup, still under a waterfall

with a sex god. He was staring at her, probably waiting for a response. Her bikini wasn't anything fancy like his designer stuff. "I got it at Target."

He laughed. "I don't care where you got it. I just like that it's on you."

"Oh."

His gaze dropped to her breasts, down to her flat stomach, her boyish hips, all the way down to her toes. He was king of the smoldering once-over. "Very nice, Kennedy."

"I'm too relaxed to be annoyed with you," she said before doing a slow turn, rinsing herself off.

He slid a hand down her wet back, stopping to rest just above her ass. "What'd I do now?"

She turned back and held up his straying hand. "Flirty, inappropriate leering and touching."

"Aww…you're too hard on me."

She dropped his hand. "I'm not hard enough."

"That makes one of us."

She glanced down to see he was plenty hard. She flushed and met his eyes. "Now why do you look proud?"

"I'm proving my virility," he quipped.

She rolled her eyes. "I'm going for that soak." She turned to go, and he snagged her by the elbow. Water ran down his beautiful face, his golden muscular chest, over the, *gulp*, bulge. She tore her gaze away.

"Kennedy, you do realize we're supposed to soak together."

She hadn't. "I'm sure it's a big tub."

"Doesn't matter how big. It's still a tub." He stroked her jaw. "Our body parts might touch. Think you can handle it?"

She lifted her chin defiantly. "I can handle whatever you dish out."

His dark blue eyes sparked with challenge. "I haven't even begun to dish anything out."

"Let's do this, Reynolds."

He smiled like he'd won some big victory. Ha! He gestured for her to step out of the spray first. "After you, Ward."

Sure, he sounded like a gentleman, but he was probably just checking out her ass. Not one to back down from a challenge, she turned and stepped out. Two neatly folded white towels waited for them on a nearby bench. Their previous pile of towels and her hair band were nowhere to be seen. She grabbed the fresh towel and wrapped it around her. He tied the other around his waist, and they headed down the path together.

"Hi, Ken!" Candy called, waving, as she approached from behind a small sand dune on the Long Island Sound side of the property. Kennedy had been to the Sound before, though not on private property. The beach was mostly gritty sand with some rocks and broken shells. She liked the Sound because the water was calmer than the ocean, with gently lapping waves. A mix of salt water from the nearby Atlantic Ocean and fresh water from the Catawan River on the other side of the property fed into it.

Bentley was at her side. "Hi, Luke! Hi, Ken! Are you feeling relaxed yet?"

"Absolutely," Luke said.

"It was wonderful," Kennedy said. "We're about to soak."

"Enjoy!" Bentley said. "We'll catch up with you at lunch. We're going to have our massage now."

Luke entwined his fingers with hers, and they continued down the winding stone path to the far end of the spa. "They're nice people."

"They are." She lowered her voice. "I don't know why people give Bentley a hard time. His heart's in the right place."

"You need more than heart to be a smart investor," Luke said under his breath. "He's not."

"That's why he'll need me."

"That's why he'll need *me*."

She pressed her lips together. The tension that had been massaged out of her started to build again.

Luke squeezed her hand. "Sorry. I promised no business until the last day. I can feel you tensing already. Relax."

He picked up the pace toward their destination and opened the side door. They stepped into a dimly lit, tiled room with an enormous heart-shaped tub full of bubbles and surrounded by glowing votive candles. Two flutes of champagne stood on the edge of the tub. Slow jazz played through some speakers in the ceiling.

Luke rubbed his jaw. "So this is romantic."

She turned to him. "Yeah." She'd never seen anything like it in real life. Only on TV.

"We should get in, I guess." He suddenly seemed nervous, which made her want to laugh. He was afraid of a little bubbles?

She slipped into the tub, leaving her bikini on and relaxing into the steaming hot water. "It's great. Come in."

He slipped in on the opposite side from her and stretched out, resting his head on the back of the tub. "This is nice. Just don't come over here."

"Why not?"

"It's a little too romantic. I'm afraid you'll get the wrong idea." He winked.

She rolled her eyes. Then she picked up a flute of champagne and took a sip of the bubbly crisp drink. Damn, she could get used to this kind of life.

He stretched out his hand like he was grasping for the other champagne flute, which was near her, a good four feet away. "Could you pass me the champagne?"

She got his flute and scooted over by him. He took it, set it on the side ledge, grabbed her and settled her on his lap.

"You tricked me," she said over her shoulder.

"I got lonely way over here."

She sipped her champagne, set the flute on the side, and rested her head back against his shoulder. His arms wrapped around her. She could feel his hardness pressing against her hip, but she was too relaxed to move or complain.

"Did you ever think when you met me on the golf course on Monday that by Saturday you'd be sitting in a love tub with me?" he asked in her ear.

A hot shiver went through her. "That's how all my business meetings end."

He chuckled. "I like you. I didn't want to, but I sure do."

"I like you too," she admitted. She took another sip of champagne and then she just floated, relaxing against him. The music changed from jazz to a sexy hip-hop beat, the lyrics quite explicit. *Fuck you hard, fuck you on the inside...*

"It's Candy and Bentley's sex playlist," Luke quipped.

She burst out laughing. Then she had a horrifying thought. "You think they did it in this tub?"

"Probably."

She tried to leap up, but Luke held her in place. "Don't worry. I'm sure they have staff that cleans everything."

She shuddered. "What else do you think they have planned for us?"

"I have no idea." He rested his chin on her bare shoulder. "How do you top a coconut scrub, hot towels, massage, shower, and soak in a tub?"

"Sex?"

He pushed her hair to the side and kissed the nape of her neck, sending electric frissons of sensation down her spine. "You think they have an official sex time around here? A prelunch appointment?"

She giggled.

"The whole house shaking to the rafters." He moved his legs, shaking her a little on his lap. "Ooh, yes. Bennie! Oh, Candy. Oh-oh-oh!"

"Luke!" she said on a laugh.

He stopped the shaking, and she turned in his arms. He grinned. She couldn't help herself, she stroked one hand over his cheek and jaw, which felt a little rough with stubble. His smile dropped.

"I just wanted to feel without the beard," she said softly.

"Anything else you want to do without the beard?" he asked in a husky voice. His gaze dropped to her mouth. It felt like the most natural thing in the world to lean forward and press her lips to his.

He took over the kiss, pressing closer, and then his tongue slipped in, tasting hers. She moaned and wrapped her arms around his neck. He kissed her deeper, his hands sliding down her back, pulling her so she straddled his lap. His hands slid up to cup her head, one hand tangling in her hair as he kissed her into a druggingly relaxed state of pure surrender. He broke the kiss and stared at her, his dark blue eyes smoldering.

"This doesn't mean we're getting involved," she quickly said.

"We're not getting involved," he agreed before claiming her mouth again.

She tore her mouth away. "It's just not a good idea."

"Terrible," he agreed, leaning in for another kiss.

She slammed a hand on his chest. "Terrible?"

"I, uh, thought we were on the same page." He kissed her jaw. "Weekend of fun."

She slid off his lap.

"What's the problem?" he asked with an edge to his voice.

She stood and stepped out of the tub, quickly snagging her robe and yanking it on. She'd nearly lost sight of her goal. Hooking up with Luke was not a good idea. He was her competitor. Bentley had narrowed it down to just the two of them, and she couldn't afford to give Luke any advantage. Already she'd forgotten the need to prepare for her lunch meeting with Bentley and Candy.

"This weekend is business," she told him before hurrying to the door. She'd nearly made her escape when she heard him holler after her.

"We agreed to fun!"

CHAPTER SEVEN

Kennedy had only made it halfway down the stone path back toward the house when she saw Bentley, Candy, and an elderly bald man wearing round spectacles standing on the veranda as if they were waiting for her. She slowed her steps, thinking they'd want to know where Luke was and why she wasn't with him, when Luke appeared at her side, out of breath.

"Hi, honey," he said in a low voice. "What's with the posse?"

She let out a breath of relief that she wouldn't have to explain anything to Bentley and Candy. "I have no idea," she said under her breath.

Bentley beamed at them as soon as they reached the veranda. "Ken, Luke!" he called. "Meet Master Johnson."

Kennedy stepped forward, greeting him and shaking his hand. Luke followed suit.

"We ran into him before our massage," Bentley said, "and knew we had to wait on our massage so that you and Luke could meet him as soon as possible."

Kennedy shot Luke a look. Had Bentley and Candy known what was going on in that soaking tub? Had they changed the music on purpose to move things along? Luke lifted a brow as if to say *who knows?*

Bentley went on. "He's our love guru, and we're so lucky he was available this weekend at the last minute. He's going to give you the same session that Candy and I had before our marriage."

"Kennedy and I are fine," Luke said firmly. "We don't need counseling. Thanks anyway, we're going to—"

"Oh, he's not a counselor," Candy said. "He's a spiritual guru. He's going to get to the heart of your true path and help guide you into a marriage that keeps you both fulfilled."

Kennedy piped up. "That's very generous, but really not necessary."

The guru took her arm and started walking.

"Shouldn't we dress?" she asked in a last desperate attempt to avoid love counseling.

Luke appeared at her other side and took her hand.

"Don't worry!" Candy called. "You don't have to dress! The sessions are naked so you don't have anything to hide. It's sym-bol-ic."

"But I like my clothes!" Kennedy called over her shoulder. She was still pretty relaxed from the earlier massage, soak, and champagne. Just not *that* relaxed.

They walked past an infinity pool to the other side of the property where a small teepee stood.

"We're going in," Luke said in a mock serious voice. Like they were heading into battle.

She giggled. Maybe they were. When she'd imagined this weekend, naked couples therapy had never entered the picture. She briefly considered bolting, but that wasn't her. She'd see this through to the end, doing whatever it took to win.

~ ~ ~

Luke settled cross-legged on a woven mat on the canvas floor of the teepee across from the so-called guru. The man had insisted they leave their robes on a hook by the entrance. Luke sat in his wet swim trunks, refusing to strip down for a guy. He doubted Kennedy would either. Though she was pretty loosey-goosey right now.

"Please sit with your beloved," Master Johnson said to Kennedy, indicating the mat where Luke sat. "I will secure the circle with the sage stick, and then you may remove your swimsuits."

He lit a big wad of tied sticks and began an incantation in a foreign language, probably made up, swirling it in the air as he moved in a circle around the teepee.

Kennedy plopped down next to him and whispered loudly in his ear, "He can't be serious! We're not doing naked counseling."

Luke slowly shook his head.

"If you're more comfortable in wet swimsuits," Master Johnson said, "stay in wet swimsuits."

"How 'bout naked under a robe?" Luke asked. Because while he wouldn't mind seeing Kennedy naked, he wasn't too keen on Master Johnson witnessing the same. "Still very symbolic. Right, honey?"

She nodded. They both grabbed their robes and took off their swimsuits underneath. After they hung the wet suits on the hook, they returned to the mat.

Master Johnson settled cross-legged on a smaller mat across from them. "Perhaps this clinging to an outer covering symbolizes a protective shell for both of you," he said in a grave voice.

"Perhaps," Luke replied cheerfully.

Kennedy fidgeted at his side. "I like my shell," she blurted.

Master Johnson harrumphed and steepled his fingers in front of him. "So where should we begin?"

"You tell us, Master Love," Luke said. This was a bunch of hooey. But he'd do whatever Bentley wanted.

It would all be worth it to bag him as a client. Kennedy bit her lip, trying not to smile.

"What do you hope for in the marriage?" Master Love asked.

"Happiness?" Luke guessed.

Master Love considered that answer in a grave manner. "Is that a question?"

"Happiness," Luke repeated firmly.

Kennedy turned mute. She busied herself playing with the edge of her robe. He was really starting to feel alone in this marriage.

Luke elbowed her, and she jolted upright. "I agree," she said.

"I see," Master Love said, his tone dripping with disapproval. "And do you expect your partner to make you happy?"

"Yes," he and Kennedy replied in unison. At least they were on the same page. *Agree, agree, agree, and get out of here.*

"No," Master Love snapped. "You must never seek happiness from another. You must be happy on your own."

"Then why bother getting married?" Luke asked.

"Yeah," Kennedy said. "Why bother?"

Master Love looked from Kennedy to Luke. "Are you sure you wish to be married?"

"Yes," Kennedy said firmly.

"Luke?" Master Love asked.

"I do," he said, which made Kennedy jump. He bit back a smile. He loved getting a rise out of her.

"Okay, then." The love guru rubbed his hands together. "I can see I have my work cut out with you two. Let's start at the beginning. Birthday and year. I will study your astrological chart and work from there."

Kennedy raised her hand like they were in school. Luke gave her a sideways look. She dropped her hand. "I don't believe in astrology," she said.

Luke hitched a thumb in her direction. "What she said."

Master Love's face flushed red before he took a calming breath of spirituality. He folded his hands in front of him. "And what *do* you believe in?"

"Capitalism," Kennedy said.

"The free market," Luke said.

"Good one," Kennedy said. He nodded in acknowledgement of the compliment.

Master Love bristled. "Is this a merger or a marriage?"

"Both," Luke said.

Kennedy squirmed at his side. She wanted out of this teepee as badly as he did.

"How long have you been together?" Master Love inquired in a strained voice.

"Four months," Kennedy said.

"That's not long," Master Love said. "Perhaps it would be wise—"

"We love each other," Luke interrupted. "Why wait? She's not getting any younger."

"Neither are you!" Kennedy huffed.

"And do you want children?" Master Love asked.

"Yes," Luke said at the same time Kennedy said, "Maybe."

They both looked at her. "A long, long time down the road," she added.

Master Love took another calming spiritual breath. "Let's complete our circle." He reached for both of their hands so the three of them held hands in a circle. "Close your eyes," he said, closing his eyes.

Kennedy kept her eyes open. Luke knew because his were open too. They took one look at each other and nearly bust a gut trying not to laugh. But they couldn't piss off the love guru. Bentley would definitely not appreciate that.

Luke moaned. "I'm feeling it. The spirit of true love is moving within me."

Kennedy bit her lip to keep from laughing.

"What is it saying?" Master Love asked in a hushed voice. His eyes were still closed.

"It's telling me there's an aura in here," Luke said in a burst of inspiration. "Purple. For the highest, purest love." He amped up his voice. "It's surrounding us. Kennedy! Do you see it?"

Master Love opened his eyes and studied their aura.

"I see it!" Kennedy exclaimed. "Oh, Luke, it's so beautiful." She stood, pulling him with her, and started swaying.

"Is the spirit of love moving you too?" Master Love asked Kennedy.

"Yes!" She waved her arms over her head and swayed back and forth. "It's telling me the merger of our souls is destiny."

"Destiny!" Luke exclaimed before scooping her up in his arms and carrying her right out of the teepee.

"Wait!" Master Love called. "Where are you going?"

"When the spirit of love moves you like this, it's straight to bed!" Luke called over his shoulder.

Kennedy giggled. He heard a rustle behind him like Master Love had just left the teepee.

"Shh," he told her. "He's following us."

Master Love appeared at their side and took them in. "I suppose that's the physical embodiment of your love. And since you already felt the spiritual—"

"We couldn't have done it without you," Luke said. "We are in your debt. Thank you."

The man flushed pink. "Of course. That's what

I'm here for. I'm—"

"Bye, Master Johnson!" Kennedy called.

Luke picked up the pace. Once he'd cleared the corner of the house, he glanced over his shoulder to make sure they weren't being followed. "He's gone."

Kennedy laughed. "Do you think people really believe in that stuff?"

He loved seeing her laugh, looking so carefree. "Well, it works for some people. Bentley, for one."

"Can you imagine getting naked in front of Master Johnson while he's asking all those probing questions?"

"Do you think he gets down to his birthday suit too?"

"Oh, geez, I hope not!"

He kept walking, carrying her back to the house.

"Luke, you can put me down now."

"I can't. The love guru glued you in place. If I drop you, it'll break the bond."

She giggled. "Who was that guy?"

"Probably some accountant who gets off on hanging out with naked couples."

"He probably gets paid thousands just to tell them they'll be happy soul mates forever. As if there is such a thing!"

"Right?" He gazed down at her. Her expression was relaxed and happy, and she was stroking his arm. "See, this is why my idea for a weekend of fun makes sense. We both know it's not forever. What Bentley and Candy have is a fluke. A lightning strike."

She stopped stroking his arm. "Could you put me down?"

"Nope."

She sighed, but she didn't fight him on it. "If I met you any other way, I might consider…something fun, but it just doesn't make good business sense to get in bed with my only competitor. He said he narrowed it down to the two of us."

"And you think hooking up gives me the advantage?"

"Yes!"

"I already have the advantage," he said matter-of-factly. "I'm more qualified with more experience."

"That's honest," she huffed.

"Here's some more honesty for you. Whether or not we hook up has absolutely no bearing on the outcome of this weekend. So can we just have fun and put business on the back burner?"

"This side of you is so unattractive," she said through her teeth.

"What side?"

"Arrogant, overly—"

"Hush now." Elizabeth, the housekeeper, opened the French doors to let them in the back of the house.

He nodded at Elizabeth and continued on, taking

Kennedy straight to their bedroom as the love guru expected. He'd probably already reported back to Bentley and Candy about the "success" of their session.

He kicked the door shut behind them and set her on the bed. Her robe gaped open, giving him a glimpse of the curve of one breast and her smooth, flat stomach. She quickly tucked it back around her.

He sat next to her and stroked her hair back from her face. It was in wild disarray, half wet still from their outdoor shower.

She scooted toward the edge of the bed. "I'm going to get dressed."

"But the love guru thinks we're doing it," he said with a grin.

She rolled her eyes and stood.

"Come on. We should at least bounce around and make some noises so they think we're doing it. Elizabeth is probably listening to report on our progress."

"Go for it. I'm getting dressed."

He bounced a few times, making the mattress squeak. "Oh, Luke," he said in a falsetto. "You're the king!"

She rushed back. "Shut up," she hissed, her blue eyes flashing fire at him. "I don't sound like that at all! I would never call you king!"

"Glory horse?" He gestured to his groin. "Because I'm hung like a—"

"Just assume we're in quiet ecstasy," she said through her teeth.

He studied her flushed face, her blue eyes still lit up with outrage. "I don't think you'd be quiet."

She crossed her arms. "I am. I'm very quiet."

"Then your boyfriends weren't doing it right." He went back to impersonating her. "Luke, yes! Spank me! Harder!"

She slapped a hand over his mouth. "I swear if you don't stop—"

He pulled her hand off his mouth. "Then you do it." He patted the bed next to him. "If you even know what ecstasy sounds like." He smirked.

She huffed and rolled her eyes.

He opened his mouth again, and she promptly sat. He made a herculean effort not to gloat. This should be good. He bounced a bit, making the mattress squeak.

She closed her eyes and sat quietly for a moment. "O-o-o-h," she finally moaned, and he went rock hard. "Ah. Ah. Ah. Yes!"

She gave him a look of triumph.

"Continue," he said in a low voice.

"Yes, right there." She fake gasped. "Ohgodohgod. Yes!" She let out a throaty scream that sounded so real and so orgasmic that he instinctively rolled on top of her before he knew what he was doing. He stilled. He usually had more finesse, but those sounds triggered some powerful instinct.

He rested on his forearms and looked down at her. "You're awfully good at that, Kennedy."

Their gazes locked. He slowly leaned down, intending a kiss and nothing more. But the moment his lips met hers, a surge of raw lust gripped him, an aching need that made him want way too much. He eased back, breaking the kiss, but then she slid her hand in his hair, pulled him back down, and her sweet mouth opened for him. He took full advantage, kissing her until they were both breathless, and then moved to her jawline and further to her slender neck that he'd longed to taste. She tilted her head, offering more skin. He liked to dominate, to make the woman let go, so he tested the waters as he let his teeth scrape against her and slowly pulled her wrists above her head and then pinned them with one hand in a firm grip. She moaned, and he claimed her mouth, rough and urgent, and she yielded, her mouth softening, her legs spreading for him. Sweet, sweet surrender. He kept her wrists pinned and returned to her neck, working his way down, kissing and nipping and soothing with his tongue.

"Just for the weekend," she whispered urgently.

"Just sex. No business maneuvering. Promise."

He lifted his head. "God, yes." That was all he'd wanted all along. And he didn't need to do any maneuvering. This client was always his.

His mouth slammed against hers. He spread her legs further apart, fitting more firmly against her, pelvis to pelvis. She moaned in the back of her throat.

There was a knock at the door. Kennedy tore her mouth from his.

"Just a minute," she called.

He rolled off her, irritated and unreasonably disappointed. She'd agreed to a weekend fling. That should be enough, but he was having trouble waiting. He'd never wanted anyone the way he wanted her.

She leaped off the bed, tightening her robe around her as she hurried to answer the door. He heard Elizabeth's crisp tone. "Lunch is in half an hour. Bentley and Candy would like you to join them in the dining room."

"Of course," Kennedy replied. "Thank you."

She shut the door and grabbed her duffel bag, heading to the bathroom.

He sat up. "We can do a lot in half an hour," he called, half serious. "That's three times what your best guy did."

She stopped, turned, and glared at him. Maybe he shouldn't have said that last part. But, seriously, he'd nearly boasted about his own prowess when he'd heard the duration of her "relationships" were only ten minutes.

"Think it over," he said with his most charming, sexy smile.

She whirled, stepped into the bathroom, and quietly shut the door behind her.

"Don't think too hard!" he called.

He flopped back on the bed and groaned. He still had a raging hard-on. If Elizabeth hadn't knocked on the door, he was sure things would've moved forward. Though he really couldn't complain.

This fake engagement thing was working out better than he'd thought.

CHAPTER EIGHT

Kennedy dressed in a simple off-the-shoulder pink floral top with white capris and sandals. She combed out her hair and reapplied makeup. When she emerged from the bathroom, Luke was busy on his cell phone and shirtless. She tore her gaze away. There'd be plenty of time for that tonight. Nerves ran through her at the thought. Having Luke stretched out on top of her, kissing her, had made her crazy with lust, but now...well, now she had to focus on Bentley again.

"Hey, gorgeous," Luke said, looking up from the screen. "Give me a few minutes."

"Take all the time you need," she said and left, determined to get back on track with her real mission. It was way too easy to let her mind get clouded with lust in his presence. She headed downstairs and mentally reviewed her proposal for a foundation that would both provide a tax shelter and bring some good PR to Williams Oil.

She stepped into a formal dining room, where Bentley and Candy were already seated at one end of a long cherrywood mission-style table. They wore matching orange polo shirts with orange shorts.

"There you are," Bentley said with a big smile. "Don't you look relaxed? The spa was to your liking?"

"It was wonderful," she replied honestly. "Thanks so much for inviting us."

"Where's Luke?" Candy asked, peering behind her.

She took the seat across from Candy. "He's still getting ready."

"Did he like the body scrub?" Candy asked. "Bennie didn't like it the first time."

"I sure did," Luke replied, stepping into the room. His navy polo shirt brought out the dark blue of his eyes, and she fervently wished she didn't notice that kind of distracting detail about him. Somehow he blended the upper class and casual look effortlessly. The sandals looked designer. Her gaze lingered on his calves for no good reason other than that they were muscular, golden, and beautiful. She sighed inwardly. Just like the rest of him.

He stopped by her chair and leaned down to kiss her cheek. "Thanks for waiting for me," he said in a low voice. He smiled at her, a smile that didn't reach his eyes, a smile that said he was onto her, before taking the seat next to her.

She battled briefly with a pang of guilt and shook it off. This was business.

Bentley signaled and a man wearing all white as Elizabeth had (the staff uniform?) appeared with a silver tray of appetizers. The man stopped by each of them, offering the food. She watched as Bentley and Candy pointed to what they wanted and the man picked it up with tongs and placed it on their small plates. When the tray reached her, she couldn't decide between crab meat in a phyllo shell, some kind of pate on crostini, or miniature quiche.

"I'll take one of each," Luke said.

"Me too," she quickly added.

The man inclined his head. "Certainly." He set the delicacies on their plates.

She ate the crab in phyllo first. So buttery and delicious she nearly moaned. She was used to crackers and hastily made peanut butter and jelly sandwiches.

"Did you also do the full spa treatment?" Luke asked Bentley and Candy.

"We'll do it tomorrow," Candy said. "We didn't want to miss out on our time with you. We thought after lunch we'd take a sail together. And then, Ken, you and I can do mani-pedis tomorrow after I finish my spa treatments. Sound good?"

"Sounds good," Kennedy said. She'd never had a mani-pedi, but she knew this weekend was all about doing whatever Bentley and Candy wanted.

"How did you two like the soaking tub?" Candy asked with a knowing smile.

"Very nice," Luke said in a deep voice that implied more. He smiled at her, and she forced herself to smile back. He squeezed her hand under the table, which somehow made her relax.

Bentley and Candy laughed. "That's our favorite too," Bentley said, taking Candy's hand.

Kennedy suppressed a shudder and glanced at Luke, whose expression didn't change. He was good.

After the appetizers, she enjoyed a course of cold melon soup followed by a plate of fresh lobster, roasted potatoes, and asparagus. It was the best meal she'd ever had. She was so full she couldn't even eat the chocolate mousse they brought out for dessert. They were going to have to roll her out of the room.

"No dessert?" Luke asked her.

She put a hand on her stomach, which felt like it had grown. "I'm just so full."

"You're so skinny," Candy said. "I'm jealous. I could never pass up dessert."

"Ask me in a few hours and I'd eat the whole thing," Kennedy said with a smile.

"Don't forget," Candy said, "tonight's the dinner party. Not black tie, but nice, you know. Then we'll go to the beach for a bonfire." She turned to Bentley.

"Did I miss anything?"

"That's everything for today," Bentley said.

"Who's coming to the dinner party?" Kennedy asked.

"Just a few of my closest friends," Bentley replied.

"Is Prince Erik able to come?" Candy asked.

Kennedy's eyes widened. A prince?

Bentley shook his head. "Not this time. Some urgent business to attend to. Princely life isn't all fun and games. But let's see…" He then rattled off a list of names that were not at all what Kennedy had expected. Not titans of industry, not billionaires born into the family money. The guests were A-list actors, rock stars, and professional athletes. Of course, they had money, but the vibe was going to be entirely different. She had a sinking feeling she was not going to be remotely interesting to this crowd. And she had nothing glam to wear either. She put her hands under her legs so she wouldn't start biting her nails again. She might've been a little out of her league before, battling for a big financial-management client, but at least she'd had solid research to back her up. These people wouldn't care about that.

"Sounds like a blast," Luke said. And he sounded like he meant it.

"So fun!" she said, matching his tone.

Luke asked Bentley about the house, and he

launched into what was clearly a favorite topic as he told them all about having the house and surrounding property designed to his party expectations.

"Entertaining guests is so important in relationship building," Bentley finished. "Well, you two know that."

"Couldn't agree more," Luke said.

Kennedy felt like she was having an out-of-body experience, floating above it all. She'd attended an exclusive private school with the children of old-money families. She could hold her own, but this was a whole different thing with celebrities. The day's events caught up with her. The foreign experience of being near naked while strangers rubbed and squeezed her. The constant back and forth with Luke, which triggered a mighty lust that she was not at all used to. She suddenly felt exhausted.

"Excuse me," she said. "I need the ladies' room."

Candy gave her a nod, and the conversation went on without her. She went up to the guest room, quietly shut the door, and walked like a zombie over to the bed, where she promptly flopped face down.

A few minutes later, the door opened and she heard footsteps. She didn't bother to lift her head. Whether it was Luke or Elizabeth coming to check on her, she didn't have the energy. The person sat on the bed, and she immediately knew from the way the bed creaked and her whole body came to attention that it was Luke. Not to mention that delicious uber-expensive cologne he wore.

"Relaxing again?" Luke asked. He stroked her hair. "Didn't we spend the whole morning relaxing?"

She rolled over to face him. "You ever meet a celebrity before?"

"Sure, lots of times at parties in the city. They're just regular people that get their faces on TV."

She sat up. Should she confide in him? Or would her confession just make it easier for him to win Bentley over and leave her behind?

"Spit it out," he said. "Or I'll be forced to tickle it out of you."

"I'm afraid I'm going to clam up," she blurted. "I'll just stand there like an idiot and Bentley will think I have nothing to offer someone like him."

"Advantage mine."

She groaned and threw herself back on the bed, covering her face with both hands. "Augh!" She took her hands off her face. "I don't know why I told you that. Now I've just handed everything over on a silver platter."

He flopped down on his back next to her. "I've always had the advantage. I worked Wall Street for years. I have connections, lots and lots of connections, and ten years' experience. You have two as an assistant." He turned and pinned her with his dark blue eyes before delivering a direct hit to the gut. "This game was always rigged. I fully expect to walk away with Bentley's business."

Rage began a slow boil in her. He was so damn arrogant. So casually dismissive of her abilities.

She propped up on one elbow. "Well, that's honest."

He turned on his side and propped his head on his hand. "I didn't want you to get the wrong idea about what's going on. So now you know where you stand. Can you just enjoy the best night of your life? Not everyone gets invited to an A-list Bentley party."

"Enjoy the best night of my life with you?"

"Who else?"

She battled between wanting to punch him for his dismissal and, at the same time, secretly fearing he was right. She sat up, swung her legs over the side of the bed, and rested her elbows on her knees while she thought over what he'd said. Was it true? Was the game rigged? But then why had Bentley narrowed it down to just the two of them? That was before she'd announced they were engaged. There must be a reason she'd gotten the meeting, something Bentley saw in her that he liked.

Her cell rang in her purse. She leaped up to answer it.

It was her younger brother Alex. "Ken," he said in a subdued voice, "can you pick me up at the Clover Park police station? Mom's up at Frank's college for parents' weekend and Dad wants me to spend the night in jail to learn my lesson, but—" he lowered his voice, nearly inaudible "—this place skeeves me out. I'm in the basement. It looks like a dungeon." His voice cracked. "I think I saw a rat."

She groaned. "What'd you do?" Ever since their dad's accident, Alex had been acting out.

"Shoplifting."

"What was it? I told you we couldn't afford the sneakers you wanted." At seventeen, Alex's need to follow the crowd in certain brand-name clothes and shoes trumped his understanding of just how dire their family's money situation was. Though she'd explained it several times.

"It wasn't that," Alex mumbled.

"What, then?"

"Nothing. Okay? Would you please come get me?"

"I don't even have my car. I got a ride to Greenport."

"I can't spend the night in a dungeon with rats. Please, Ken." His voice came out small at the end, and her protective big-sister instincts reared up. He used to be so sweet. Of all her brothers and sisters, Alex was the one who looked to her most when he needed a hug or extra attention when their mom was overwhelmed with their other siblings.

"Hold on." She covered the mouthpiece of the phone and turned to Luke. "Can you lend me some money for a cab back to Clover Park?"

He stood. "What's going on?"

"My brother needs me."

"Let's go. I'll drive you."

She stared at him for a moment, shocked that he was willing to leave Bentley's place on a moment's notice to help her brother that he'd never met. "You don't have to come. I'll take a cab."

His gaze was direct. "I said I'd drive."

"Uh…thank you."

He nodded once.

She spoke to Alex. "I'm coming to get you. Do we have to pay bail, or will they just let you go?"

"Bail!" Luke exclaimed. She waved her hand, telling him to quiet down.

"They'll let me go," Alex said. "I'm a minor. Can you tell them you have permission from Dad?"

She sighed. She'd have to actually get her dad to call in and agree. Unlikely. In any case, her dad couldn't drive even if he wanted to, her mom had the car and he hadn't driven since his surgery because it pained him to move. She'd try her mom on her cell. She knew her mom would never directly oppose her dad, but she might be willing to call on the side in her quiet way. Kennedy would take it from there.

They quickly made their apologies to Bentley and Candy, taking a rain check on the sail, and promised to be back in time for the cocktail hour before the party.

After they got in Luke's car, he turned to her. "We headed to the police station?"

"Unfortunately."

He started the car and pulled out onto the main road. "What'd your brother do?"

She shook her head, still not quite believing it herself. "Shoplifted. I don't know what. He's seventeen. Probably some jeans or a hoodie with some sports logo on the front. I told him we can't afford that logo stuff. How's he going to get into a good college? Now he'll have a record."

"Maybe not. Maybe we can work something out with the police. The chief of police's been involved with punk kids through the Police Athletic League for years. Chief O'Hare picked up right where Chief Bailey left off."

We? For the first time she felt like she wasn't alone in her efforts to help her family. "How do you know all this?"

One corner of his mouth lifted in a wry smile. "Because I used to be one of those punk kids."

CHAPTER NINE

"You!" Kennedy exclaimed.

Luke laughed. "Yeah, me. Was it the clean-shaven look that gave you the impression I was squeaky clean?"

"You don't seem like a criminal."

"I'm not a criminal. I just used to be a punk."

"What'd you do?"

"Nothing that landed me in jail. Stole money from my dad's wallet, took a baseball bat to mailboxes, ran my mouth off, graffitied a bunch of stuff. You know, the usual acting-out shit."

"What made you straighten out?"

He didn't answer.

"You did straighten out, right?"

"More or less." He gave her a wry smile. "I'd like to say I just grew up, but the truth is I owe it all to my stepdad, Vinny. He took on the dad role for me when my own dad was an utter asshole, and, despite me being a pain-in-the-ass punk kid, Vinny stuck by me. Showed me what a real man is made of. Sometimes a boy out of control just needs a man to step up. Teach him how to be a man."

"Can I hire you?"

He barked out a laugh. "What's the deal with your dad? Not up to the job?"

She stared out the window at the expensive boutique shops and restaurants of downtown Greenport. Where to start with that one? Her dad used to be great, involved in their school and sports since they all went to the same school. She missed the car rides commuting back and forth to school, where they'd all talk and laugh. He was like a different person now.

She turned back to Luke. "He injured his back pretty badly in a car accident." Luckily, he'd been alone, so none of her younger siblings had been hurt. She said a silent thank you for that as she did every time she had the terrifying image of one of her brothers or sisters injured. She couldn't handle it if something happened to one of them.

She went on. "He had back surgery a few months ago, but he's still in a lot of pain. He can't work. He's on pain pills and going to physical therapy, He's basically miserable. He snaps at everyone to leave him alone." She let out a long breath. "Disability ran out.

My parents blew through their savings on his therapy. So. Yeah. Things are kinda tight right now. I suspect Alex stole something he wanted that we couldn't afford."

"Tell me about Alex."

And the way he said it made her feel like he really wanted to know. She fell a little harder into like with him.

"He's just starting his senior year," she said. "His grades aren't bad, but they're not great. He could get straight As if he tried. He's smart. He was in and out of detention all last semester and my mom just basically threw her hands up with him. I'm trying to pick up the slack, but I'm also working, and I can't always get through to him. He's got, you know, teenaged attitude."

"Tough guy?"

"Not so tough. I mean, he's big enough to kick someone's ass. And he'd kill me for saying this, but he's just a big mush on the inside. Beneath all that bluster, he's still my sweet little brother." Her voice cracked, and she fought back tears. She couldn't let Alex's life go down the drain just because things were tough at home.

"Hey, it'll be okay." He reached over and squeezed her hand. "Really. It sounds like the usual teenaged stuff. He's not into drugs or anything, is he?"

"No. Definitely not."

"How do you know?"

"I still live at home. I've never seen him come home looking drunk or stoned. He mostly just looks pissed off."

"Pissed off is fine. Maybe he just stole something to impress a girl. Wouldn't be the first time a guy did something stupid for a pretty girl."

"Seriously? Risk jail for a pretty face? If that's it, I'm going to let him rot in jail."

He shot her a look. "Harsh. Haven't you ever done anything crazy stupid for a good-looking guy?"

"Nope."

"Damn, I was really hoping." He grinned, and she couldn't help but laugh.

"Thanks for coming with me. You make it seem more manageable. I don't feel nearly as freaked out as I was."

"I aim to please. We'll stop by Garner's for your car. I don't have room for three." He hitched a thumb toward the back of the Porsche. "No backseat. Then I'll follow you home, and we'll drive back to Greenport together."

"Sounds like a plan. Thanks again."

"You can thank me more tonight."

"Luke!"

He chuckled. If she wasn't so grateful to him,

she'd smack him.

By the time they reached the Clover Park police station, after fetching her car, she'd succeeded in getting her mom to call in and get permission for Kennedy to pick up her brother. Her mom hadn't even known about it, but after a brief freak-out, Kennedy was able to assure her mom that she'd handle it. She hoped Chief O'Hare had let her brother know he was going free. She didn't want Alex to worry unnecessarily.

She rang the buzzer of the locked police station. Chief O'Hare let them in. She'd seen him around town when he was on duty, but she didn't know him well. He was maybe forty, tall with broad shoulders, and intimidating as all hell. He had short dark brown hair, sharp hazel eyes, and a non-smiling demeanor that said he took shit from no one. His sharp eyes landed on her, flicked to Luke, and back to her. "You Kennedy?"

She swallowed hard. "Yes."

"Come in."

They stepped inside. Before she could ask to see her brother, Luke introduced himself.

"Luke Reynolds," he said, offering his hand. "Ryan, right? My brother Gabe is friends with Shane." They shook hands. "I worked with Chief Bailey as a kid."

The tough-looking cop's face lit up with a smile. "I thought you looked familiar. How long's it been? I remember you—" he held up a hand about two feet shorter than Luke's height "—about yay high."

Luke smiled. "That's me. Maybe around fourth grade you saw me before you left town for the academy?"

Chief O'Hare turned to her, smiling and looking a lot less intimidating. "His brother Gabe is friends with my younger brother Shane." He turned back to Luke. "How ya been? You look like Chief Bailey straightened you out."

Luke laughed. "Yeah, I'm good."

"You local?" Chief O'Hare asked. "We've found the best coaches at the Police Athletic League are former juvies." He leaned in conspiratorially. "I use that term affectionately." He straightened. "My brother Trav used to be trouble, but he turned his life around. Now he's coaching the six- to eight-year-old baseball team with his friend Rico. Trav's son, Bryce, is on the team. We could use a soccer coach for the younger kids. It's guys like you that've been there that reach the kids best."

Kennedy fidgeted. It was all well and good to catch up on old times, but what about her brother rotting away in some dungeon?

"I'm in the city," Luke said.

Chief O'Hare inclined his head. "Let me know if you ever move back."

"I will," Luke replied.

"What about my brother?" Kennedy asked with some exasperation.

Chief O'Hare's eyes narrowed and he returned to intimidating-cop mode. "He stole a book from the bookstore. It wasn't the first time. Rachel and Shane, the owners, talked to him several times, but he just keeps doing it. Finally they called me in, hoping I could make him see reason. He cursed me out and took off with the stolen property. I had no choice but to haul him in."

"He's stealing books?" Luke asked. "What's wrong with the library?"

Chief O'Hare shook his head. "Don't know. Maybe you can get it out of him. He's stealing picture books. You know, the kind for little kids."

Kennedy's brows drew together. That was so odd. "No one at our house is young enough to read picture books."

"Just tell him to stop and this all goes away," Chief O'Hare said. "Rachel and Shane don't want to press charges, but you have to nip it in the bud. We don't want him branching out to stealing other things." He lowered his voice. "The only reason he's in the dungeon is because your dad wanted him to be. I figured it wouldn't hurt to give him a taste of what happens when you break the law."

It really was a dungeon! Kennedy nodded. "I'll talk to him. Can you bring him up?"

Chief O'Hare turned and went through a door in the back to fetch him.

"That is the lamest crime I've ever heard," Luke said.

"It doesn't make sense," Kennedy said. "Our youngest sister is thirteen."

"Maybe there's a girl he likes with a younger brother or sister."

"Not everything's about sex!"

Someone cleared their throat. She looked up to see Chief O'Hare with her tall, athletic brother with his shaggy dark brown hair covering his dark brown eyes, staring at the ground.

"Hi, Ken," Alex said in a small voice.

She rushed over and hugged him, her head only reaching his chest. She used to be able to carry him around. Those days were long gone, but he was still her sweet little brother. He hugged her back tightly.

She pulled back and stroked his hair out of his face. "You okay?"

"Yeah," he muttered, his cheeks flushing pink as he glanced under his lashes at the other men witnessing her motherly display.

"Come on," she said, turning to go. She stopped and turned back. "Thank you, Chief O'Hare."

"You got it," the chief replied. "Hey, Alex."

Alex met his eyes. "What?"

"Don't let me see you in here again," he ordered in a voice that brooked no argument.

"No, sir," Alex mumbled.

She walked with him out the door. Luke followed behind after saying goodbye to the chief.

Once on the sidewalk outside, Luke extended his hand to Alex. "Hey, Kennedy forgot to introduce us. I'm Luke Reynolds."

Alex shook his hand. "Hi," he mumbled.

She unlocked her car. "Get in."

"Unless you want to ride in a Porsche," Luke said, gesturing to his car parked a few spaces down.

"Holy shit!" Alex exclaimed, sounding more like his old self. "This is your car? This is awesome!"

Luke grinned. "Yeah."

Kennedy frowned. "Luke, you can't reward him with a ride in your car after he's been in jail."

Luke inclined his head in acknowledgment, then turned back to Alex. "So who's the girl?"

Alex's ears and cheeks turned bright red. "What? I don't know. No one." He looked away.

"Who's the girl you're stealing picture books for?" Luke pressed.

Alex kicked a rock down the sidewalk. "Who told you that? I'm not stealing stupid picture books." Alex didn't know that Chief O'Hare filled them in already.

"Yeah?" Luke asked casually. "What'd you steal, then?"

Alex lifted his chin defiantly. "Cigarettes."

"Alex!" Kennedy exclaimed. She marched right back to where her brother stood next to Luke. "We know what you stole! Stop trying to act cool with cigarettes. I told you how bad smoking is for you. Remember those awful commercials of people with emphysema that can barely breathe?"

"He's not smoking," Luke said, "are you?"

Alex clamped his mouth shut.

Kennedy blew out a breath, reaching for a rapidly vanishing patience. "The bookstore isn't pressing charges now, but if you keep doing it, they might. This year is so important for college applications. You can't afford a criminal record."

"I'm underage," Alex said sullenly. "It doesn't count."

"It does count!" she exclaimed. "It's still going on your record. Do you want to end up in a juvenile delinquent center?"

"Whatever," Alex mumbled.

He was not taking this seriously enough for Kennedy's liking. "I can't always come to your rescue!

You have to get your head on straight!" She worked hard to control her voice. She had to get through to him, not push him away. "Just study hard, follow the rules, and you can move on to college. You won't always be stuck at home." She put a hand on his arm. "Just stick it out one more year. Okay?"

Alex didn't respond, merely shook her hand off.

"Answer your sister," Luke snapped.

"Okay," Alex mumbled.

A beat passed in silence. She looked from Alex to Luke and sighed. "Get in my car, Alex."

"You know what girls like?" Luke asked Alex out of nowhere.

Alex turned to him skeptically.

"Luke, don't," she started.

"They like a good compliment," Luke said. "Doesn't cost you a cent. Just one of those you're so cute or pretty or beautiful, depending on the girl, you see. You don't want to push the level of credibility." He leaned against his Porsche, looking like the poster boy for picking up hot women. "Girls have a near perfect bullshit meter."

Alex slowly nodded.

"You can build from there," Luke went on. "Nice dress, nice skirt." He waved a hand. "You know, whatever they've got on. And whatever you do, never answer *do I look fat in this* with anything other than a no. That's a trick question no matter how many times she says she wants the honest truth."

Alex grinned and then quickly stopped. "Are you Ken's boyfriend?"

"Just a friend," Luke replied easily.

"Cool," Alex said.

He was kinda cool, Kennedy thought. And this time when she looked at Luke, it was with pure admiration for the way he took the unexpected in stride, the way he believed in the goodness of her little brother, the way he just casually spoke to him man-to-man. Though now that she was onto his wily ways, she certainly wouldn't be falling for any of his false compliments.

"You ask her out yet?" Luke asked her brother.

Alex shook his head.

"Women love talking," Luke advised. "Just talk to her. It'll naturally lead to more."

"That's enough, Luke," Kennedy piped up. Next thing you knew he'd be giving her brother sex advice.

Luke raised a brow. "Excuse me, Ms. Ward, we're having a little man-to-man talk here that doesn't concern you."

"Yeah," Alex said.

She rolled her eyes.

"All right, let's go," Luke said, straightening up. "Go ride with your sister and thank her for hauling your sorry ass out of jail."

"Thank you," Alex mumbled.

"You're welcome," Kennedy said. "And I never want to do that again!"

Alex slunk over to her car. He was silent and sullen on the ride home as she lectured him about how he was the oldest boy and had to set an example for their younger brother, Quinn, who worshipped him. She saw Quinn shooting hoops with a few other kids on the basketball court by the entrance to the apartment complex and honked the horn at him on the way in. He lifted a hand in the smallest of acknowledgements because he was, at fifteen, too cool for the likes of his big sister. That was outside. In the house, he turned to her for everything he needed. She'd encouraged her siblings to come to her from an early age, responding immediately to whatever they needed, from a sandwich cut in four pieces to help with their math homework, which her parents found puzzling with the new methods, to how to deal with problems at school. Being the oldest by six years and well aware of where she stood in the family, she'd worked very hard to be needed.

She parked near her family's apartment. Luke pulled into the space next to her.

"Bye," Alex said tersely. He got out of the car, and she did too, heading over to the passenger side of

Luke's car.

Alex stopped next to Luke, and Luke powered down the window. "Nice to meet you, Luke," Alex said in a much more friendly voice. "You ever…"

"What?" Luke asked.

Kennedy slid inside and fastened her seatbelt.

"You ever think I could take your Porsche for a spin?" Alex asked.

"No," Luke said.

Alex's face fell back into his sullen expression again. He backed away. "Figured."

"Go home!" she hollered. "You're grounded!"

He rolled his eyes and swaggered away. Dammit. She didn't have time for this. She had to get back to Bentley's place for the party. Actually now that she was home, she wanted to grab her little black dress. She'd packed a sundress, which wasn't glam enough for a celebrity party.

Luke turned to her. "Ready?"

"Hold on. I need to go inside for a minute."

"You want me to come in with you?"

"No! I mean, that's not necessary."

A flash of hurt crossed his face before he pulled out his cell and started checking for messages.

She studied him for a moment. His expression was neutral, but she knew she'd hurt his feelings by not inviting him in. Why would he want to meet her family anyway?

She put a hand on his arm. "You were really good with him. Thanks."

"No problem," he said, not even looking up.

She made her way to the apartment and let herself in. Her dad sat in his old ratty beige recliner chair, watching TV. The accident had aged him. It pained her to see her formerly vibrant, athletic dad looking beat down. He had lines on his face that hadn't been there before, his previously thinning dark brown hair had gray in it, and his dark brown eyes were always clouded with pain.

"Hi, Dad."

"You shouldn't have bailed him out," he snarled. Her dad used to be nicer. The chronic pain had made him short-tempered.

"He was scared. I talked to him."

His eyes flashed at her as he pinned her with a hard look. "He should be scared. You break the law, you pay the price. You don't do him any favors babying him." He narrowed his eyes. "Where you been anyway?"

"I told you I was spending the weekend at a client's estate. It's a working weekend. I'm networking with a lot of important people."

"Sounds like a fancy place."

"It is."

"Don't sleep your way into money."

She stiffened. He had no filter now, and she hated the change in him. Maybe he'd always had this cynical hard view of the world, but she'd only heard this harshness from him after the accident.

She shook her head. "How can you say that to me?"

"I'm just giving you advice. Be smart, Ken. Rich old guys like pretty young things."

"Bentley's not old and he's married besides."

He winced as he turned back to the TV. "Could you get me the whiskey?"

"We're out."

"Dammit. Can you pick some up?"

"I can't. I just have enough time to grab my dress and get back. There's a party."

"Well, don't worry about your old dad here suffering," he snapped. "By all means, go to your fancy party."

She bit back any further remarks, reminding herself he was in pain, that he wasn't himself when he was like that. She went to the bedroom with its double bunk beds that her siblings shared. She'd always slept on the living room couch. The three sisters shared the bedroom closet, and the boys shared the hall closet. Her thirteen-year-old sister, Jamie, lay on her stomach on the top bunk, with headphones on, drawing in her sketch pad.

Kennedy rummaged through the closet for her one nice dress and pulled it out. She gasped and turned to Jamie. "Did you wear my dress?" They wore the same size, though Jamie was taller than her already.

Jamie didn't notice her. She marched up to the bunk and smacked the frame, making it shake. Jamie's dark brown eyes widened. She pulled off the headphones. "Hey, Ken, when'd you get home?"

"Five minutes ago. Did you wear my black dress?"

Jamie twirled a lock of her long, dark brown hair. "No."

"Liar! There's a giant stain on it." A red stain bloomed on one side. She shoved the dress in her sister's face.

Jamie wrinkled her nose. "It looks worse in daylight, doesn't it? I tried to get it out with club soda, but cherry pie really sticks."

"You little rat. You know not to touch my stuff! I have a very important party and this is the only thing I have to wear to it!"

Jamie's lower lip quivered. "But it was my first dance. Robbie asked me. I couldn't say no. He's the cutest guy in the entire school!"

"Then you should've worn one of your dresses or at least asked me!" She stared at the stain. There was no way she could get this out. "They had cherry pie at your dance?"

"No, after. We walked over to the café for dessert."

"Why didn't you tell me when it happened? Maybe I could've fixed it."

Jamie looked contrite. "I thought I fixed it. I put Mountain Dew on it right away. That's like club soda. Right?"

"Augh!" She threw the dress on the bottom bunk. Then she went back to the closet and rifled through it. She had three business suits, some skirts, and a yellow sundress that was nicer than the one she'd packed, but not right for the occasion. She snatched the sundress. "Don't take my clothes without asking ever again!"

"So-rry," Jamie said with a roll of her eyes. She put the headphones back on.

Kennedy stalked out of the room. "Bye, Dad."

He grunted.

She stalked outside, grumbling to herself, and got into Luke's car.

He straightened and put his cell phone away. "Uh-oh. What's wrong?"

"Nothing."

"Yeah? Why do you look so pissed off?"

"I'm fine." She folded her stupid dress in half and avoided his eyes. "Let's just go."

"Uh-uh. I know what 'fine' means in female talk. Tell me what's wrong."

"My parents are idiots, my sister's a jerk, and I have nothing to wear! This dress won't work at all!" She shook the dress in the air.

He raised a brow. "I can fix one of those things."

"You're not buying me clothes."

He crossed his arms. "You think I want to show up with my fiancée at an A-list party in that thing?" He indicated the dress with a look of disgust.

She hugged the dress to her. "What's wrong with it?"

"You tell me."

"Nothing."

"Then wear it."

She set it in her lap and stared at it. She met his dark blue eyes. "It's not dressy enough."

He studied her for a moment, making her squirm. She knew she wasn't making sense. But she was stuck between pride and embarrassment over showing up at a fancy party, looking out of place.

"All right," Luke finally said. "Here's the deal. If you let me buy you a dress, I'll let you show a lot of skin in it."

"That makes no sense. Why would I want—"

His gaze was heated, his words unmistakably erotic. "To please me."

She went silent, tired of the way he tried to rattle her with his sexual innuendo.

He started the car and pulled out of the lot. They drove in silence, except for the radio tuned to some classic rock station.

Finally Luke pulled into one of the fancy boutiques she'd admired earlier in downtown Greenport. The same wealthy community where Bentley had his summer "cottage."

She stared at the designer dresses in the window display. Gorgeous. Out of her reach.

She sank down in her seat. "Luke, those dresses must cost at least a week's pay at your salary, not mine. I could never repay you."

"You can pay me back tonight." At her silence, he went on. "I want what any guy wants. Starts with a B."

"I'm not giving you a blow job!"

He barked out a laugh. "I meant a beautiful woman. But hey…either one works for me."

She gritted her teeth. "You purposely made me say that."

He grinned. "I really can't help it if you have a dirty mind."

Grr…

His dark blue eyes sparked with amusement. "Settle down now."

"You just love messing with me."

He inclined his head. "I do. Ready to buy a dress, beautiful?"

And even though she knew the "beautiful" was probably a line he used all the time, she couldn't help but warm to the compliment. He took her hand, never breaking eye contact, and brushed his lips across the backs of her fingers. She tried very hard not to show how it affected her. She would never be a swooning, lovesick fool for any man.

She pressed her lips together tightly. He was still holding her hand. Their gazes locked in a battle of wills.

She caved. "Okay, fine, you can buy me a dress."

"You're very generous," he said with a straight face.

A few moments later, she stepped inside the boutique and was instantly out of place in the elegant atmosphere. Soft jazz played, the air was scented with jasmine, and the shop was filled with gorgeous cocktail dresses and evening gowns. Designer purses lined one wall and designer shoes were displayed on shelves on the opposite wall. The kind she could only stare at online and quietly drool over.

A refined brunette woman in a form-fitting light blue skirt with matching blazer approached. "How can I help you?"

Kennedy was momentarily speechless. She didn't even know where to start.

Luke spoke up. "We're looking for something as beautiful as she is."

"I see," the woman said with a smile for Kennedy.

Kennedy's cheeks heated. She found her voice again. "I'm looking for a cocktail dress for a party."

"Do we have a price range?" the woman asked, looking from Kennedy to Luke.

"Whatever she wants," Luke said, shocking her. He didn't stick around and headed for a cushioned settee in the center of the store, where he sat and pulled out his cell phone.

"Very good," the woman said to her. "Right this way."

A short while later, Kennedy was in the dressing room, trying on dresses that the saleswoman continually refreshed with even more dresses. She couldn't decide. She kept veering toward the classic little-black-dress style she was used to, but then she'd change her mind. Either because it was too simple or too expensive. Sometimes the price was relatively reasonable, but she just didn't love it. Sometimes she liked it, but the price was a jaw-dropping two grand.

She'd occasionally step out and gesture to Luke for his opinion. He shook his head no each time. Finally, she tried on a scarlet dress that she loved. She beamed and twirled in front of the mirror. It was the perfect compromise between elegant and edgy. A sleeveless sheath that ended above the knees. The jeweled collar above a deep V neckline with crisscrossing straps in the back were what sold it for her. It was a Roberto Cavalli with a hefty price tag. Five grand. She was torn between serious love and serious angst over the price.

She stepped out to look in the three-way mirror.

"This is the one!" the saleswoman exclaimed.

Kennedy stepped into the showroom. "Luke?"

He looked up from his cell, smiled, and nodded.

"I guess I'll take it," she told the saleswoman, trying to restrain her glee.

"Wonderful. I'll wrap it for you." She left the dressing area and Kennedy followed. "Do you need shoes?"

She immediately thought of the expense of the dress. "No, this is plenty."

"Get the shoes," Luke called.

And that was how she walked out with her first ever pair of Jimmy Choos. Open-toe metallic glitter wedge sandals with crisscrossing straps. They were to die for, and she pushed down the guilt over the money and just reveled in it. One day she could afford designer clothes and shoes. And the first thing she'd do, after paying Luke back, was go on a monster shopping spree.

After Luke put everything on his credit card, he carried the two boxes tied with pink ribbon to the car for her. Even the packaging was expensive and beautiful.

"You know I'm going to pay you back one day," Kennedy said.

"A simple thank you will do," he replied as he stashed the boxes in the trunk.

"Thank you."

He shut the trunk. "You are quite welcome."

"Why did you say yes to the scarlet dress and not the others?"

He stopped in front of her. "Because I knew you liked it best. You looked lit up. The other dresses you didn't."

She studied him. "Are you always this perceptive?"

One corner of his mouth lifted in a wry smile. "Honestly, you're an open book. I'm just reading the large print."

"I am not. No one's ever said that about me."

"You must've gone out with idiots."

"I've dated some very smart men."

"With very little experience with women, I'll bet." He opened the passenger-side door for her. "Ready to party?"

"Ready as I'll ever be," she said.

He peered at her. "Are you nervous? The woman who had the balls to go after a billionaire client with nothing but book smarts to back her up?"

"I'm not nervous. I'm sure it'll be great."

"You're a terrible liar."

She slipped into the car. She had to cover her nerves a lot better if she was going to hold her own tonight. As soon as Luke got in the driver's seat, she took the offensive. "If I'm such a terrible liar, then why do Bentley and Candy believe we're a couple?"

He gave her a look she couldn't interpret. "Isn't it obvious?"

"No."

He cupped her jaw firmly, which made her entire body heat. "You look at me like you want to eat me for breakfast."

"What! I do not!"

His fingers stroked down the side of her neck. "Maybe I look like I just ate you out for dessert."

She went damp. "L-Luke," she sputtered. She wasn't used to such raw language, especially not from a gorgeous man who was even now stroking lower, his fingers brushing across her exposed collarbone.

He gave her a lopsided smile. "It's my cat-that-ate-the-canary look."

She swallowed hard. "We should go."

His fingers trailed back up her neck, coming to rest over her rapidly beating pulse point.

She licked her lips. "We really need to get back."

He stared at her mouth. "Kennedy—" he leaned close, and she held her breath "—I can't wait to have you."

"Stop talking about sex." She glanced at his sensuous lips that curved into a sexy smile. "Is that all you think about?"

He dropped his hand and leaned back. She was ridiculously disappointed.

"No, I don't always think about sex." He started the car and turned back to her with a slow, sexy smile. "Sometimes I think about sports."

"Then think about sports!"

He shook his head sadly. "Doesn't work when a beautiful woman is next to me."

She jabbed a finger at him. "I know that's a line. You told my brother to call women beautiful."

His dark blue eyes burned into hers. "Use your bullshit meter. Am I lying?"

She sucked in a breath. "No."

He inclined his head. "It's especially hard not to think about sex when it's a sexy woman next to me."

She huffed. "You just love teasing me. I'd be mad at you, but I'm too grateful for everything you did for me and Alex."

He finally put the car in gear and pulled out of the lot. "That was my devious plan all along."

"Was it?" She was still trying to figure him out. Was he a ruthless competitor? A seducer with an ulterior motive? Or a decent, kind man with a strong belief in family?

"You tell me."

It would be so much easier to put him in the enemy category, but her gut instinct was telling her Luke was exactly the kind of man she could fall hard for. And that was the last thing she needed. *Depend on no man.*

"Kennedy?"

She sighed. "You were just being yourself."

"And…" he prompted. When she didn't respond, he finished the sentence for her. "You like myself. A *whole* lot."

"I do," she admitted forlornly.

He smiled and her heart did a little flip-flop. "I do too." He grinned. "Like me, that is."

"Luke!"

He stopped at a traffic light and met her eyes. "Honestly, I like you too much."

That warmed her like nothing else he'd said. She gazed back, just taking in the man, the good looks, yes, but also the good heart.

"Keep that up," he said, "and we'll be doing the naked tango by sundown."

"What'd I do?" But she knew. Her eyes must've given away her softening thoughts toward just how wonderful he was.

He brushed his thumb across her lower lip, and her lips parted on their own. "That's a promise."

She believed him.

CHAPTER TEN

Luke paced the length of the guest bedroom he shared with Kennedy. He couldn't hold out much longer. The minute Kennedy emerged from the bathroom in that sexy dress, her blond hair loose and flowing to her shoulders, he knew his usual smooth talk and slow seduction weren't going to happen. He wanted her fiercely, greedily, and from the look she'd given him earlier, she did too. Still, he had to at least get through poolside cocktail hour with Bentley, Candy, and any early arrivals. He couldn't completely blow off the necessary networking to pull in the client he needed. The party with the A-listers wouldn't really get started until late tonight. Maybe he could bring Kennedy back to their room between cocktails and the party.

She slipped into the heels and turned to him, looking a little unsure of herself. For some reason, she was intimidated by the fact that some of the party guests were famous.

He wolf-whistled in appreciation, and she blushed. Even in the high heels, she was a petite thing. He instinctively wanted to wrap her up and protect her from the world. Though she'd kill him if she knew. She was strong and independent. He liked that about her. He could relax and be himself without worrying he was hurting her tender feelings.

"Gorgeous," he proclaimed, closing the distance between them. The deep V-neck of her dress showed off the curve of her breasts and also a hint of her ribs. He'd noticed that earlier when she wore her bikini, but hadn't wanted to bring it up and embarrass her. He hoped she wasn't one of those women who starved themselves to look good. Now that he was on more solid ground with her—she'd admitted she liked him, putting him firmly out of enemy territory—he wanted to make sure she was okay.

"You look nice too," she said, almost shyly as she looked at him from under her lashes.

"Not as good as you." He was dressed business casual tonight—a white button-down shirt with dark gray tailored pants and Italian leather shoes. He put a hand low on her back just above her ass as he guided her out of the room. "You always been this thin?"

"What do you mean?"

"I can see your ribs a little bit. You getting enough to eat?"

She grabbed his hand and slid it up higher on her back. "I've always been petite. I guess I'm just bony."

He stopped walking and met her eyes. "You skip meals?"

"Sometimes."

"Why? You don't need to diet. I'm sure you'd look just as sexy filled out a bit."

She tried for a teasing smile, but he saw the worry in her eyes. She was hiding something. "Trying to fatten me up?"

He took both her hands in his. They were still in the upstairs hallway, alone. "How often do you skip meals?"

"Not a lot. Just once or twice a week. I'm not starving."

"Why are you skipping?"

She looked away. "It's nothing. Sometimes Alex and Quinn are really hungry. They're growing boys, so I give them my portion."

"You can't afford enough food?"

She pulled her hands from his and stepped back. "I'm not growing. I don't need it as much as they do."

"Kennedy, that's not right." She went hungry for her younger brothers' sakes? It was simultaneously honorable and alarming. "We're going to fix this. You need to eat."

She started to walk away, but he snagged her hand

and stopped her.

"I don't need help," she insisted. "I'm not a charity case."

"You do need help."

Her blue eyes flashed. "It's none of your business. Let's just go to the party."

"I'm not going to sit by and watch you starve yourself."

"I'm not starving myself!"

She yanked her hand from his and headed downstairs. He followed, determined to get to the bottom of this. He wasn't going to sit idly by while Kennedy worked herself literally to the bone for her family. She was too young and the burden was misplaced on her petite shoulders.

"Good evening," Elizabeth said, meeting them in the large foyer. "Cocktails are poolside off the veranda." She pointed toward the back of the house.

"Thank you," Luke said.

"Beautiful dress, Miss Kennedy," Elizabeth said.

"Thank you," Kennedy said graciously.

As soon as they were out of earshot, he told Kennedy, "I want to see you eating tonight."

"Just drop it," she hissed.

She tried to hustle ahead of him, but he snagged her hand, entwining their fingers. He spoke in a low voice. "Don't forget we're happily engaged."

"Not for much longer," she returned, blue eyes flashing. A jolt of lust gripped him. Why did he find her so appealing when she was pissed off at him? Maybe it was because she was such a worthy sparring partner. He really had to stop antagonizing her.

"You love being my fiancée," he told her.

Her jaw clenched. He fought back a grin.

"You'd better wipe that smirk off your face before I smack it off," she threatened.

He barked out a laugh.

"There's the happy couple!" Bentley proclaimed, greeting them by the open French patio doors with a tall drink with a mint leaf sticking out of it.

Candy stood next to him, sipping a glass of white wine. "We missed you sailing today. Mojito?"

"I'd love one," Kennedy said.

"Just one," Luke put in. "She's a lightweight." Both with alcohol and with her weight. That last was not going to be true for much longer. He'd make sure of it.

Bentley and Candy laughed. "He sure looks out for you, honey," Candy said. "I love your dress. Is it a Stella McCartney?"

The two women walked away, talking excitedly. He found himself smiling, glad he'd been able to help her with her dress problem. So far, it looked to be just the four of them.

Bentley pushed his messy brown hair out of his blue eyes. "You want a drink?"

"I'll wait until later, thanks."

"Everything good with your stay?"

"Yes, it is. We're looking forward to the party."

Bentley grinned. "I hope you like dancing. I got Griffin Huntley to play. He's a friend."

"Seriously? That's awesome! Wow. I'm a huge fan." Luke had been a fan of Griffin Huntley's music going way back when he was in Twisted Star, but ever since Griffin went solo three years ago, he'd exploded on the music scene with his unique combination of rock, country, and some indescribable Griffin heart. Songs that made you really feel, even when they weren't ballads. His songs were on the radio all the time, and he'd just finished a world tour. He'd heard Griffin had made an appearance in Clover Park several years back, but Luke had missed it, already living in the city. He was beyond excited. "Kennedy!"

She appeared from just around a column, holding a mojito. "What?"

Candy appeared next to her and looked at him curiously. The two women were a study in contrasts, tall and short, buxom and athletic, bubbly and serious, yet they seemed to click.

He crossed to her. "Griffin Huntley is playing live here tonight."

Kennedy gasped. "I love him."

"Oh, he's a sweetheart," Candy drawled. "I'll introduce you. His girlfriend's a riot. You'll just love her, Ken. She's a sharp businesswoman like you. His manager."

Kennedy lit up at the compliment. "Cool." She slurped her mojito.

"Let's get you something to eat," Luke said to Kennedy.

"There's hors d'oeuvres coming around soon," Candy said. "Let me go check on catering."

She headed back inside. Bentley followed quickly behind her, pinching her ass. Candy squealed, and they ran inside, laughing.

"Stop acting like my mother," Kennedy snapped.

"I'm just looking out for you."

"Well, knock it off. If you have any hope of a naked tango by sundown…" She gave him a pointed look. His cock strained against his pants in response. "Then you'd better let all this food business go."

He snagged her around the waist and pulled her close. "You been thinking about that naked tango, huh?"

She met his eyes matter-of-factly. "Yes."

"And?"

She gazed at him with a serious expression. "It's inevitable, isn't it?"

He dropped his hands. "Don't sound too excited."

She huffed. "We're sharing a room, so..." She slurped more mojito. "Plus we agreed to, you know, just for the weekend."

Somehow this wasn't as much fun as he'd thought it'd be. She seemed almost resigned to sleeping with him. He was about to say *don't do me any favors* when he had an even better idea—taking her upstairs and showing her just how exciting it could be. A vision of Kennedy pinned under him, begging for the release only he could give her, had him grabbing her hand.

Bentley suddenly appeared, pulling him from his lusty fantasy when he asked, "What's just for the weekend?"

Kennedy startled and whirled around, looking guilty. Luke dropped an arm around her shoulders. "We agreed no wedding talk for the weekend. I just needed a break. Ya know?"

Bentley shook his head with a big smile. "I know. Candy had me running around to all these crazy venues, dress shops, caterers. You name it, I was there! Actually, I should have Candy set you up with some of that info. Unless you've already booked everything." He looked from Luke to Kennedy.

"Not yet," Kennedy said.

"Well, good!" Bentley exclaimed. "I'll get you set up. Maybe we can help you plan everything." He winked. "After the weekend."

Kennedy stiffened. Probably because they'd agreed to calling the whole thing off after the weekend. Luke wasn't worried. They'd cross that bridge when they came to it.

"Very generous," Luke said.

Candy appeared and Bentley filled her in on the wedding planning. "Ooh, yes!" Candy exclaimed. "I have a scrapbook full of information. Let's go!"

Which was how they spent the next exhausting hour oohing and aahing over Candy's scrapbook jam-packed with wedding info at the dining room table instead of tearing up the sheets in their room like he'd hoped. Kennedy warmed to the topic, especially on the pages with wedding gowns, showing genuine enthusiasm. As the groom, he merely said, "Whatever she wants," which Bentley and Candy wholeheartedly approved. Finally guests started to arrive and they were spared a look at Candy and Bentley's three wedding albums. They headed back outside to mingle.

Kennedy pulled him to the far corner of the veranda while Bentley and Candy greeted some old friends, wrapped her arms around his neck, and whispered urgently, "What're we going to do? They want to plan our wedding with us! I just know Candy's going to follow up."

He wrapped his arms around her waist, enjoying

having her close again. "So we'll plan our wedding."

"Be serious," she hissed.

He placed a kiss on the tender spot just below her jaw. "I'm not worried about it."

"That's because you're the groom! I have to actually do stuff."

"I guess you'll have to fake marry me," he teased.

She smacked his arm. "This isn't funny."

"It's just for the weekend." He kissed his way up her neck and spoke directly in her ear. "Then we'll break up and this all goes away."

She shivered. "Okay, okay. You're right. I just feel so guilty. Candy's being so nice."

"Don't feel guilty." He leaned down, wanting to jolt her back to the present, and nipped her neck. She gasped. "Just enjoy right now."

"I need a drink," she said, pulling away. He joined her at the bar. They both got a drink and wandered back to a spot on the side of the veranda where they could watch guests arrive. He'd barely gotten two sips of his beer when Kennedy said in a hushed voice, "Is that Chase Thompson?"

He turned and saw the young actor who used to star in one of those teenaged shows on the squeaky-clean network. Chase stepped outside along with his entourage of four male friends. The guy was in his twenties now. Tall and overly muscled like only working with a trainer four hours a day could do. Perfect face, perfect blond hair, bright blue eyes, tanned. Typical Hollywood. He glanced at Kennedy, who set down her second mojito on a nearby table and smoothed her hair.

He'd barely muttered, "Want to meet him?" when she took off.

He caught up with her at the bar, where Chase and friends were ordering up drinks. Kennedy stood right next to Chase, staring, obviously starstruck.

"Hey, do I know you?" Chase asked her.

She remained mute.

Luke stepped in. "Hi, this is Kennedy. She's a fan."

Chase smiled widely, revealing teeth that shone blindingly white. "Always nice to meet a fan." He shook her hand. "Would you like a picture?"

Kennedy nodded enthusiastically. Luke pulled out his cell and snapped a picture of the two of them.

Kennedy resumed staring. He was simultaneously embarrassed for her and irritated. He wrapped an arm around her shoulders. "Thanks. We'll see ya." He guided her away and sat her down on a cushioned outdoor sofa.

She finally snapped out of it and turned to him, blue eyes wide. "I had his poster on my wall as a teenager. I can't believe I met him."

"Pretty exciting," he said dryly.

She grabbed his hand. "I'm so glad I was with you. I couldn't utter a word."

His irritation vanished. "I'm glad I was with you too. If you told him you had his poster on your wall, woo-ee! He'd be all over you. Easy lay."

She smacked his arm. "Luke! I'm not an easy lay."

"Shh, you're way too loud."

He followed her gaze back to Chase Thompson. "Don't be so obvious in your ogling. You're going to make people feel uncomfortable."

She snapped her gaze back to him. "I was not ogling." She frowned. "Was I?" She stood abruptly. "I have to go check my makeup."

"You look fine."

She took off. He resigned himself to a long night as the third wheel in Kennedy's celebrity oglefest. More guests arrived. He sipped his beer. Kennedy was taking a long time. By the time he finished his beer, he was getting worried. He stood to go fetch her from wherever she'd gotten off to, but then she stepped out on the veranda, her hair done up in a sophisticated twist that showed off her delicate jawline and her slender throat. He strode toward her a little faster than he'd normally move for a woman. He couldn't help it. He just wanted to be with her again.

"Hey," he said.

She looked over his shoulder and said in a hushed voice, "I think I just saw the guy from the Tommy Hilfiger ad campaign."

He tamped down his irritation. He was the one she was sharing a room with tonight. He was the one she needed by her side so she didn't embarrass herself with her mute ogling.

"No!" he said in mock excitement, clapping a hand over his mouth.

She didn't notice his teasing. "Yes!"

She looked at him for the first time. God, she was beautiful. Her face with the delicate cheekbones, the jawline leading to her stubborn, defiant little chin. The soft creamy skin that made him ache to touch and—

"You're not jealous that I'm drooling over these gorgeous men?" she asked.

Her reminder snapped him out of his lusty dream. "Why would I be jealous? I'm the one you're *inevitably* going to sleep with."

She nodded absently. "True. Okay, let's go meet McDreamy."

Could she at least *pretend* to be excited by the prospect of sleeping with him? Geez.

They joined a small group of actors and models poolside. More celebrities arrived gradually throughout the evening. Kennedy grabbed his arm in an iron grip at each new arrival. It was kind of cute, actually. She was clearly starstruck, but also just as clearly wanted him at her side. He smoothed over her awkward silences because as much as she wanted to meet everyone, she couldn't seem to get a word out.

By the time she met Griffin Huntley, the rock star he also admired, he was done introducing her to other good-looking men. He didn't pretend he could compete with the cool swagger of a rock star. Griffin's charisma alone kept him the center of attention in a revolving circle of admirers. His black hair was close cropped with a few spikes on top. He'd dressed casual in a white T-shirt and jeans with hiking boots. His arms were muscled and covered in tattoos. Kennedy alternated her ogling between his arms and his face with its five o'clock shadow while they waited to get close enough for an introduction. By the time they stood in front of Griffin, Kennedy was beside herself, crushing Luke's fingers in her grip.

"Hi, Griffin," Luke said. "We're big fans."

Kennedy squeaked and nodded.

Griffin smiled. "Nice to meet you both." He chucked Kennedy under the chin. "Want me to sign something?"

Kennedy turned to Luke, eyes wide and beseeching. He snagged a cocktail napkin off a nearby table and handed it over.

"Who should I make it out to?" Griffin asked.

Kennedy stared mutely again.

"Kennedy," Luke supplied.

A petite brunette woman with a short, choppy hairstyle and startlingly blue eyes appeared at Griffin's side. "Relax, sweetheart," the woman said to Kennedy in a strong New York accent. Brooklyn or Queens, maybe. "He leaves the toilet seat up just like every other man."

Griffin's face lit up as he turned to the woman. "I'm working on it," he growled before hauling her close and kissing her. He turned back to them. "This ballbuster is my manager Christina."

Christina preened. "I'm his muse."

Kennedy finally found her voice. "I'm Kennedy." She reached out and shook Christina's hand. "Candy said we should meet. She said you're a sharp businesswoman."

"Aww…" Christina craned her neck. "Where'd she get off to?"

Griffin lifted Christina by the waist to see above the crowd. "Candy!" she called with a big wave. "Hold up, we're coming to see you!" She looked over her shoulder at Griffin. "Thanks."

He set her down. "My pleasure."

Christina stroked his scruffy jaw. "You gonna be okay without me for a few?"

He pulled her close, wrapping his arms around her

waist. "I'll come get you when I can't bear it anymore."

"Sign her napkin before we go," Christina instructed.

Griffin leaned on a nearby table and signed the napkin, handing it back to Kennedy with a flourish.

"Thank you," Kennedy breathed.

"See ya," Christina said, looping her arm in Kennedy's and taking her to go see Candy.

The crowd closed in on Griffin again. Luke stepped away and mingled with the party guests, making small talk with one eye always on Kennedy. She was chatting with Candy and Christina in a small seating area by an outdoor fireplace. Nearly an hour passed before Bentley grabbed the mike at a makeshift stage area with a chair and a spotlight and announced Griffin was about to play.

Griffin spent a few minutes tuning his acoustic guitar. Christina headed to the stage area, so Luke moved in to fetch Kennedy.

Kennedy was still starstruck. "I can't believe I met him," she breathed. "And his girlfriend is so cool. I really like her. She invited me to come to their next show and go backstage to meet the band!"

He grabbed her hand, eyes wide. "Can you believe you met me?"

She scoffed. "You're just a regular guy."

"Would you sleep with a guy like Griffin?" He could've kicked himself for letting his jealousy show. But, come on, she'd spent half the night staring at other men.

"He's wrapped around Christina's little finger. Did you see the way he keeps an eye on her even when he's talking to other people?"

He grunted, embarrassed that he'd done the same thing. He stroked a hand down her bare back. "I do love this dress."

She shivered. "Should we hit the bar?"

Griffin started playing a ballad, one of his most famous, "Crazy Thing." Christina danced nearby, and Griffin frequently gazed over at her.

"Come on, we're dancing." Luke pulled her to the area cleared for dancing, where several couples already swayed in time to the music. He stopped and pulled her close, his hands resting on her lower back, and felt himself relax. She belonged in his arms.

She slipped her arms around his neck. "I really appreciate you filling in all my dorky silences tonight."

"No problem." It was nice to be appreciated. His earlier irritation and embarrassing pangs of jealousy eased up.

"And for helping with my brother earlier. That means a lot to me."

"Yeah, well, guys aren't that complicated. Some

basic needs and urges. Especially the teenaged variety. It all comes down to sex."

"I'm sure it's more complicated than that. I told you the deal with my dad and how tight money is."

He turned her slightly so she couldn't see Chase Thompson looking in her direction. He was done sharing her with other men. "Trust me, he's trying to impress a girl. Why do you think he wanted to drive my car?"

"Because it's a Porsche?"

Luke lowered his voice. "You'll see. If money's tight, you should leave some condoms in his room. Don't leave that up to a shoplifting trip." He chuckled. "Security! Condom robber on aisle three!"

She ducked her head. "Omigod, I'm not buying my brother condoms!"

"Then just give him the cash and tell him to." He turned her again as the Tommy Hilfiger model checked out her ass. "Trust me on this."

She rested her head on his chest. "I do trust you."

The admission felt like a gift. He rested his hand on the back of her head, just holding her, feeling unexpectedly tender toward the woman that had dragged him into a fake engagement only to make him actually enjoy it.

If only he'd met her under different circumstances. If only there could be two winners in this game. Her family's financial situation worried him, especially where it concerned her not having enough money for the basics. But if he wanted to keep his job, he needed this client. He pushed those thoughts right out of his head. This was business. Bentley would choose only one of them. Most likely him based on his experience. And Kennedy would walk out of his life.

She sighed, and his chest ached. They still had the weekend, he reminded himself, and he intended to enjoy every minute.

~ ~ ~

Kennedy walked hand in hand with Luke back to their shared bedroom after the party and bonfire on the beach. She was exhausted but also wired with energy. "That was fun."

"Not bad," he said. "Would've been better with more Bentley time, but he was a little busy dancing on a table in his tightie whities."

She laughed. "I noticed."

They reached their room, and Luke held the door open for her. "After you."

Nerves raced through her as she stepped through the doorway.

He followed and eyed her. Like he was waiting to see what she'd do next.

She waited in breathless anticipation for him to

pounce. He'd been flirting and touching her all night. At the bonfire, Luke had set out a blanket and settled her in front of him so he could wrap his arms around her. He'd made her crazy with his hot breath whispering over her ear every time he spoke, and his occasional stroke along her neck or jawline. Nothing too aggressive, just constant reminders that he wanted her.

"Welp," he finally said. "Guess I'll go brush my teeth before *the inevitable*."

And with that he went into the bathroom and shut the door.

She stood there for a moment, thoroughly confused. Brush his teeth? After all the touching and flirting? Unsure what to do, she took off her heels, hung up her dress, and wrapped herself in a robe, waiting for him to finish.

He stepped out in a T-shirt and shorts a few minutes later. "Your turn."

She grabbed her duffel bag and got ready too. After she brushed her teeth and her hair, she contemplated whether she should put on the pajamas she'd packed, wear the robe with nothing under it, or just step out naked. While she'd only known Luke for a week, after today, she definitely knew she wanted to be with him. Beneath the polished exterior was a soul she could relate to, one who cared deeply about others.

Just look at how he'd helped out with her brother. And how he'd made sure she felt comfortable tonight, both with the proper dress and with hobnobbing with celebrities. As they'd left the beach tonight, talking easily, she was completely on board with a weekend of fun. Business would wait. A natural end to their time together. It made things simple and easy. But now she feared she'd jumped to conclusions. Was she just assuming their tumble into bed was inevitable? Wouldn't it be embarrassing to step out naked and find him still wearing his T-shirt and shorts?

She stepped into the bedroom in her T-shirt and fuzzy polka-dotted pajama pants.

Luke was already in bed, lounging shirtless with the sheet half covering him up to his waist. Was he naked or wearing shorts? Damn, his chest was beautiful, golden with pecs and washboard abs.

"Hey, polka dots, get over here." He let out a loud put-upon sigh. "Might as well get *the inevitable* over with."

She crossed her arms, annoyed that he seemed put out. "Not if it's any trouble."

He patted the mattress next to him. "If it's what you want, I'll deal."

"Don't do me any favors," she snapped.

"Come on, polka dots," he said in a jaded, I-do-this-all-the-time tone. "Time's a-wasting. Show me what you got."

She crossed to the side of the bed next to him, glanced down at his gorgeous golden chest and back up to his dark blue eyes that she now saw were sparkling with amusement.

She stiffened. "Your idea of seduction is *not* working for me."

"You're the one who said us sleeping together was inevitable. You sounded real excited about it too." He did an exaggerated eye roll.

"Forget it." She stepped away, and he snagged her by the hips. "Luke! Let go. It turns out it's not inevitable!"

He turned her to face him and sat up so she stood between his legs. His head was very close to her breasts and though he made no move, she heated, her nipples tightening into points at his nearness. He noticed.

One corner of his mouth lifted in an overly confident sexy smirk. "You're happy to see me."

"You tease me too much." She pushed at his hands, but he wasn't letting go.

"Don't worry," he said, pulling her with him as he laid down on the mattress. He settled her on top of him. "I'm very happy to see you too." He palmed her ass and thrust to show her.

"Is this how you seduce a woman?" she asked. "Your technique could use some work."

He cocked a brow. "Oh, yeah? Let's see your technique. You seduce me."

"It doesn't work that way." She'd never seduced a man before. All she had to do was let her boyfriend know it was time and he'd just go for it.

"Chicken."

Her hackles rose. She rolled off him. "Get naked," she ordered.

"Already am." He slid the sheet to the end of the bed. His massive erection sprang up proudly, waiting for her. "And I've got a strip of condoms in the nightstand with your name on them."

She swallowed hard.

He eyed her still standing on the side of the bed, taking him in. "I'm ready when you are," he said. "Obviously."

She looked up and down his body, so hard and male, unsure where to start.

"You need a hint?" he asked, folding his hands behind his head, all relaxed like it was just a day at the beach. "Your mouth just about anywhere sounds real good. Or you could just keep looking, but that means I get a turn at just looking too."

That got her moving. She wasn't prepared to lay naked while he studied her every flaw. She started at his calves, first stroking with her hands, then kissing and nipping and tasting, working her way up. His scent, fresh and clean and pure Luke, drew her in; his taste made her bold. By the time she reached his inner thigh, he wasn't nearly so relaxed. His hand slid into her hair, cupping her head. "Kennedy," he groaned.

She ran her tongue up and down the length of his erection. His hand tightened in her hair. She took him in, just a few sucking strokes, before she released him and moved further up his body, continuing her slow exploration. His hand was still tangled in her hair, his other hand sliding firmly down her back. She could feel the tension in him and knew it was just a matter of time before he took control. Luke was not the kind of man to give over the advantage for long.

But he surprised her. Though his hands gripped her and he groaned a lot, especially when she swirled her tongue around his flat nipples, he let her keep going. She kissed up his neck and along his stubbled jawline before finally landing with a soft kiss on his lips. She lifted her head and gazed down at him, still a little surprised he'd let her have her way.

"You're an animal." He threw his arms to the sides. "I feel ravished."

She found herself smiling. "You never stop."

His eyes went to half-mast as he stared at her mouth. "Don't you stop."

She kissed him again, her tongue sliding in to taste. He pushed her hair away from her face and held her head as she kissed him deeply, reveling in the feel of him, all hard planes under her. The kiss went on and on with her in the driver's seat. She rubbed herself against him restlessly, wishing she'd stripped naked too, suddenly needing to feel skin on skin. An urgency to feel more of him made her aggressive for the first time in the bedroom. She slid one hand down to cup him and nipped his bottom lip. That was all it took.

He grabbed her and rolled her under him, kissing her long and hard and deep, with an urgency that told her he was just as turned on as she was. She was lost in a haze of sensations, his hard body pressed against hers, his mouth demanding, his hand cupping her jaw, holding her in place. She grabbed at him frantically, unbelievably needy, her fingernails digging into his shoulders. But that wasn't how Luke wanted things to go between them.

He pinned her wrists above her head with one hand and deepened the kiss, claiming her mouth hard and rough, demanding total surrender. She softened and gave in to his silent demand, her body on fire as she waited for him to give her what she desperately needed. He made her wait, kissing her ravenously as his hand nudged her legs apart. She immediately opened and he rocked against her while he dominated her mouth, her arms still pinned above her head, the hold making her crazed. The need for release overwhelmed her. She mewled in the back of her throat, begging for him to take her in the only way she could.

He lifted his head with a wicked smile. "Still my turn."

She shivered.

He got off her, slid his hands under the waistband of her fuzzy polka-dot pants and pulled them off. Her panties went right along with them. "Much better," he murmured.

She sat up, peeled off her T-shirt and tossed it across the room. She lifted her chin and met his eyes in challenge. "Do your worst."

He chuckled softly. "Do my worst." He held her chin firmly. "Look at this defiant chin. What's my worst mean for you, Kennedy? You like the soft feather touch, the firm handling, or rougher? I'm flexible. Whatever brings you pleasure."

She swallowed hard. "I was teasing. Like you do."

He slid a hand into her hair and kissed her tenderly, his fingers stroking lightly down her throat. One finger did a light swirl over her shoulder before dipping lower to palm her breast. It felt good, like sex usually did.

He pulled back and gave her a knowing smile. "You like that?"

"Yes."

He pulled her onto his lap, making her straddle him, and kissed her again, harder this time, one hand cupping her jaw, the other hand holding her breast firmly as his thumb stroked back and forth over her hard nipple. Heat pooled between her legs. His hand left her breast and slowly slid further south. She held her breath, desperate for his touch. His tongue thrust in her mouth as his hand cupped her sex firmly, making her ache. He pulled back, still holding her firmly, and studied her expression. "You like that better."

It wasn't a question.

"Yes," she said softly, hoping he'd do more.

"Let's see what else you like better." He set her back on the bed, grabbed her by the ankles and gave a tug, making her lie flat on her back. Her breathing ratcheted up. "Now you get to feel ravished."

She waited in breathless anticipation. But then he just looked his fill, still lightly holding her ankles as he gave her a slow once-over, starting at her mouth, moving to her neck, then her breasts, her nipples still tight, aching for his touch. She heated as his gaze lingered on her sex, and when she started to squirm, his hold on her ankles tightened. That ignited her. She didn't know why. She'd never been restrained. She only knew she wanted with an intensity that she'd never felt before. He slid her heels up and apart, opening her to him, his hands firm on her ankles. His gaze on her most private parts was intense. He licked his lips, his grip on her ankles tightening.

"Luke," she begged, "please. Inside me."

His heated gaze flicked up to her eyes. "Do you feel ravished?"

"I want to."

He gazed back at her exposed sex. She whimpered and tossed her head side to side. Then he settled down low, between her legs, pushed her legs over his shoulders, and slid her slick folds apart with his fingers. He held her like that, taking her in, and the anticipation made her tremble. Finally he lowered his head, his tongue rasping over her most sensitive spot. Her hips came off the mattress. He used his shoulders to push her legs further apart, and she began a fervent plea, *please, please.* His fingers slid inside her, pressing up and stroking her on the inside as his mouth worked her at times rough and then soft. She exploded, bucking against him while he continued as if nothing had happened at all, making her wild.

"Luke!" she cried. "I'm done."

He lifted his head, his fingers still stroking her on the inside. She bucked uncontrollably against him, the white-hot intensity too much to bear. His hand clamped around her hip, pinning her to the mattress. "Again," he growled before lowering his head and suckling her.

She immediately came, electric shocks of sensation arcing down her legs, leaving her quivering. She panted, trying to catch her breath, as he finally released her.

He sat back and stroked a hand idly up and down her inner thigh. His voice was low and raspy and commanding. "On your belly."

She hesitated, unsure what he had in mind. "Luke, you ravished me enough."

His hand stilled. "You like what I did so far?"

"Yes."

"You trust me?"

She immediately thought of all he'd done for her both tonight and earlier today. "Yes."

He flipped her over and shoved her legs apart. "I say when it's enough."

She trembled at the words and not because she was scared. Though maybe she should've been because Luke being in charge in bed was the most turned-on she'd been in her life. She went on all fours and lifted her hips, offering herself to him, and was rewarded with a masculine groan. But he didn't touch her. She wondered if he was just going to stare at her some more from this position. She heard him move off the bed and then a rustle and realized she'd finally gotten to him and he was getting the condom. A thrill of victory went through her.

That was short lived.

He grabbed her by the hips and yanked her to the end of the mattress where he was standing. She lifted her head in surprise, and he pushed it down to the mattress and held her there. Heat flooded her, drenching her as she waited head down, bottom up. She trembled with excitement as he positioned himself at her entrance. But he gave her just a little, pulling out again, teasing her. Her entire body protested, clenching around him as he pushed in the tiniest bit, trying to hold him, and then he'd pull out again. She clamped her jaw shut. She wouldn't beg. That was exactly what he wanted.

He pushed in a little more and she nearly cried with relief before he pulled all the way out again. The word was on the tip of her tongue. *Please.*

He slid in again, giving her an inch, and stilled. She arched her hips back, silently begging. He slid halfway in and stopped, making her want to scream. His warm hand on her head stroked her hair to the side, exposing her neck. He pulled nearly all the way out and she tried to push back onto him, but his hand on her head held her in place. She started to shake, her body in overdrive, needy and on edge. He slid slowly in again, inch by inch, as his other hand stroked lightly down her spine, drawing arcs of electric sensation toward the one spot that ached for him to fill her. His hand rested on the dip in her lower back, his other hand kept her head pinned to the mattress. His cock was halfway home. He waited.

"Please," she whispered.

His hand slid from her lower back to her hip, which he held in a firm grip. She held her breath. His other hand released her head only long enough to shift lower and squeeze the nape of her neck in a primal hold. She surrendered with a shuddering breath and then gasped as he thrust fully within her, going deeper than she'd thought possible, making her ache. He thrust hard and fast and deep, taking what he needed, and she felt breathless as her body spiraled with sensation, tightening around him.

"Luke," she cried out, though she didn't know what she was asking.

He did. He slid one hand to her shoulder, pinning her down, while the other hand slipped around and stroked her center gently. The contrast of the alternating hard thrusts and gentle strokes made her crazed. "Luke," she cried out again. He knew. He knew what she needed. She just needed him to give it to her.

"I know," he said as if she'd said her thoughts out loud. "But I'm not done with you."

He gentled his touch, feathering light strokes over

her before thrusting hard again. She whimpered, she begged, she shook with her need. He didn't care. He kept her pinned by the shoulder while he played with her body, stroking lightly with his fingers, thrusting deep, and then changing it up with rough strokes and a gentle slide in and out. She gave up anticipating and let him have his way, alternately moaning and whimpering incoherently. She felt dizzy, beyond speech, lost in electric jolts and waves of sensation all controlled by this one man.

"You get me so hot," he said before yanking her by the hips onto him, making her take him deeper. She could do nothing but pant and take it. "Kennedy," he growled in a voice that revved her up further, "you break when I say so. On my command."

She trembled, feverish and soaked in waves of never-ending pleasure. He thrust hard, both hands on her hips, holding her in a firm grip. He kept going, more and more, both of them panting. The pressure built up and her mind screamed for her release. His hand slid around, pressing firmly against her hard nub. She felt it, the edge of a white-hot—

"Not yet," he growled, still holding her firmly as he thrust again.

She trembled uncontrollably. He kept a firm hold and thrust deep, making her cry out. Oh, God, she couldn't hold back.

He dropped his hand. *No!*

He squeezed the nape of her neck again as he thrust faster and faster. Her entire body surrendered with a shuddering sigh. No more begging. She rode the wave of pleasure he gave, under him, which was exactly what he must've wanted from her because his wonderful fingers were back, stroking her firmly, taking her higher and higher as he pounded into her. She struggled to hold back, to wait for his command. He'd know and he'd stop. Her body clenched around him involuntarily, bearing down as he thrust. He groaned and pushed them both for more. Her breath caught as the release she craved threatened to pull her under.

"Come for me," he said, and she broke hard in a shattering, heart-pounding release as she clenched and unclenched around him helplessly. She would've collapsed except Luke still had her firmly in his grip, both hands on her hips, pulling her back onto him as he pumped deep, faster and faster. A second orgasm threatened. She felt light-headed. It was too much, she couldn't hold back.

"Luke," she cried out desperately.

"Yes," he said, giving her permission as he thrust deep, slamming her over the edge. She exploded with a harsh cry, and he finally let go, pumping into her with a long, silent release of his own.

He pulled out a moment later, and she just lay there boneless and thoroughly satisfied. More satisfied than she'd ever thought possible. He'd wrung every last drop of pleasure out of her body.

He rolled her over, leaned down and kissed her gently. "You look good when you're ravished."

She pried an eye open and took in his cocky grin. Her ravishing of him had nothing on what he'd done to her. "Shut up."

He gave her another cocky smile. "I know how to shut you up."

She shivered. How could he still get her worked up at this point? He slid onto the bed and pulled her to his side, settling the sheet and comforter over both of them. Then he arranged her arm and leg over him, tucking her head against his chest.

"Luke?"

"Hmm…"

"Was it…" she trailed off. She suddenly felt unsure. Was it as good for him as it was for her? He'd said he was flexible. Maybe he liked it a different way better. She hated that she felt insecure, but she'd never been with a man like Luke. Gorgeous, confident, take charge. Her boyfriends fell far short of him in every possible way. "Nothing."

"Was it good for me?"

She ducked her head, embarrassed beyond belief.

"It sucked."

She sprang up in outrage, and he pulled her back down, but not before she saw the gleam in his eye. He settled his hand on her head, making her rest on his chest.

"Try again tomorrow, Kennedy." His chest shook with laughter. "Try real hard."

"You try again tomorrow," she snapped.

He palmed her ass and pressed her close. "I will. That's a promise. That was fucking awesome."

She let out a sigh.

He squeezed her ass. "Tomorrow night I'm going to tie you up."

Her heart raced. "What?"

"So just dream about that."

He sounded entirely too arrogant. She lifted her head. "What makes you think I want to be tied up?"

He pulled her close and his voice rumbled in her ear. "You like when I'm in charge."

She shivered, hot and cold at the same time. Who was this man? Teasing to tempting in the space of a breath. She could barely keep up. Yet she was turned on beyond belief. Almost restless in her need for more.

She let out a shaky breath. He chuckled.

She was beyond outrage at the way he played with her. "Maybe I'll tie you up instead."

"Sure."

"You don't mind giving me control?"

"Nope, but…"

She propped up on his chest to look at him. His eyes were closed. He had a small, satisfied smile on his face. "But what?"

"Nothing."

"Luke!"

"Damn, I'm tired. Night."

She shook him by the shoulder. "You can't fall asleep yet. What were you going to say?"

He let out a long-suffering sigh. "Can't a guy get some sleep after all that orgasming business?"

She climbed on top of him, stretched out, and propped her hands on his chest to look at him. "Not until you explain yourself."

"Mmm…" Both his hands slid to cup her ass. "This is nice."

"Luke!"

He didn't bother to open his eyes. "I don't care who gets tied up. But you're the one who's going to go off like a firecracker." He yawned. "It's the strong women who like to hand over the reins the most."

"You've done this before?" She was torn between outrage and intrigue. Also, he'd sort of complimented her there, calling her strong. Her petite size often made people not take her seriously.

He slid her up his body and kissed her. It wasn't a

demanding kiss. It was deep and all consuming, but tender. The outrage over his other women slipped away as she returned the kiss, lost in sensation once more.

"Night," he mumbled, scooting her back down to rest her head on his chest. His hands settled firmly on her ass. A few moments later, his breathing deepened into sleep.

She lay there, worrying over the way she liked him taking control. She never let a man have the upper hand. In truth, she feared turning out like her mom, just letting the man run her life. And what happens when that man falters, suddenly you have nothing. No savings of your own, no direction, just lost and helpless. Luke was the first lover to ever take over like that. The first time she'd ever had orgasms of that shattering magnitude. Not to mention multiple times. He was a take-charge kind of man. She'd known that from the first time she'd met him.

He's done this before. It's just a game to him. He didn't really know her. So that meant he couldn't take over her life. Depend on no man, she reminded herself.

Feeling a little better, she relaxed in his firm, if slightly indecent, hold. Sleep claimed her as soon as she closed her eyes.

CHAPTER ELEVEN

Luke woke the next morning feeling refreshed and energized. He often struggled with insomnia, his mind too full of things he had to do for work, but that bout with Kennedy and having her even now sleeping on top of him like a warm kitten had worked fantastic. He looked down at her sleeping so peacefully and idly stroked a hand up and down her back, noticing again how thin she was. Now he knew why he felt that protective instinct toward her. She was simultaneously strong and vulnerable. The vulnerability made him want to keep her close. The strength turned him on.

He'd meant it when he'd told her he was flexible in the way he made love. He was open minded, willing to do whatever brought a woman pleasure because it inevitably increased his pleasure. But what he enjoyed the most was when the woman completely and totally put her pleasure in his hands. Only with Kennedy, he'd wanted more, wanted her to wait for his permission to come. He'd never done that before, had no idea where that had come from, but it worked for both of them. And now he only wanted more. More sex, yes, but also more of Kennedy. More spit and fire by day, more shuddering sighs of surrender by night. He'd never wanted someone more the morning after than the day before. That fact should've troubled him, especially knowing once Bentley chose him, Kennedy wouldn't let Luke touch her at all. She'd be pissed off and rightly so.

But none of that seemed to matter right now.

Last night had been so much more than just a game. Though he'd tried to brush it off, teasing her after, he knew exactly why it had been the best sex of his life. He cared about her deeply. She sighed in her sleep, and his chest ached. Why did the one woman he actually felt something for have to be the one woman he couldn't have?

He glanced at the clock on the nightstand. It was late. They'd have to meet Bentley and Candy soon. Kennedy was scheduled for a mani-pedi with Candy. He and Bentley would be lounging by the pool with mimosas. After lunch, Bentley wanted them to go for a sail since they'd missed it yesterday. He slid Kennedy to the mattress, deciding to quietly take his turn getting ready and let her sleep. After his usual morning routine, he stepped into a steaming hot shower. It was like showering in a huge walk-in closet. He'd have to get Kennedy in here later. Maybe tonight. He worked the shampoo through his hair, closed his eyes and tipped his head back in the water to rinse. When he opened his eyes, he startled. Kennedy was standing naked, hands on her hips, glaring at him through the glass. He went rock hard.

"Were you just going to sneak out and meet Bentley without me?" she demanded.

He pushed the glass door open. "Better grab a condom from my bag." He indicated the black toiletry bag sitting on the bathroom counter. He always kept one in there for just such an occasion.

She lifted her defiant little chin.

He held her chin. "I do like this strong chin." He reached past her, snagged a condom, then pulled her in.

She sputtered as he shoved her under the spray. He rolled on the condom while she shoved her wet hair out of her eyes. "Why didn't you wake me?" she demanded.

"Good morning to you too."

"Luke!"

He pulled her flush against him and kissed her. She resisted for a moment, stiff in his arms, and he deepened the kiss, one hand gripping her hair, his arm banded around her waist. She melted against him.

That only made him want more. He turned and pinned her against the shower wall, pressing his body against her soft curves as he claimed her mouth. She wrapped her arms around his neck, and he lifted her so she could wrap her legs around him too. Once he had her how he wanted, he stopped briefly to set things straight because he didn't want angry sex. He wanted her to finish up happy.

"I was being considerate," he said in a low voice, stroking a finger over the rapidly beating pulse point on her neck. "Letting you sleep a little longer. I definitely wasn't planning on meeting Bentley without you. Are you kidding? He'd think I was scum if I left my fiancée behind for all the planned festivities."

"We need to—" She sucked in a breath as he pinched her nipple.

"We really do." He carried her to the long bench conveniently placed in the back of the shower stall and sat down with her straddling him. He gazed deep into her blue eyes, which had darkened and dilated, then lifted her up, slid halfway in, and held her there. "Say when."

"When," she whispered.

He dropped her onto him, taking her fully in one deep thrust. She cried out, and he nearly did the same. Sweet glory, she felt like heaven, hot and clasping him tightly. He lifted her again, and she whimpered. He dropped her, letting gravity sink him in deep. He groaned as she clenched around him. He felt like he was going to explode. She started to lift herself, wanting more, but he stopped her, grabbing her by the hips and holding her there, his cock halfway in. She went wild, trying to move, grabbing him everywhere. He waited her out, watched her struggle with her need and his want, and then she gave him what he most wanted.

"When," she said softly.

He dropped her onto him, giving them both what they needed. She keened, and he felt the pleasure ripple through her. He dropped her again, and she screamed. He covered her mouth with his to keep her from bringing too much attention to their morning activities. She thrust her fingers in his hair, returning the kiss passionately. He stroked her center and guided her slowly up and down the length of him, gripping her firmly by the hip. She mewled for more, but he held her to his pace, wanting to let it build, wanting to watch her break hard, uncontrollably. He felt himself grow thicker just thinking about it. He gripped both of her hips and lifted her, pushing her nipple to the roof of his mouth, sucking hard and then letting his teeth scrape over her as he released her. She panted. He did the same to the other breast. She moved restlessly against him. He slowly lowered her onto him as she clenched and unclenched around him. She was close; he could feel it.

"Don't come until I tell you to," he rasped near her ear. He wanted it as badly as she did, but he also wanted her crazed. A full body shudder racked her.

"Please," she said softly.

The soft voice, the plea, made him want to give her more. He gripped her hair and claimed her mouth in a hard kiss while his other hand moved her up and down on him, faster and faster. She was hot, mewling with need, clenching around him every time he ground her down. She tore her mouth from his. "Luke!" she cried.

"Not yet," he told her, and angled her so he could stroke her on the inside. She screamed, and he muffled her with another kiss. He kept going, slowing things down so he'd last longer, so he could prolong it for her.

She threw her head back in total surrender, exposing her throat. He sucked on the cord of her throat as he pumped. She clamped down on him. He made her take more. She mewled and trembled and keened, waiting for his command, making him thicker and harder.

He thrust again, one long stroke. "Now." She broke violently, her body racked with pleasure, which set him off. He pumped once, and she gasped. Twice, and she spasmed around him, still riding that wave, and the third time he let go. He came so hard his ears rang. When he landed back in reality, Kennedy was collapsed on him, her head resting on his chest, her arms loosely around his waist, still seated fully on him.

He kissed her temple. "I don't think I could ever get enough of you."

She looked up at him with a satisfied smile. "I hope you do."

He stroked her cheek and cupped her jaw. "What does that mean? You want me to finish with you?"

"I want you to take everything you want from me," she said simply.

His cock pulsed inside her. He placed a kiss on the side of her neck and scraped his teeth lightly over her. She shuddered.

"I can't believe I want you again," he growled in her ear.

"Take what you want," she said softly.

His fingers curled into her hips. The soft voice, the open surrender made him want her more than he'd ever wanted anyone. Even after everything they just did.

He really couldn't get enough of her. And his only thought was, how could he get more time with her?

But they didn't have time. They had to meet Bentley and Candy. They had to finish this business deal. And then they'd be finished.

She bit his lower lip, the movement giving him a nice stroking. "If you have the stamina, Grand—"

He swatted her bottom. "Don't you dare." She was not going to get away with calling him Grandpa. Not after he'd showed her his much-longer-than-ten-minutes prowess.

She lifted her chin. He kissed that defiant little chin tenderly. Then he set her off him, stood, and grabbed one of the handheld shower nozzles. "Guess who's about to get really clean?"

She grabbed for the other nozzle but he caught her wrist in a firm grip. Her breath came harder and her eyes dilated. He grinned and began a thorough soaking that had her first sputtering and then pleading and finally calling his name like a fucking halleluiah.

As she should be.

~ ~ ~

Kennedy had a mani-pedi with Candy, who she discovered was surprisingly astute when it came to Bentley's business dealings. Was she, in fact, the one making decisions? Was that why she was at all of his business meetings? She didn't know how to ask, but Candy had successfully run a luxury spa in Manhattan, where she'd started as a masseuse, built up her wealthy clientele, and then took over when the former owner retired. Candy had been toying with the idea of expanding the spa to other cities, but since getting married, her focus had been on Bentley.

"Don't you want to go back to work?" Kennedy asked as they walked outside and down the path to the pool to meet the men.

"I'm still thinking about it," Candy replied. "Marrying Bentley gave me different options. Right now I'm just having a good time."

"I think I'd still need to work."

"I've been working since I was five years old. I grew up on a farm in upstate New York. Chores before dawn, chores after school, chores all summer long." She shook her head. "All that work and we were still dirt poor. I appreciate what I have now even more."

Kennedy could relate to that. Her chores were different, but there had been many both before and after school. Not assigned chores, but work, nonetheless, that she took on at an early age in her quest to be wanted and needed by her family.

"There's my beautiful wife," Bentley called, heading for them.

Candy tossed a smile to Kennedy before rushing into his arms. They hugged and kissed like they hadn't seen each other in days instead of just hours. Luke lay stretched out in a chaise lounge in his country-club attire—polo shirt, pressed shorts, and designer sandals.

He raised a hand and gestured for her to join him.

She made a return gesture for him to come over to her.

He let out a sigh and made a big deal out of getting out of his chaise lounge that made her laugh. He crossed to her and stood in front of her. "Happy? You got me at your beck and call."

She grinned. "Better than the other way around."

"Did you get hot pink like I told you?"

She held up her hand to show him. "Pale lavender."

"Toes?" he asked, scooping her up and cradling her in his arms to check for himself.

"Luke! Put me down!"

He checked out her toes. "Just clear, huh?"

"I don't take toenail polish orders," she said.

"No?" he asked with a devilish grin before tossing her over his shoulder. Her cheeks burned. What must Candy and Bentley think seeing her tossed around like a doll? At least she was wearing shorts and not the sundress. She smacked his back to no effect. "How about fingernail polish orders?"

"Put that poor girl down," Candy called. "Her face is bright red."

Luke walked with her back to the pool area, flipped her back to her feet, and grinned, looking mighty pleased with himself.

"Don't do that again," Kennedy said, giving his chest a shove.

He staggered back like she was extremely powerful, which gave her an idea. She gave him another shove. "Ever," she added.

He staggered back again. One more step, and she'd have him where she wanted him.

"Uh, Luke," Bentley started.

Luke turned. "What?"

Kennedy gave one final shove when he was distracted, and he toppled into the deep end fully clothed. He came up sputtering.

"Guess who's coming in with me?" he asked.

"Not me," she said, backing away.

"Run!" Candy hollered.

Luke swam toward the side of the pool and Kennedy took off for the house. He caught her around the waist, halfway to her destination, his soaking-wet clothes soaking her.

"Gotcha!" he said.

She fought like crazy and his arms just gripped her tighter. She went limp, strangely relaxed. "Luke, come on. I was just getting you back."

"What'll you give me?" he asked, his voice a suggestive rumble in her ear.

She turned in his arms to face him. "What do you want?"

"Information."

"What kind of information?"

"Did you and Candy talk about Bentley's financial future?"

She glanced back toward the pool area. Bentley and Candy were snuggled together on a chaise lounge, Candy sitting between Bentley's legs. They seemed to be out of hearing range. "No."

"Learn anything?"

"She's a smart lady."

He leaned down to her ear and whispered, "What else?"

"That's it. What'd you and Bentley talk about?"

He pulled back and met her eyes. "We talked about his favorite things—Candy, sailing, and parties."

"Anything on the financial front?"

He stroked her cheek. "Nope. He doesn't want to talk about that."

She took a deep breath. "Tomorrow we have to pin him down."

"But today's for fun," he said with a grin before scooping her up in his arms and heading back to the pool.

Halfway there, she got a bad feeling. "Don't you dare toss me in that pool, Reynolds!"

He grinned devilishly. "What's it worth to ya, Ward?"

She lowered her voice. "I'll let you tie me up."

"Ha! You were going to let me do that anyway."

"No, I wasn't."

He stopped abruptly. "Why not? You said you trusted me."

"I do."

He smiled at her tenderly. "Good." He kept walking and stopped by the edge of the pool. "You a good swimmer?"

"Don't!" She started a wild struggle, but he just held her tight.

"So feisty," he said and jumped into the deep end with her in his arms. She came up sputtering and dunked him. Bentley and Candy laughed at their antics and jumped in with them fully clothed.

"Look what you started!" Luke accused her.

"Me!"

"You pushed me in first."

She grinned and splashed him in the face. He splashed her back before lifting her and tossing her further into the pool. She swam under water and pinched his butt on her swim by, making him jump and whirl. She popped up on his other side for air, and he grabbed her, hauling her in and kissing her, before they both sank. For a moment the world was only the hot press of his mouth on hers. No sight, no sound, just a floating moment tethered to him.

They came up for air, swam over to the side of the pool, and hung on.

"When's the happy day?" Bentley asked from where he and Candy were hanging out on the steps of the shallow end, not seeming to mind sitting there in dripping wet clothes.

"It is a good day," Kennedy replied.

Luke lifted her by the waist and set her on the side of the pool. "He means our wedding day," he said quietly before joining her.

Kennedy's heart pounded. She'd almost forgotten her stupid lie. The entire reason she'd been invited for the weekend. "Oh. We haven't set a date yet."

"June is nice," Candy said.

"You could have it here if you want," Bentley offered with a smile. "Good memories of your stay with us, and we have plenty of space."

Guilt stabbed at her. Here they were pulling the wool over these nice people's eyes to score a business deal.

Luke stepped in. "That's a very nice offer, but a church wedding is important to us."

Kennedy nodded mutely. Luke stood, peeled off his shirt and wrung it out. She couldn't even appreciate the view because she was racked with guilt. She stood too. They needed to make an excuse to leave before the lies got too thick.

"What about the reception?" Candy asked. "Did you like any of the brochures I showed you in my scrapbook? Ooh! You could tour Stone Haven if you don't want it here. Remember that place?"

"It has to be inexpensive," Kennedy blurted.

Candy and Bentley exchanged a puzzled look.

Luke dropped an arm over her shoulders and grinned. "She wants to blow a wad of cash on the honeymoon."

"Ah, that makes sense," Candy said. "Our honeymoon was fabulous!"

"I barely let her leave the hotel room," Bentley added before they started sucking face.

Luke gripped her hand. "We're going to change. Meet you back here for that sail."

Candy waved over her shoulder while she continued kissing her billionaire husband.

Kennedy waited until they were nearly at the house before saying quietly to Luke, "We should tell them the truth."

"The truth will only hurt them," he said in a low voice.

"But they think we're all friends."

"We are friends."

"But if they find out..." It wasn't just losing the business. It was hurting two people who'd been nothing but generous to them.

He stopped and looked at her. "It doesn't matter. They only have to believe until the end of the weekend. Then the deal is done."

And so are we. The unspoken words hung in the air and a chill settled over her. She crossed her arms, hugging herself.

Luke's mouth formed a grim line. "You're getting a chill from those wet things. Let's get you inside."

"You don't have to take care of me."

"I'm not. I'm being practical. I want out of these wet things too. You're the wench who tossed me in the pool first." He tickled her, but she couldn't laugh. An overwhelming sadness crashed over her. He lifted her chin and kissed her gently. "We still have two more days and one very naughty night."

"You're not tying me up."

His hand squeezed hers. "Kennedy, by the end of tonight you'll be begging me to do exactly that."

"You wish."

His dark blue eyes danced merrily. "I know."

She found herself smiling. Why did his arrogant confidence make her happy? She should be irritated. But underneath all that, he was playing with her, and she'd had precious little playtime in her life.

Just enjoy this last bit, she reminded herself. *Don't think about the end.*

He held up her hand. "You ruined your nails."

The color was a little chipped. She put her arms around his neck and angled her body in a silent request to carry her again cradled in his arms. "You should see my toes."

He scooped her up and carried her inside. "Just as bad, I'm afraid. Though you have to admit it's all your fault."

They argued back and forth happily all the way inside.

~ ~ ~

Luke refused to think of the end of his time with Kennedy. They still had two days before she'd want nothing to do with him. Two days where he could enjoy her and pretend she was his. Maybe it was exactly that time limit that made him feel so much for her. If he thought he was stuck with her for real, he'd probably be dying to cut ties. He'd always been that way. Always started to feel boxed in and needing his freedom.

They boarded Bentley's sailboat and put on the requisite life vests. Bit of a disappointment because it covered Kennedy's black bikini. They'd found their swimsuits freshly laundered and waiting for them when they got back to their room. Bentley was quite the sailor and they sped along, the sleek white boat leaning nearly vertically on the side where they all sat.

Kennedy gripped his arm tightly. "Are we supposed to be dipping this far into the water?" she hollered.

Bentley grinned and adjusted a rope on the sail. "It's a racing sailboat. Don't worry! The *Sweetcakes* is stable!"

"It's named after me!" Candy added. She scooted closer to Bentley, who launched into a long explanation of which rope they should work to take advantage of the wind.

Kennedy white-knuckled the boat and him. Besides the fact they were about to get dunked in the Sound, it was a gorgeous breezy day out on the water.

"You do know how to swim?" he teased.

"Why? Am I going to fall in?"

He leaned his head back. "We're practically dipping our heads in the water." And going at a good clip too.

"I know!" she hollered, eyes wide.

He gave her a wicked grin. "I should *tie* you to the boat so you don't fall overboard."

She huffed, immediately onto his teasing about tying her up.

Of course, that just encouraged him. "It's *knot* going to be easy to survive this. Get it, *knot*?"

"Ha-ha."

He slid a hand over, gripping both her wrists in

his. "We'll be all tangled up. Don't worry I know all the best knots to tie and untie."

She flushed. "Would you stop?" she hissed.

He grabbed a nearby rope and twined it around her forearm. "How's it feel?"

She yanked her hand and the rope went with her, making the sail buckle and the boat pitch.

"What'd you do!" Bentley hollered, rushing to fix it. "Duck!"

They ducked in time for the beam to just miss all of them. The boat tipped the other way.

"Candy!" Bentley hollered. "Grab that rope. Hold on!"

Kennedy sank to the deck of the boat, tucking her knees up and ducking her head, making herself as small as possible. "It's all my fault!" she cried.

He joined her and pulled her close, wrapping his arms around her from behind. She relaxed, sliding her legs down. "It's my fault," he told her. "I was messing around. Bentley's got this."

"I got it!" Bentley crowed. The sail billowed out again and the boat resumed its angular cut through the water.

"See?" he said in her ear.

Bentley high-fived Candy. "Good teamwork, Skipper!"

Candy saluted. "Aye, aye, Captain."

He kissed Kennedy's temple. "Can you call me captain?"

"Bite me."

He did, sinking his teeth into her neck. She sucked in an audible breath.

"I can't wait for your wedding," Bentley said, looking back and forth between them, a curious expression on his face.

Kennedy stiffened. Luke lifted his head. "Of course you're invited," Luke said smoothly. "As soon as we set a date."

"Yes," Kennedy said woodenly.

He turned her and kissed her because he was afraid her guilty conscience was going to blow their cover. She snuggled into his neck and clung to him. "I'm getting a bad feeling," she whispered right into his ear.

Now was not the time for this discussion. Bentley and Candy were too close. He kissed her again before dragging her back to join Bentley and Candy on the side of the sailboat that forever felt like it was going to dump them into the Sound.

~ ~ ~

Kennedy made it through the rest of their day with a guilty conscience. Bentley and Candy had really grown on her and she felt horrible for her deception. Luke was extra affectionate with her, and she was sure it was to put on a good show for their benefit. And he kept razzing her with rope jokes—getting tied up, tangled up, hands were tied, many, *many* references to knots. Always with a wink. She was so busy trying to keep him from embarrassing both of them she didn't even have a chance to figure out the best way to let Bentley and Candy know the truth.

They enjoyed a quiet dinner on the veranda, just the four of them, followed by an after-dinner drink and a game of pool in a gorgeous billiards room all done in a dark cherry paneled wood. Kennedy played on Candy's team. They beat the men, and she and Candy high-fived each other in triumph.

Bentley, always good natured, cheered Candy on the entire time and congratulated her at the end. Luke informed her he would "knot" be congratulating her.

Candy turned to them, smiling. "You see why I love him?"

"I do," Luke said. He turned to Kennedy. "What do you love most about me, sweetheart?"

"Your modesty."

"You are *knot* making this easy," he said in his one hundredth knot joke of the night.

Bentley and Candy hugged and kissed in the corner.

"You are *knot* getting any tonight," she whispered, which only made him laugh.

"We're going to turn in," Candy announced, dragging Bentley with her.

"Are you sure?" Bentley asked. "It's early."

"I need you upstairs," Candy said with a significant look.

Understanding dawned on Bentley's face. "Sorry, have to go. It's, uh, later than I realized."

Kennedy smiled. "Go on, you horny devil," Luke said.

"Toodles!" Candy called in a way that only she could get away with.

"Toodles!" Kennedy called back with a grin.

Candy laughed, and they left.

Luke's gaze turned predatory. "So," he drawled, advancing on her. She held her ground and he just wrapped an arm around her waist, backing her up until she hit the wall. "Looks like it's time for us to play."

She lifted her chin. "You've been obnoxious all night with your rope and knot jokes."

"I know." He pinned her wrists to the wall on either side of her head and kissed her until she was breathless. "I don't even have any rope."

"You jerk! You put all these ideas in my head and you don't even have rope?"

He smiled against her mouth. "I knew you'd be into it." He kissed her long and deep, and her knees went weak. His next words whispered across her mouth. "Let me be creative." He pressed his entire body against hers, pinning her against the wall, the tight hold between his hard planes and the hard wall igniting her.

"Yes," she hissed out before he kissed her in a fierce possession, and she clung to him, her body revved and ready for whatever he had in store.

CHAPTER TWELVE

At least she thought she was ready. Until Luke pulled out two silk ties, returned to her lying naked in bed, and wrapped one around her wrist.

She swallowed. "M-maybe we should just do this the regular way."

He kept tying, moving to the bedpost. "This is just for convenience. This way I can restrain you the way you like and still have my hands free for that sexy little body."

"Maybe you should go first."

He finished tying and snagged her other wrist. "Just relax."

She gave a little tug. It was kinda tight, which made her squirm. "I am relaxed. I just really think you should go first."

He stopped and met her eyes, studying her face. "Let's do a little experiment." He untied her and put the silk ties on the nightstand. She should've felt relieved, but the experiment part was also making her nervous. "Ready? Pin my wrists above my head, straddle me for the bonus humping, and kiss me. Then report back how hot it makes you."

He laid down on his back and settled his wrists above his head.

He was teasing her again, trying to show her how easy it was, goading her into it. He knew she couldn't resist a challenge.

She stalled. "An experiment? Really? Let's just do it."

"Come on." He grabbed her and settled her in position on top of him. "Now pin my wrists."

She leaned forward, pinning his wrists above his head firmly, and kissed him. It was good. She lifted her head.

"You forgot to hump me at the same time," he said helpfully.

She rolled her eyes.

"Bring it," he dared. "Pin and hump, baby. Show me what you got."

She pinned him and kissed him hard just to shut him up, rocking her pelvis against his hardness. Heat spread through her limbs. As soon as she lifted her head, he asked, "How was it? Did it make you hot?"

"Yes, your kisses always make me hot."

"Thank you." In one quick move, he flipped her

onto her back, wedged a leg between hers, and pinned
her wrists above her head. His mouth slammed over
hers. Heat flooded her, and she ached for more. Long
moments later, he lifted his head. "Now did that make
you hot?"

She was breathless. "Yes."

He kept her wrists pinned. "It's more than that."
His mouth went to her throat, kissing and scraping his
teeth against her. "Your pulse picks up." He met her
eyes. "You're breathing hard. Face it, you like when I
pin you. So just let me tie you up. You'll like me
having my hands free. Gives me more to work with."

"I don't think I can take you having more to work
with," she replied honestly.

He grinned. "Well, let's find out." He snagged the
ties off the nightstand.

She grabbed one. "Let's find out on you."

"Fair enough."

He laid back down and let her tie his wrists to the
bedposts. She got a little crazy then, wanting to have
the kind of control over him that he had over her. First
she went slow, kissing and nipping him in all of his
most sensitive spots from his neck down to his chest
and stomach, where she stopped and worked her way
back up. He groaned. Then she went fast, working
him over with her hands and mouth, making him jolt
and groan as she went down the same path, stopping a

breath away from his thick cock, which pulsed toward her.

"Don't come until I tell you to," she growled before taking him fully in her mouth. He hissed out a breath.

She quickly got him to the point where he was moaning and thrusting up in time to her rhythm. When she felt him jerk, felt he was right on the edge, she stopped.

She lifted her head and held him firmly with one hand. "Not yet."

He thrust up and down in her hand and exploded.

She stared at her hand and then at him. "Luke! You were supposed to wait for my command."

He grinned widely. "I'm not as strong as you."

She got off him, cleaned up, and returned to where she'd left him tied to the bed. She straddled his stomach to speak to him face-to-face. "That's not how it works. I was in control."

He was still smiling, eyes closed. "Sorry. Once I'm close, ain't nothing holding it back."

"Well, I'm going to do the same thing next time."

"Difference is, you like having me hold you back."

She frowned. "I do not. It's very difficult."

He opened his eyes, those dark blues pinning her even though he was the one tied up. "Have you ever come so hard in your life? Full body shudders? I've never seen a woman come as hard as you do."

She swallowed, tight and hot and about to burst into flames.

"Untie me," he ordered. "It's your turn."

She got off him and stared at him, still not sure if she was ready for that.

"It's just a game, Kennedy. I know you want to play."

She said nothing.

His voice dropped, rough and raw. "You want to feel the silk tight against your wrists. You want to feel my hands and mouth all over your body, controlling your movements, controlling your response, controlling your orgasm. Making you come over and over—"

"Okay! Okay!" She untied him.

"Lie down, sweetheart," he said with a hint of a gloat.

"You don't have to sound—" Her retort was cut off as he kissed her, easing her down under him at the same time. She really was too easy for him, but he made her feel so good she got sucked in every time.

He lifted his head, grinned a wicked smile that had her somewhere between raw lust and nervous anticipation, and quickly tied her up. He tied kinda tight. Not enough to hurt, but enough to keep her aware of the binding. Her heart pounded, and her throat went dry.

"Give a pull," he said.

She tugged at the ties, and they held her tight. She wasn't going anywhere until he let her. Panic welled up, and she pulled hard at the restraints. Luke quickly held her wrists in place, stilling her as he kissed her in the rough and demanding way that overwhelmed her. Her body overrode her brain, and she melted into the mattress. He released her wrists and kissed lower, his mouth trailing to her jaw and neck as his hands moved to cup her breasts. Oh, God, he really was going to make her crazed. She was already throbbing, hot, wet, and ready. She tilted her head, giving him open access. He nipped her and soothed with his tongue as his fingers rolled and tugged on her nipples. The familiar surge of lust and sharp pleasure that only he brought out returned. She was strapped onto the ride and there was nothing to do but let him take her whatever way he wanted. The slow climbs and exhilarating free falls; the crazy, dizzy loops and sharp, white-knuckled turns. She let out a shuddering sigh of surrender.

"Now that's what I like to hear," he said, rising up to nip her bottom lip as he pinched her nipples. She gasped, her insides tightening with need. "My turn," he growled in her ear. "Open your eyes and watch."

He leaned back and made sure she was watching. But then instead of touching her, he just looked. His eyes trailed all over her body, lingering in places that heated under his gaze. She moved her hips restlessly, and he pinned them down with one hand. By the time he actually touched her, stroking from her throat straight down to her sex, she ignited.

"You're mine tonight," he told her as his fingers thrust inside her.

"Yes," she hissed.

"Fuck yes," he instructed as the heel of his hand pressed against her where she needed it most.

"Fuck yes," she hissed, watching him.

Luke's gaze heated, and his hand on her sex tightened in a possessive hold that made her see stars. "Let's see how many more fuck yeses I can get out of you."

It turned out as many as he wanted.

~ ~ ~

The next morning Luke woke at the crack of dawn with a naked Kennedy sleeping on top of him. She was warm and light, his little sex kitten. He'd worn her out last night, worn himself out too. He'd wanted their last night together to be long and hot and memorable. Today was their last day and the thought had weighed so heavily as he drifted off to sleep that he woke up early thinking about it. Likely Bentley would make his final decision today. The thought should've been welcome. Instead he felt an overwhelming sense of loss.

He stroked her soft blond hair, over her slight shoulders, down her back, her bony shoulder blades and ribs familiar to his hands, yet still worrying him. He had to find a way to make sure she had enough food. That her family was set so she wouldn't sacrifice herself. He simultaneously hated that she did that and loved that she cared so much for her family. It was something he understood. Family ties were important to him too. He tightened his hold on her, and she sighed in her sleep. As always, a firm grip relaxed her.

He wasn't ready to let her go.

And then in one blinding moment of clarity, he knew what he had to do. He slid her to the mattress, made sure she was covered with the blanket, and slipped out of bed. He quickly dressed and went in search of Bentley. He knew that early bird would be up.

The housekeeper, Elizabeth, met him at the foot of the stairs. "Bentley and Candy are taking their breakfast on the veranda. Would you like your breakfast sent out to you?"

"Just coffee. Thanks." He headed to the veranda, took a deep breath, and pushed through the French doors. "Good morning."

Bentley and Candy beamed from where they sat at

one side of a glass-topped patio table. "Morning!" Bentley said.

"Join us," Candy said, gesturing to the seat across from them. "Where's Ken?"

"I let her sleep in."

"She's missing this gorgeous sunrise," Bentley said, gesturing to the horizon where the sun was rising over the water.

"Another time," Luke replied. Elizabeth appeared with his coffee, black the way he liked it. "Thank you."

She nodded once, asked if anyone needed anything else, and left.

Luke took a fortifying sip of coffee. "I want you to choose Kennedy as your financial manager. She's underappreciated at work and needs the boost for her career." And she needs it for her family, he added silently.

"I do like her incredible record at golf," Bentley said. "What a handicap! And her college golf record is impressive."

Luke started, nearly knocking over his coffee as he realized what Bentley had meant during their first meeting at the golf course when he said he liked Kennedy's incredible record. Knowing that, Bentley must've known Luke wouldn't win that golf game. Which made him wonder why exactly Luke had been called at all. Bentley had mentioned his reputation.

"And what exactly was it about my reputation you liked?" Luke asked.

"Everyone knows you on the Manhattan party scene," Bentley said. "I like to work with fun people. Friends mostly."

Luke couldn't believe this whole time he'd thought his experience gave him the advantage when it really just came down to golf and parties.

"It would mean a lot to both Kennedy and I if you chose her," Luke said.

"Gosh, it's a lot to think about," Bentley said, turning to Candy in question.

"We'll take that into consideration," Candy said to Luke.

"There's something else I'd like you to consider," Luke said. "A foundation to help families with overwhelming medical bills. Kennedy's parents are having a hard time because of the bills that piled up after her dad's accident, but they don't want us to help out. A foundation that families could apply for based on need would be well worthwhile. I could help you set it up if you'd like. I've done similar before."

"I had no idea Kennedy's parents were having trouble," Candy said. "I'm so sorry. What happened?"

He told her what he knew about the accident and them coming up short on the basics like food. Something that was difficult with all her brothers and sisters to feed. He left out that Kennedy was the one who bore the brunt of that. Candy teared up, which had Bentley holding her close.

"She's very sensitive," Bentley said.

Candy wiped her eyes. "I definitely want to meet about this very important cause. I'll have Bentley's assistant, Anita, set it up."

He stood, eager to get back to Kennedy before she woke. "Thank you. We both really appreciate it."

"Of course!" Candy said. "That's what friends are for!"

A pang of guilt hit him over the small deception he and Kennedy still had going. He pushed that down. "Okay. Thanks again. I'll be back a little later with Kennedy."

He headed back inside and climbed the stairs. He was playing the long game, and he hoped it would all be worth it in the end. Now he just had to find another job because the moment his boss heard he'd lost this big client to someone with as little experience as Kennedy had, he'd be toast.

He managed to slip back into the room, strip down, and join Kennedy without her waking.

~ ~ ~

Kennedy woke on top of Luke, her own warm mattress, as his hand stroked lightly up and down her back. She lifted her head, still sleepy. "You're up. Do I have to wake up now?" She dropped her head back to his chest and closed her eyes before he could answer.

"Not yet," he said, his voice rumbling in his chest. "We have some time."

She sighed and relaxed again. But she had trouble going back to sleep because he kept touching her, stroking from the nape of her neck down her back over her hips and up her sides.

She lifted her head again. He seemed wide awake.

He pushed her hair out of her face. "We're leaving today."

"I know."

He cupped her face with one hand, and she closed her eyes, leaning into his hand. "Bentley will make a decision soon. Maybe today."

"Maybe."

"We're here for business, and he needs to let us know one way or the other who he wants." She stiffened, and he hugged her tightly. She relaxed against him, resting her head on his chest when he spoke. "I want to see you again...after this."

She lifted her head. "What are you saying?"

His dark blue eyes burned into hers. "I'm saying I want you for more than one weekend."

She bit her lip. The business part of their relationship would always come between them. "I wish

I'd met you under different circumstances."

"You say that like it's hopeless to be with me."

"In some ways it is."

He stroked her back. "In *no* way."

She sighed. "If he chooses me, you'll be upset."

He got serious. "I'll probably lose my job. They're downsizing all but the upper-tier team. My boss would cut me loose anyway for letting Bentley slip through my fingers to an assistant with two years' experience."

"Omigod! That's even worse. And if he chooses you, I'll be upset."

He grinned.

"Why are you smiling?"

"Because if he chose me, you could come work for me as my assistant. Win-win." He winked.

"You as my boss? That sounds all kinds of forbidden." Luke would make her his plaything at the office. Her body his playground.

"That's me, the forbidden fruit." He stroked her hair back from her temple in a tender gesture that made a lump form in her throat. "Wanna take a bite, Eve?" He snapped his teeth at her, making her laugh.

"I really don't think that's a good idea," she said.

He rolled on top of her, the hard heat of his body bringing her to an achy, needy state. "Alright, forget working for me. Move in with me for a month."

She felt dizzy from the change in gears. "What?"

"Just hear me out." His mouth grazed her earlobe, his words hot against her skin. "Here's what's in it for you. You'll get your own space—"

"With you." He drew her earlobe between his teeth and tugged. A hot shiver ran through her.

"More space than you have now at home." He kissed the sensitive spot on her neck just below her ear, then kissed a hot trail down her neck. She stroked his warm muscular arms that she loved to feel hold her tight.

He lifted his head. "And I'll pay off your family's debt. How much is it?"

She stiffened. "No, Luke—" He kissed her hard, making her forget everything but his marvelous body pressing against hers, his invading tongue, the firm hands that were even now stroking and massaging her, wearing down any protest she might have. She moaned as his hand cupped her jaw firmly.

He broke the kiss, his fingers stroking down her throat. "Tell me how much your family's in debt."

"Don't," she said.

"Just tell me," he urged.

"My family's not a charity case! And neither am I!" She lowered her voice with great effort, not wanting anyone to hear them fighting. "I know you mean well, but don't."

He stared at her for a long moment before he said

gruffly, "I'm not ready to let you go."

"I can't move in with you! You can't—you're not thinking clearly. Just because we had fun—"

"Let's just see how things play out." He stroked her cheek. "Can you at least give it a little time?"

She swallowed, still worried that Luke was going to try to take care of her and her family. She didn't want charity.

She pushed at his chest. "Let me up."

He rolled off her, and she sat on the side of the bed. He joined her, sitting side by side, and took her hand.

"Kennedy?" he prompted. "Can you give us a little time?"

"I guess."

"I guess?" he mocked. "Way to commit."

"I'm not required to commit to you."

"Our engagement says differently."

She stared at the floor. "I think you're getting playtime confused with reality."

He held her chin and turned her back to face him. "They're one and the same for me."

She sighed. "It's just a game. Right? Just a game."

"One that I'll win," he said all smug-like.

Her temper flared. "You make me *so* mad."

"You make me *so* hot." Then he cupped her jaw and kissed her so tenderly she felt like she was going to cry.

She pulled away. "Don't do that again."

He eyed her speculatively. "What'd I do?"

"Kiss me like that."

"Like what?"

"You know." She turned from his heated gaze.

He turned her back to face him, his fingers holding her chin firmly. "You just want me to be that guy, huh? The one who takes you rough and makes you surrender."

She couldn't answer. She was heating everywhere at his firm hold on her and his words. She'd never felt this kind of electric attraction to anyone before. But she didn't dare admit the truth. That he could get to her so easily with a tender touch. Could destroy her. She needed to keep this a game between them.

His fingers softened, stroking along her jaw. "And what if I'm not that guy? What if I'm this guy?" He brushed his lips across hers before sinking into a kiss that overwhelmed her for all the wrong reasons. His touch was firm, cupping her jaw, but the kiss was tender. She tore her mouth away.

"Don't," she said almost desperately. She stood abruptly and stumbled back. Luke followed so quickly she barely had time to comprehend what came next. One minute she was standing there trying to compose herself, the next she was airborne. He tossed her over his shoulder, his hand connecting with a smack on her bottom and staying there, holding her firmly. The blood rushed to her head and her entire body relaxed in his hold. Tender Luke was gone.

"Shower time," he said, striding toward the bathroom. "Guess who's getting every nook and cranny clean?"

"Bentley?" she asked.

He barked out a laugh. "True, but not by me. You and I are going to practice."

"Practice what?" she asked, almost giddy they were back to the game, which meant only pleasure and no heartache, no hard feelings.

He stopped in front of the shower stall and set her back on her feet. He turned on the water, reaching in and feeling the temperature.

"What are we going to practice?" she asked again with a smile.

He turned back to her, his eyes alight with mischief and mayhem again. "We're going to see if you'd be a good assistant to this boss." He raised a brow. "Or would you rather be my student?"

"I—ah!" He grabbed her and pulled her under the spray.

She sputtered, shaking her head. He pushed her hair out of her face and wrapped his arms around her. "Kidding. You don't get a choice. It's my game."

She beamed. He slowly shook his head; then his hand gripped her hair and he kissed her in a rush of possession. She sank against him in equal parts desire and relief that he wasn't pushing the issue of them as a couple. Yet this time was different, as she soon discovered. There was an edge to his voice and his handling of her that hadn't been there before as he became the demanding boss to her assistant. First with the shower hose then with his devious hands and wicked mouth. She gladly gave everything he wanted, everything he demanded, until they were both panting and frenzied in a frantic joining that had her pinned against the shower wall, her heart pounding against her rib cage as hard as Luke was pounding against her. An eternity of hazy, steamy ride later, he let her break. She surrendered to a shattering release, her legs quivering with it as electric shocks radiated through her.

"Yes, so good," he praised her as he did whenever she broke on his command. Then he took what he needed, hard and fierce the way she liked. The way that kept her heart safe.

And when they finished, he wrapped her up in a towel, her overly sensitized, overly clean body a limp noodle. He cupped the back of her neck in a firm hold and looked deep into her eyes. "We're not done, Kennedy."

She didn't like the look in his eyes that spoke of

emotion that would never work. "You mean assistant, sir," she said in an attempt to bring him back to the game. The way he used her full name killed her. No one called her by her full name and especially not the way he did, making it sound beautiful.

He squeezed the nape of her neck, somehow knowing his words would sneak past her defenses that way. "I mean it." Something in his dark blue eyes reached in, grabbed her heart, and squeezed. She was momentarily dazed, mesmerized by that look in his eyes. No man had ever looked at her like that, fiercely loving. But that couldn't be. "We're not finished. Not by a long shot."

She just stood there, unable to speak past the lump in her throat.

His lips met hers in a tender kiss, his hand cupping the back of her neck. He pulled back, and her eyes welled up. She closed them, trying to hold the unexpected tears back. He held her face in both hands and kissed her closed eyelids gently before pulling her close, wrapped in his arms. She stiffened, knowing he was pulling her into dangerous territory, but his arms tightened around her and her body melted despite her brain's protests. She wrapped her arms around his waist tightly.

"Don't break my heart," she whispered.

He kissed the top of her head. "I won't."

But she feared it was too late. She didn't know how she'd survive Luke. How could she pick up the pieces once things fell apart?

Chapter Thirteen

By late afternoon, Kennedy was settled on a chaise lounge on the patio by the pool, sipping a fabulous chardonnay, which she'd bet cost a fortune, with Luke, Bentley, and Candy. They'd be leaving soon, and it was time to find out if she stood a chance as Bentley's financial manager.

"It's been an amazing weekend," Luke said, taking her hand and entwining their fingers together. "Kennedy and I want to thank you both for being such generous hosts."

"Yes," Kennedy chimed in.

Bentley beamed. "Glad you enjoyed yourselves. Nothing like a weekend at the cottage."

"It was wonderful," Kennedy said. "And that party! Best I've ever been to. I especially liked hearing Griffin Huntley live."

"He's good and so cute, isn't he?" Candy asked Kennedy.

"Hey!" Bentley protested.

"Not as cute as you," Candy cooed. They rubbed noses in their cutesy way.

Luke crooked his finger at her and did a little head shake like he wanted to rub noses. She shook him off. He pointed a warning finger at her with a mock stern expression that made her grin despite her nerves over Bentley's final decision.

"Honey, we should invite them to the harvest ball!" Candy exclaimed.

Luke glanced at her questioningly. She hadn't intended on prolonging their fake engagement beyond this weekend. The guilt was killing her.

"It's a charity ball," Bentley said, "to benefit the Long Island Sound." He gestured to the water of the Sound reaching out to the horizon. "A cause near and dear to me, obviously. Would you like to go?"

Luke looked to Kennedy. She sat in silent horror.

Bentley turned to Candy. "It's in what? Two weeks?"

"Three Saturdays away," Candy said. She turned to them. "It's fun. Black tie, dancing. You like dancing, right? I saw you two on the dance floor."

"Sure do," Luke replied jovially.

"Then it's settled," Bentley said. "Back to the grindstone tomorrow. I've got a board meeting."

"Speaking of which, have you given any thought to

future wealth management?" Kennedy asked.

Bentley's mouth curled into a look of distaste. "Wealth?"

Dammit. She'd forgotten the number one rule of rich people. Never talk about how rich they were.

Luke spoke up. "You definitely want to choose someone who will make sure your legacy multiplies. You'll be set for years to come and for future generations." He took in Candy with this last remark.

Candy and Bentley exchanged a look.

"We're expecting!" Candy exclaimed.

"Congratulations," Luke said smoothly. "Even more important to have things set up. I'm sure you'll want a trust and a diversified portfolio moving forward."

"If you drop some of the dead weight like that hockey team," Kennedy started.

"I like my hockey team!" Bentley protested. Shit. She couldn't seem to connect right with him.

"There are several areas of your portfolio we could look at together," Luke said, taking in Kennedy with his remark and shocking the hell out of her. Like they were an actual team instead of rivals. "Our job is to make it as easy as possible for you."

Bentley smiled. "I like easy."

"Don't we all?" Luke said with a laugh. "What do you say, ready to move forward with a financial manager?"

Bentley's brow furrowed. "What do you think, Can?"

Candy considered thoughtfully. And Kennedy realized her mistake. She should've been running her ideas past Candy this whole time, not Bentley. The beautiful bubbly woman was the decision maker here.

"Let's see their proposals," Candy said. "Mail them to Anita. That's his assistant. Then we'll look them over and make a decision." She smiled brightly. "The nice thing is, no hard feelings because if we choose Luke, Kennedy still benefits as his wife. And if we choose Kennedy, same thing."

Luke was silent. He must be so upset. He wanted this client as badly as she did. She, on the other hand, was secretly elated to still be in the running.

Candy turned to Kennedy. "Call me, and we'll go shopping for dresses for the ball. Unless you already have one?"

"I do need one," she replied honestly. "That'd be great."

The rest of the afternoon passed uneventfully as they chatted and enjoyed the last bit of the weekend, finishing with a delicious dinner of paella out on the veranda. After they said their goodbyes, Kennedy drove home with Luke, both of them silent. She because she realized she had to extend the charade of a fake engagement at least one more time. He, most likely, because he was pissed that he didn't get the client he assumed would easily go to him.

She finally broke the silence as they neared her apartment building. "I guess you're pissed."

"I'm fine."

"I know things didn't go down like you wanted."

He snorted. "Don't you see? Bentley's just stringing us along. He doesn't want either of us."

"I don't believe that. I think he's just not the kind to jump into doing anything that might require work or research. He just wants to have a good time."

"Whatever," he muttered.

"Now you sound like Alex." Except he wasn't a sullen teenager, he was a pissed-off full-of-himself man.

He met her eyes, his gaze trailing to her mouth before he returned to looking at the road. "You can't afford to go shopping for a gown."

"I'll put it on a credit card and pay the minimum every month."

He frowned. "That's stupid."

"I know credit card debt isn't smart, but it'll pay off with the connections I'll make. It's part of the game."

He scowled.

She let out a breath of frustration. "I really don't

get why you're so pissed off. This weekend couldn't have gone any better. Bentley and Candy love us. We have even more opportunities to find new clients."

At his silence, she went on. "I'm having a talk with my boss tomorrow, and I'm going to leverage what I've got for more access, more opportunity, and a corporate credit card to make it all happen."

He shook his head. "Damn, Kennedy, even I wasn't that ballsy starting out."

"It's more competitive now. Less money to go around. More players on the field."

He gave her a slow, sexy smile. "You're making me hot."

She bit back a smile. "Seriously."

He snagged her wrist and stroked the underside. "Come back to my place. Please."

She pulled her wrist from his grip. "I need to go home. It's a school night and I need to make sure lunches and backpacks are packed. All homework completed. My life is not meant for fun for long."

"You sound like their mom."

"My mom has her hands full with my dad and her bookkeeping business. Things fall through the cracks. Besides, I know my family wants to see me tomorrow. It's my birthday. They probably bought me a birthday breakfast cupcake already."

"A cupcake, huh?"

"Yeah."

When they got to her apartment complex, Luke pulled into a dark corner of the lot behind the building. She got a very uneasy feeling that Luke was going to make a move, and she would cave as she always did when he got her going with his demanding kisses and firm hands.

"What're you doing?" she squeaked.

He didn't reply until he'd turned off the car. Then he thrust his fingers in her hair, cupping her head and pulling her close. "I want to give you a birthday gift. I'll make it so good for you."

Her breath caught. "In your Porsche?"

"On my Porsche. Right on the hood." He kissed her, a coaxing kiss, before taking things deeper, hotter, a carnal invitation.

She shoved at his chest, her heart beating way too fast. "You're acting crazy. Go home and prepare your proposal."

His teeth flashed in a wolfish smile. "It's already prepared."

"So's mine." She didn't want him to think she was a rookie. She'd prepared hers the minute she'd gotten the go on the golf invitation.

"So what's the problem?"

She blew out a breath. "I guess my life is the problem. It's back to reality."

He was silent.

"I'll see you at the charity ball." She undid her seatbelt.

He let out a curse, grabbed her seatbelt, redid it with a firm click, and drove her back to her apartment.

She let herself out. "Bye. Thanks for…everything."

He scowled. "Thanks for—you know what? I'm done pretending with you. When I see you at that charity ball, it won't be as your fake fiancé."

She'd work around that. He was just pissed that Bentley hadn't picked him right away like he thought he would. "See you then!"

She'd barely reached the sidewalk when he peeled out of the lot with a squeal of tires. So much for driving like an old man.

She congratulated herself on resisting temptation, on enjoying what little life allotted her for fun, and headed inside to turn family chaos into order once more.

~ ~ ~

Luke took a long pull on his beer and stared at a crack in the back patio at his parents' ranch house in a full-on sulk. He glanced up at the dark red roses blooming along an archway leading out to the wide expanse of grass and thought again of the dark red dress he'd bought for Kennedy. How beautiful she'd looked.

How happy she'd been that night. He kicked a rock. Everyone was inside getting Sunday dinner ready and talking over each other like usual. He needed some alone time to stop pretending everything was okay. It wasn't just that Bentley hadn't responded to his second request to please choose Kennedy (so Luke could stop worrying about her). It was that Kennedy met his invitation to hookup at his place this weekend with a polite refusal and a reminder that she'd see him at the charity ball.

They were very compatible in bed, and he didn't see why they couldn't sleep together some more, seeing as how they were pseudo-engaged and going to a formal ball together like a real fucking couple. It had been a week since that weekend of insanely good sex with her, and he wanted more. Not just wanted, more like craved it. He couldn't stop thinking about her. She should *want* to hook up with him. He'd told her they weren't done and thought she was on board. The charity ball was two weeks away at this point, and he didn't think he'd make it that long.

"What crawled up your butt and died?"

He didn't need to look up to know which of his five brothers that voice belonged to. The brother that always had a sixth sense about him because they'd been close for so many years.

His stepbrother Nico joined him, beer in hand.

They were about the same size, but where he was
light—dirty blond hair and fair skinned—Nico was
dark—dark brown hair, dark brown eyes, and olive
skin like his Italian dad.

"Nothing." Luke took another long pull on his
beer.

"Woman problems?" Nico asked with a smirk.
Luke didn't even sock him one because he'd razzed
Nico enough when he'd been dealing with his hard-to-
get Lily through one helluva long road trip that ended
with Nico devastated and in love. Now the happy pair
were three weeks away from getting married. He knew
Nico was letting him off easy with just a smirk.

He met his brother's dark brown eyes. "Okay,
what would you do if—"

"Nail her." Nico grinned.

"Ha. Yeah." He shook his head. "Okay. I've got
this weird situation where we're going for the same
client, pretending to be engaged."

"And you got caught?"

"No. So we spend the whole weekend at the
client's estate, things go well, you know…"

One corner of Nico's mouth lifted. He lifted the
beer bottle to his lips and spoke around it. "Yeah, I
know." He drank.

"Now she's like, see you in two weeks at the
charity ball."

"She's not into you."

"Dammit."

Nico slapped a hand on Luke's shoulder. "Sorry. If she was, she wouldn't think a two-week separation was nothing."

Luke stared at the label on his beer. "But we were good together," he said quietly.

"Maybe she faked it."

Luke's head snapped up. "No! No way."

Nico lifted one shoulder up and down. "Just saying. It happens."

"Not to me."

"Well…"

"Well what?" Luke snapped.

"It has to happen to someone."

"I know what I'm doing!"

Nico chuckled and raised a palm. "Hey, no one's questioning your manhood. Maybe you just didn't float her boat."

"Oh, I floated it all right." He remembered everything. Every last scream and shudder and orgasmic cry wrenched from her throat. That was not fake. He'd heard her fake it when they were joking around in bed before the first time they hooked up.

Nico raised a brow. "You know what worked for getting Lily where I wanted her?"

"Begging." His brother had been a wreck. Nearly

collapsed at their older brother Vince's bachelor party in his gloom and doom that he'd lost his true love. Now that he had her, he was a smirky know-it-all.

"Ha-ha. No, I was very firm with her." He raised his beer bottle. "Told her how it was going to be."

"You did not. She's got you wrapped around her little finger."

Nico sliced a hand through the air. "I told her stop stalling and get with the program. And she did."

Lily came out then, her red hair swinging with her sassy walk. "Did I, Nic? Did I finally get with the program?"

A flush crept up Nico's neck. "Lily! How long you been standing there?"

She wrapped an arm around his waist, and he tucked her against his side. "Long enough." She turned to Luke. "Don't listen to him. Just be yourself. If it's meant to be, it will be."

Nico nuzzled into Lily's neck, and she tilted her head to give him more skin. Luke let out a breath of disgust. These two were constantly all over each other. Sure, their wedding was three weeks away, and they were all happy for them, but did they have to see it *all* the time?

He walked back into the house. Not that Nico or Lily noticed. He glanced back over his shoulder. They were kissing passionately. He left, giving them privacy.

Luke was quiet during a family dinner of lasagna, salad, and garlic bread. Nobody noticed. He was often preoccupied during Sunday dinner with checking his cell so he could return messages or urgent texts from clients, but this time he was just sitting there among a whole lotta love and happiness, feeling like the ugly duckling. There were his stepdad and mom in a googly second-honeymoon phase ever since his stepdad had been given a clean bill of health after a cancer scare. His older brother Gabe and his bubbly wife, Zoe, in love with their baby, Miles, and each other. His oldest stepbrother, another dark-haired Italian, Vince, and his wife, Sophia, worked and lived together, the respect and open affection between them a tangible thing. And now Nico and Lily, always beaming at each other, seeming to be in on some secret joke that none of them were let in on.

His gaze caught on his younger brother Jared laughing and teasing their youngest stepbrother Angel. Jared resembled Luke both in looks and in his happy, carefree bachelor status. Well, Luke was still a bachelor, just not happy. Angel, with his dark brown rumpled hair and angelic dimples, was, for reasons none of them could understand after so many years, seemingly contentedly devoted in a platonic way to a woman friend. Luke secretly thought Angel was pulling a fast one and sleeping with her on the sly.

He picked at his food, thinking of Kennedy and how she didn't get enough to eat on account of her brothers. He could at least fix that. They wouldn't take charity, but maybe he could just pop in with food on a regular basis. Or was that too weird?

"Luke's got PMS," Jared pronounced. He grinned, laugh lines forming around his green eyes. "My professional diagnosis is pretty moody syndrome." He was an orthopedic surgeon and liked to throw around his doctor status.

"What's up, son?" his stepdad asked.

"Nothing," Luke said. "Just thinking."

"Big mistake," Vince boomed. "Don't think, just do."

"Don't think, just do," Jared mimicked in a Yoda voice.

Vince jabbed a finger at Jared from across the table. "You're lucky I can't reach you."

"He's got woman troubles," Nico put in helpfully, grinning like a loon. Luke knew very well this was payback for the hard time he'd given Nico over Lily yanking his chain.

Vince slapped a hand on the table. "You came to the right place. Me, Gabe, Nico, we know how to handle our women."

"Oh, really?" Sophia asked. "Handle your woman?"

Vince got quiet. Then he seemed to remember himself and pinned her with a hot look. "Yeah."

Sophia licked her lips, then tore her gaze away. She looked to Zoe, with her bright brown eyes, who was grinning, and over to Lily with a nod. Luke got a chill at the sisterly bonding. Any more females at this table and they'd all be in deep trouble.

"Luke," Sophia said, "take advantage of the wisdom from the women in this family. We wouldn't steer you wrong, and believe me, we understand the female psyche a lot better than your brothers." She gave Vince a significant look.

This was likely true.

Vince shrugged, conceding the point.

"So…" Zoe prompted.

Luke shook her off. "Nothing. No problem."

"She's not that into him," Nico offered.

"Ooh, sorry, Luke," Sophia said with a wince. "There's not much you can do in that case."

"But that doesn't mean you won't find someone wonderful that is into you," Lily offered. Nico took her hand and kissed the back of her knuckles.

"Absolutely!" Zoe exclaimed. "And P.S. any woman would be lucky to have you. If she's not into you, don't give up. Someone special is out there for you."

Now he felt worse off than when he started. His

sister-in-laws were giving him the pity talk. He turned to his youngest brother, Angel. He was a school social worker and sort of specialized in feelings.

Angel lifted one shoulder. "That pretty much sums it up."

"Did you get the signal?" Vince asked, referring to the woman's signal that she'd like you to touch her. It was a leaning toward you, touching her own body, looking up under her lashes. Vince had told them all about it when he'd discovered it in high school.

"What signal?" their mom asked.

Luke shook his head, hoping he'd drop it.

"If you didn't get the signal, what'd you make a move for?" Vince barked. "I told ya, get the signal and *then* break the touch barrier."

"I broke the touch barrier!" Luke exclaimed. His cheeks burned as his brothers had a good laugh at his expense. His sister-in-laws looked at him with some concern.

Vince shook his head. "If you broke the touch barrier, and—" he jabbed a warning finger "—you'd better had waited for the signal, and she don't want nothing to do with you, move on."

Luke stared at his plate forlornly. Everyone was quiet for once, probably feeling sorry for him. The one time he cared about someone she wasn't into him.

"Would you like to invite her to Sunday dinner?"

his mom asked.

His brothers snickered. That was his mom's code for *bring the woman home so I can do some matchmaking*. She'd embarrassed the hell out of Vince, telling Sophia all about his virtues.

"No," he said firmly.

"Couldn't hurt," his stepdad said, gesturing to his married or soon-to-be-married sons, who'd brought their loves home for his mother's notorious Italian wedding soup and Italian wedding cookies—a ridiculous superstition that his family believed. If the woman ate the wedding food, supposedly a marriage would be in their future. *Please.* It was pure coincidence that Sophia had eaten the soup and cookies and later married Vince. Lily didn't even eat a wedding cookie until Nico was about to propose.

"Is there any leftover lasagna?" he asked his mom.

"I have half a tray in the kitchen," she said. "Do you want seconds?" She looked to his plate. "You didn't even finish what's on your plate."

"Not for me. I just know a family that might appreciate it. They're having a hard time financially."

"Oh, if I'd known, I would've made an extra tray."

His stepdad wiped his mouth with a napkin. "I think we've got stuffed shells in the freezer. They still there, Allie?"

"Yes. I'll take them out to start defrosting. Just

twenty minutes at three fifty, and they're just as good."

"Thanks, Mom." His appetite returned and he dug into his lasagna.

She stopped on the way to the kitchen and kissed his cheek. "Always happy to help."

~ ~ ~

He should've just asked Kennedy out on a date, Luke reasoned as he left his parents' house. He'd played this all wrong, basically propositioning her, and what woman wanted that? She had to know he cared about her. That it wasn't just the amazing sex. He left Eastman and headed straight to Clover Park to the apartment complex where Kennedy lived. He took the stuffed shells with him along with half a loaf of garlic bread left over from dinner.

Kennedy answered the door, and he was momentarily speechless. She looked beautiful in a simple T-shirt and jeans, her blond hair loose around her shoulders.

"Luke, what are you doing here?"

The door opened wide, and he got a peek at her family sitting in a neat but small apartment.

"Hey, Luke!" her younger brother Alex called.

"Hey, Alex," he returned.

"Who's that?" her dad called from where he sat in a beige recliner. He looked like Alex probably would in his later years with dark brown hair shot with gray and dark brown eyes. The small TV tray next to him held prescription bottles, water, and the remote.

"I brought you some stuffed shells," Luke told Kennedy.

She pulled him inside. There were hooks by the door with a row of jackets and backpacks lined up underneath. He'd bet Kennedy was the one who made sure everything was all set for school tomorrow.

She took the food from him. "Thank you." She gave him a quizzical look.

He went and introduced himself to her dad, who wouldn't shake his offered hand. "Can't move much due to my back," her dad said.

Her mom came in, a petite woman with light brown hair and hazel eyes. She greeted him warmly with a quiet voice and a weak grip when they shook hands. He saw immediately where Kennedy got her delicate features. But her mom was all whispery softness, whereas Kennedy was all feisty strength despite her size. Her other siblings wandered in to check him out. He met her younger brother Quinn and her youngest sister, Jamie, who kept staring at him starry-eyed. She was at that peak teen-crush age. Her brothers and sister were dark haired and dark eyed like her dad. Even her mom had hazel eyes not blue. For a minute he wondered if Kennedy was adopted, but her delicate features did resemble her mom.

"Can we talk?" he asked Kennedy.

She nodded once. "Sure." She looked to her family. "I'll be right back."

She stepped outside with him, and they sat on the bottom step of the stairs leading to the second floor of the apartment building. Now that he was here, he didn't know what to say. She seemed just fine without him. She didn't even seem excited to see him, only surprised. Maybe Nico was right, and she just wasn't into him. *Dammit.*

"How's it going?" he asked.

She tucked a lock of hair behind her ear. "Great. My boss liked my initiative and now I'm an associate. Well, I'm still his assistant for now, but as soon as I bring in a big client, I'll be doing more."

He snapped his fingers. "Just like that."

"Well…if I land Bentley or one of his friends."

"A contingent promotion."

"That's what I'd always expected. It's good."

He stared straight ahead. "I thought we were on the same page. I said we weren't done. You said don't break my heart. That means we're supposed to keep seeing each other."

"On a date?" Her voice hit a high note.

He turned to find her somewhere between surprise and disbelief. "Yeah."

"Why?"

Not the response he'd been hoping for. He grabbed her hand and took a deep breath. "Because I'm into you," he admitted.

She eyed him suspiciously. "But you kept inviting me to hook up. On top of your car. At your apartment."

"So? I like hooking up."

She stared at their hands clasped together and said in a quiet voice, "Why did you bring my family food?"

"It was just an excuse to see you." *And to make sure you were fed.*

Her eyes narrowed. "Why exactly are you into me?"

He let out a breath of frustration. "Can't we just go on a date? Why do I have to have a bunch of reasons for it?"

She huffed. "I'll see you at the ball."

He grabbed her head and kissed her long enough to remind her what they had together. He pulled back. She looked satisfyingly dazed. "That's why."

"Luke...I agree we have chemistry—"

"It's more than that and you know it. Otherwise you wouldn't be scared I'd break your heart."

"I'm not scared!"

"Liar. Saturday night. I'm taking you to dinner and a Broadway show. Our first official date." He stood and glowered down at her. "Okay?" he barked.

She stood and smiled. "Okay."

He nearly sagged with relief. "Great. I'll pick you up at six. No, five. Four." He pointed at her. "Be ready by four."

She beamed. "How about three?"

"Even better." He headed to his car, stopped and turned back to find her just standing there watching him go. He stalked back to her, kissed her hard, and let her go before he begged her to come back to his place and hook up again. He had to do it right this time.

So he left with only one more backward glance.

She was still standing there. She lifted a hand and waved.

He waved back. "Go back inside before I take you home with me!" he hollered.

She just stood there grinning. Woman drove him crazy.

He finally left, smiling like a fool.

～ ～ ～

Kennedy went with Luke to dinner in the city followed by a Broadway show, *Chicago*, for their first date. Both were fun. Luke was charming and easy to talk to. By the time it was over, it was late.

"You want to come back to my place for a drink?"

he asked as they walked hand in hand down the sidewalk.

She eyed him. "Is that code for fucking?"

"Yes."

"Okay."

He laughed. "You're easy." She smacked his arm. "Ow." He rubbed his arm. "Watch that right hook, Ward."

She followed him into a beautiful two-bedroom apartment with high ceilings and hardwood floors. Modern white sofas and a few lounging chairs, along with glass-topped end tables and a coffee table, were arranged around a modern geometric area rug. Vintage advertising posters hung framed on the walls. He always dressed nice and had an appreciation for the finer things.

They didn't fuck at all this time. They made love. Which was all Luke's doing. She kept trying to amp him up with a bite on the neck or nails down his back, but he'd pin her wrists over her head and return to a tender, slow lovemaking that just about did her in.

The next morning Luke was more aggressive, giving her the ride she craved, and she collapsed happily on top of him when he was done making her crazed. She traced his chest with one fingertip. "I think I like you too much," she admitted.

"I hate when that happens," he replied, stroking a

warm hand down her back.

"It's just…I told myself not to fall for a man that will just take over and take care of everything. Never put everything in a man's hands."

"Hey." He tipped her chin up and met her eyes. "I never asked you to."

"I know. It's just my dad, well, he was that for us. Larger than life, directing everything, taking care of everything, and the minute something happened to him, everything went to shit."

"So you're afraid I'll take care of you?"

"I'm afraid it will be too easy to let you."

He kissed her hair. "I would. That's who I am. I take care of those I love."

She startled. "What?"

"Nothing. That just slipped out."

"Luke—"

"Calm down. I didn't mean it."

She got off him and shoved a hand in her hair. "I'm terrified, but I think I'm falling for you too."

He gave her a slow smile and pulled her back on top of him. "We really screwed up this fake engagement thing, didn't we?" He scoffed. "Falling in love. Now we'll have to get married."

She stiffened. "I can't."

"Joking. We barely know each other. I mean we just met three excruciatingly long weeks ago. Right?"

He closed his eyes. "Forget I said anything."

"It's not you. Well, it is you, but it's me too."

"Yeah, I get it."

"You do?"

"You're afraid."

"I'm not."

"You are." He slid her to the mattress, rolled out of bed, and pulled some jogging pants on. "You're too young for me anyway."

She covered herself with the sheet. "I'm not that young. I'm twenty-four." She didn't know why she was arguing with him. He was letting her off the hook.

He stared at her, his eyes cool and distant. "You're still figuring out who you are, what you want from your life. I don't want you moving from your parents' house to my place. You need to be on your own for a while." He shoved a hand in his hair. "Stop me if I'm wrong."

"No, you're right. I do need to try living independently. So where does that leave us?"

"Fake engagement fuck buddies?"

She stood, hurt and vulnerable and full of regrets. "I can't do this." She grabbed her clothes off the floor. "I'm going home."

"You're just going to walk out after I said stuff?" he barked. "Deep shit from the heart!"

"Yes!" she cried.

He snagged her clothes right out of her hands, tossing them to the side, and pulled her flush against him. "Don't go." His arms wrapped tight around her. "Please."

She took a deep breath. "Don't call me your fuck buddy ever again."

He kissed her and pulled back to look in her eyes. "I won't. I promise. I'm new at this love stuff."

Her lower lip trembled. "So am I."

"Hey, we'll figure it out." He scooped her up and carried her back to bed. "Okay?"

"Okay," she said softly.

Later, after a long morning makeup sex session and breakfast, Luke drove her back home. They kept smiling at each other, and she felt a little giddy. He'd invited her to his family's Sunday dinner tonight. Only when they pulled up to her apartment building, her good mood vanished.

A police cruiser was parked in front of her apartment.

CHAPTER FOURTEEN

She turned to Luke. "I really hope that's not for Alex."

"You want me to come in with you?"

She nodded. He got out, laced his fingers with hers, and walked with her to her apartment.

As she feared, Chief O'Hare was standing in their living room, a serious expression on his face. Alex sat on the sofa, looking scared. Her dad sat in his chair, pissed off. Her mom stood by her dad's chair, fighting back tears. Her siblings were hiding down the hallway, listening in.

"What happened?" Kennedy asked.

"Your brother stole a car," her dad barked.

"I was going to give it back," Alex cried. "I just needed it for a few hours."

"He got in an accident," her mom said stiffly. "Luckily, no one was hurt."

Alex had his license at least. But he didn't have insurance; they couldn't afford to add him to the policy. She released Luke's hand and crossed to Alex. "How? Where did you get the keys?"

"He hot-wired the mayor's car," Chief O'Hare said.

Kennedy stared at Alex. "You stole from the mayor! What, are you an idiot? How did you even know how to do that?"

"I looked it up on the Internet," Alex mumbled. "Besides, I didn't know it was the mayor's. It was just sitting in the parking lot by Baldwin Park."

Chief O'Hare let out a dry laugh. "It was a 1985 IROC Camaro. Bright yellow. Very recognizable. The mayor is kind of fond of it. It was his first car and he keeps it around for the occasional Sunday drive. Today he drove it to the park." He moved to stand directly in front of Alex and peered down at him intimidatingly. "So, Alex, what's it going to be? The mayor says a year of community service would cover it, or we can take things to the next level and get you in front of a judge in juvenile court."

"I think a year of community service is very generous," her mom said.

Her dad harrumphed.

"Alex, be smart," Kennedy said. "Do the service."

"What do I have to do?" Alex asked.

"Whatever we tell you to," Chief O'Hare said sternly.

"What is this, the military?" Alex muttered under his breath.

"You ought to be glad they're offering you this chance!" her dad roared. "Do you want to end up in jail? What's wrong with you?"

Alex stood, hands in fists. "What's wrong with you, Dad? You just let this family go to shit because you feel sorry for yourself."

"I'm recovering from surgery!" her dad barked. "I'm in a lot of pain. Not that anyone around here gives a shit."

Kennedy stiffened. They all tiptoed around her dad because of his pain.

Alex and her dad glared at each other.

Luke's hands settled on her shoulders and squeezed, making her relax a little.

Alex jerked a chin at Luke. "What's he doing here?"

"Watching you make the right decision," Luke replied easily.

"Fine, I'll do the stupid community service," Alex said.

"Great," Chief O'Hare said. "We'll see you at seven a.m. Saturday at the station for your first assignment."

"Seven a.m.!" Alex exclaimed. Her brother often slept until noon on the weekends.

Chief O'Hare fixed Alex with a level stare. "I make the hours, I say if you've fulfilled your obligation, I ride your ass until the job is done. If you have a problem with that, I'm happy to turn the case over to the juvenile court."

"Thank the officer," her dad said.

"Thank you," Alex mumbled.

Chief O'Hare inclined his head and left.

Alex stormed out the door right after.

Her parents started arguing over Alex and what to do about his punishment. Her dad was for grounding him for a year. Her mom felt maybe counseling was in order and grounding for a month. Kennedy grabbed Luke's hand and pulled him out the door. Alex was marching down the sidewalk. She was about to holler for him to get back here when Luke asked, "Mind if I hang with your brother for a bit?"

She stopped short, shocked that he'd want to. "I don't mind," she said slowly. "He won't be much fun right now, though."

Luke whistled. "Alex!"

Alex turned. "What?"

"C'mere."

Her brother stalked back and asked belligerently, "What?"

"You just earned yourself a big brother," Luke said. "Sunday dinner at my parents' house tonight. Actually, you just got six big brothers. Just what a little brother needs."

Alex stuck his chin out mulishly. "I'm not little."

Luke grinned. "You are to me. Now you got someone who'll kick your ass when you need it, get your back when you need it, and keep you from making an idiot out of yourself."

"Whatever."

"Alex!" Kennedy said.

Luke held up a hand, nodding to her in an *I got this* gesture. "I'm sure you have a better vocabulary than just '*whatever.*'" He said the word with all the world weariness of a teenager with major attitude. "You want to drive my Porsche?"

Alex's eyes lit up. "Yeah."

"You have to earn it. Good grades, good attitude about your community service." He held up a warning finger. "No trouble."

Alex looked from Luke to Kennedy and back. "Are you Kennedy's boyfriend now?"

"Yes," Luke said.

Alex took a step forward. "You'd better not hurt my sister. She's overly generous. And sometimes that makes her end up not getting as much as she deserves."

"I'm well aware of that," Luke replied. "You'd better stop hurting your sister."

"I don't hurt her!" Alex protested.

"It hurts her every time you get in trouble." Luke said. "She wants the best for you." He turned to Kennedy. "I can't fit both of you in my car, so I'll text you the address. Five o'clock."

She nodded and turned to her brother, who didn't look nearly as upset as she thought he should be given the circumstances. In fact, he looked happy. "Really, Alex, what were you thinking?"

"I just wanted to take someone out in a nice car," Alex muttered.

"Who?" she asked.

He looked away, a pink flush to his cheeks. "Forget it."

Luke sent her a look. Omigod, he was right. It was all about a girl.

"You should've just asked," Kennedy said. "You could've borrowed my car."

"I didn't want your crappy car."

"It's a Mustang!" A surge of frustration and anger rushed through her. "Do you want to go to jail?" she hollered. "Do you want to ruin your life?"

"No." Alex shoved a hand in his hair. "I...she said she really liked Camaros."

"Use your brain, Alex! Really!"

"Later," Alex said before taking off down the sidewalk again, heading toward the other side of the apartment complex.

"Agh!" she exclaimed. "What is wrong with him?"

"I think he's in love," Luke said.

"What?"

He pointed to where Alex was at the door of someone's apartment near the end of the building. The door opened and a petite brunette stepped out and then ushered him in.

Omigod. She knew that woman. Carla Gomez was a single mother with a three-year-old.

~ ~ ~

Luke was surprised at how easy it was to bring Kennedy home to meet his family. He'd always thought if he brought a woman home, it would feel like a momentous occasion, but it just felt natural. Just like bringing Kennedy back to his place last night and sleeping with her on top of him felt natural. He never slept better, actually, than when he was with her.

He rang the doorbell of his parents' house and dropped a hand on Kennedy's shoulder in a firm grip to relax the nerves he felt radiating off her. Alex shifted uneasily next to her.

His mom, a petite blond woman, answered the door with a big smile. He'd given her a heads-up with an earlier phone call.

"So nice to meet some of Luke's friends," she said warmly to Kennedy and Alex.

Luke made the introductions. "Kennedy is my girlfriend. This is her brother Alex. He's the oldest brother and desperately in need of an older brother to kick his ass."

"Language," his mom warned.

"Butt," Luke amended as they walked inside.

"My husband will be back shortly," his mom said. "He stopped to pick up a few things at the grocery store."

"Ha!" his older brother Vince barked. "You'd know about getting your butt kicked, little bro." He put Luke in a headlock and Luke just grinned. Vince had never hurt him even once when they were kids. He was all big threats and loving headlocks. Except with Gabe. They'd gone a few rounds as kids over who was the ringleader of their band of brothers.

Vince let him go and shook Alex's hand, man to man. "Good to meet ya." He shook Kennedy's hand and said the same.

"Hey, Alex," Vince said, "wanna beer?"

"He's underage," Kennedy said.

"I'm old enough," Alex said, puffing out his chest. "Almost eighteen."

"He's seventeen," Kennedy said. "And doing hardcore community service for stealing a car, among other things."

"We'll get you some of the hardcore stuff, then,"

Vince said with a wink that said he'd been teasing all along. "V8. Gotta build you up." He squeezed Alex's bicep, which was pretty scrawny.

"Angel here?" Luke asked.

"Not yet," his mom said. "He's coming."

He introduced Kennedy to his older brother Gabe, a former lawyer and now manager to his wife Zoe's music career, and their nine-month-old son, Miles. It was pretty clear in his family which of the men were Reynolds—him, Gabe, and Jared, with their blond to light brown hair, light skin, and light eyes (blue or green in Jared's case)—and which were Marinos— Vince, Nico, and Angel, with their dark-haired Italian looks. Vince's wife, Sophia, was an Italian beauty too. Kennedy was the only one in her family that really didn't fit looks-wise. He made a mental note to ask her why. Maybe she was a stepsister or something.

Sophia came over to meet Kennedy. Then Nico and Lily arrived. After Luke introduced them, Nico started ribbing him.

"So this the one who's not into you?" Nico asked with a smirk.

"I told you she was into me," Luke boasted. "You can't fake the way she—"

"Luke!" Kennedy stood there, red-faced. Nico grinned.

He and Nico ribbed each other some more, until

Lily put a stop to it.

"Enough, guys," Lily said. "You're embarrassing the poor girl. We get it. Luke's manhood is well established."

Luke's chest puffed out and he slid an arm around a blushing Kennedy. She elbowed him in the gut.

His younger brother Jared arrived next. Kennedy chatted with Jared a bit about her dad, since Jared was an orthopedic surgeon. Even with all the conversation, Luke only half paid attention as he watched the door for Angel. He knew Angel's school social worker background could be a big help with Alex. As soon as Angel walked through the door, Luke introduced him to Kennedy and Alex, and then pulled Alex out to the back patio to talk to Angel.

"I got this, Luke," Angel said, holding up a hand. "Give us a few minutes in privacy."

He heard Alex ask, "Are you a cop?"

"Not at all," Angel said in a soothing tone. "Here, have a seat."

Luke glanced over his shoulder to see Alex taking the patio chair across from Angel. Alex crossed his arms over his chest and slouched down in the seat. Angel leaned forward, elbows on his knees, and spoke in a low confidential tone. Luke went inside, knowing Alex was in good hands.

Everyone was gathered in the kitchen, talking.

Kennedy met his eyes, a worried expression on her face. He crossed to her. "He's fine. Angel's a social worker. They're talking."

"Your brother in some kind of trouble?" Jared asked.

Kennedy sighed. "He's been acting out ever since my dad got injured. Things are a little tense at home." She glanced around at his brothers and sister-in-laws, who waited patiently for her to go on. Luke took her hand and held it firmly.

She went on. "Medical expenses piled up after his accident. I understand what's up with Alex, but it's so frustrating. It's his senior year. If he would just settle down long enough to get into a good college, I could breathe again."

"Angel's at the elementary school, but he worked with families before that," Jared said. "He'll know what to do."

Several minutes later, Angel and Alex stepped back inside.

"Everything okay?" Kennedy asked, looking back and forth between Angel and Alex.

Alex jerked his chin. Angel nodded. Both of them looked serious.

"Of course everything's okay," Luke said. "Angel's taking him to a strip club after this to get his fill of looking at naked women."

Angel turned scarlet. Alex burst out laughing.

His brothers chuckled.

"You guys are terrible," Sophia said. "I'm sure Angel's above all that." She had a soft spot for Angel.

"What a saint!" Vince exclaimed, raising his hand and wiggling his fingers. "Floating above us all in heaven."

"I'm no saint," Angel muttered.

"Yeah?" Vince asked with an elbow to the gut. "What kind of sin you guilty of? Gotta be lust." He jerked a thumb at Angel. "He's practically a virgin at this point."

Angel's face turned a mottled red, his hands in fists.

"Vince!" Sophia exclaimed.

"Shut up," Angel snapped in a rare show of temper. "It's none of your damn business."

"Or lack of business," Jared put in.

Luke shook his head. Jared never knew when to quit with the teasing.

Angel stalked out of the kitchen and kept going. The front door slammed behind him. Sophia pulled Vince out the back door, probably to give him an earful for upsetting Angel. Not that Angel needed her to. He could handle himself.

"So!" Zoe said brightly. "Anyone want a drink?"

A chorus of agreement had them popping open

bottles of beer and pouring the wine. Alex had lemonade.

Vince returned, Sophia hot on his heels. "Where's Angel?" he asked in a subdued voice.

"He took a walk," Luke said.

His mom walked in, her arms full with a grocery bag, followed by his stepdad and Angel helping her carry them in. They set the bags down on the counter. Angel went about quietly putting things away.

"Hey, Angel," Vince said, "sorry. I crossed the line."

Angel shook his head and kept putting groceries away.

"What happened?" his mom asked.

"Nothing," Vince said.

"Vince made fun of his chastity," Jared supplied helpfully.

His mom narrowed her eyes at Jared and then at Vince.

"Just drop it!" Angel barked before storming out of the room.

His mom sighed. "You both know exactly why he's the way he is, and when it's the right time, he'll move forward."

Kennedy looked to Luke in question, but he just shook his head. No good could come from bringing up that topic now.

"Someone needs sensitivity training," Luke announced with a significant look at Jared. At least Vince had Sophia keeping him in line. Jared ran at the mouth with nothing holding him back.

"Who?" Jared mouthed. The smartass.

"The real issue is," Luke drawled, turning the topic away from his saintly brother, "Alex here has girl problems."

It was Alex's turn to turn scarlet.

"What kind of girl problems?" Jared asked.

Everyone looked to Alex, who remained silent.

"This is a sympathetic-to-love group," his stepdad said. "Each of these guys has had their share of hard knocks. You can tell them."

Alex said nothing, just stared at the ground, blushing. Luke was surprised he didn't bolt from the room. Maybe he actually wanted to talk about it with a bunch of strangers. A little easier than telling his friends or family, who might judge him for wanting a single mother.

Zoe gave Alex a sympathetic look. "Maybe we can help. I mean us women." She indicated Sophia, Lily, Kennedy, and his mom. "What kind of problem?"

Alex remained silent, so Luke got the ball rolling. "He's in love with an older woman."

Kennedy's mouth formed a grim line.

"What's her name?" Zoe asked. "How old?"

Alex looked up, meeting only Zoe's eyes. "Carla."

"She's a single mother with a three-year-old," Kennedy said. "Omigod. That's why you were stealing picture books. Oh, Alex."

Alex's chin jutted out, reminding Luke of Kennedy's stubborn look. "Carla's only three years older than me. She got pregnant in high school."

"Alex, you're seventeen," Kennedy said. "You are not ready for that kind of responsibility."

"I love her!" Alex hollered.

The room fell silent.

Alex swallowed visibly. His brothers and sister-in-laws exchanged quiet looks.

Lily broke the awkward silence. "Does she love you back?"

"I don't know," Alex muttered. "I haven't told her yet."

"Wait on that," Nico advised.

"I agree," Vince said. "Wait until you're old enough to do something about it. After you graduate high school at least."

"Eighteen is too young to get married and be a father," Kennedy protested. "He's supposed to go to college."

"Everyone has their own path," his stepdad said. He'd married his high school sweetheart. She'd died when Angel was only five, and he knew his stepdad was glad he'd had that early time with her.

Kennedy put her hands on her hips and glared at them all. "I have to say this has been very unhelpful." She turned to him. "Luke, the only reason I let him come here was because I thought you'd straighten him out."

"I am looking out for him," Luke said.

"I don't need anyone straightening me out," Alex snarled.

"Hey, you like cars?" Nico asked Alex.

Alex jerked his chin.

"Come on," Nico said. "I've got a beauty out front to show you."

Alex followed at a slow saunter, all macho bravado.

Kennedy paced the room.

"He'll be fine," Luke said.

"He like ball?" Jared asked.

Kennedy stopped pacing. "Baseball? He loves it."

"We'll play a game of pickup after dinner," Jared said. "There's a field a couple blocks away. We'll talk some sense into him between plays. You want to join us?"

She shook her head. "No, thanks."

"You hang with us women," Sophia said with a smile. "We'll tell you all of Luke's dirty secrets."

"Don't you dare, Soph," Luke said, pointing a warning finger at her. He didn't have any dirty secrets, just embarrassing childhood stories his family liked to tell. Like the time he ran away from home on his bike, determined to take the train to the city to move in with his biological dad. He'd been fearless and determined even as a kid. Ten years old and he was running away to big scary New York City on his own. He'd skidded out on the road to the train station and broke his arm. Then he'd sat on the side of the road and bawled his eyes out, partly in pain and partly in frustration that he couldn't run away after all. He'd been pissed at a new stepdad taking his real dad's place. A car pulled over and helped him call his dad in the city. But guess who showed up to help? His stepdad, Vinny. His real dad had passed the torch, calling his mom to take care of the problem. Vinny had sat with him at the hospital, held his hand, and wiped his tears. Then he'd taken him out for ice cream and told him how glad he was to have him for a son. Not a stepson. A *son*. Taking him in right along with his three biological sons, Vince, Nico, and Angel. It wasn't the first time Vinny had said that to him or his brothers, Gabe and Jared, but it was the first time it really got through Luke's thick skull. He shook off the memory. There were plenty more punk-kid stories Sophia could spill.

Sophia grinned cheekily. "What's it worth to ya?"

"You're as bad as Vince," Luke said.

Vince hauled her close and kissed the top of her head. "I'm rubbing off on her."

"We're doomed!" Luke exclaimed.

~ ~ ~

Kennedy felt right at home with Luke's noisy, loving family over dinner. It reminded her of how her family used to be before her dad's accident. After dinner, the men headed with Alex to the field for baseball. She stayed at the table with the women. Mrs. Marino brought out tea for everyone and some wonderful crescent cookies covered in powdered sugar.

"These are delicious," Kennedy said, helping herself to a second cookie.

"So glad you like them," Mrs. Marino said, hiding a smile by sipping her tea.

Sophia, Lily, and Zoe exchanged amused looks.

"What?" Kennedy asked.

Lily smiled. "Nothing. We all like them too."

"I'll have to get your recipe," Kennedy said.

"Sure, honey," Mrs. Marino said. "I'd love to share it."

"So what's the dirt on Luke?" Kennedy asked Sophia.

"His dirty little secret?" Sophia asked. She waited for a dramatic pause before admitting, "He has none. The little rat. He's as good as they come."

"Luke has a real soft spot for kids in trouble," Mrs. Marino said. "He's a Big Brother."

"We all knew that," Zoe said.

Mrs. Marino shook her head. "No, I mean he volunteers with the Big Brothers Big Sisters program in the city. He's been doing it for years, ever since he moved there. He has two little brothers that he sees on alternate weekends. How old are they now?"

Sophia answered. "Mateo just shot up. He's thirteen. Luke's been with him since he was five. And…" She thought for a moment. "I think Tony is seventeen now. Luke's been with him since he was fourteen. Mateo is a total sweetheart. Tony took a little more work to break through, but Luke persisted. Vince and I met up with them one time at the Bronx Zoo." She turned to Kennedy. "Hey, maybe Tony would like to meet Alex since they're the same age."

Tears sprang to Kennedy's eyes as that last little piece of her heart she'd kept closed to Luke opened in a rush. Why hadn't he ever mentioned this?

"Luke never said," she choked out. "He comes off like this slick finance guy."

"With a heart made of money?" Lily asked. "He's got a heart of gold. All of these guys do. It's their wonderful family that made them this way." Her voice choked up. Mrs. Marino walked around the table to hug her.

Mrs. Marino stroked Lily's red hair. "Lily's still a little new to the family. She keeps getting choked up because she fell so hard for Nico her heart's sitting right out on her sleeve." She patted her sleeve.

"I love you guys!" Lily exclaimed, dashing the tears from her eyes.

"Aww," Zoe said. "We love you too!" She turned to the other women. "It'll only get worse once she's pregnant. My sister and I were so-o-o emotional when we were pregnant. All those hormones bouncing around." She stopped abruptly. "Lily, are you pregnant?"

"No," Lily said with a watery smile. "Though we do want a big family. I'm just in love with all of you."

"Aww!" the women chorused. Sophia squeezed her hand.

"Let's get her married first," Mrs. Marino said. "One thing at a time." She turned to Kennedy. "They're getting married in two weeks. Did Luke invite you to the wedding?"

"No," Kennedy said, a little embarrassed to admit it.

"Oh, well," Mrs. Marino said.

"You're welcome to come," Lily said.

"That's okay. I'm not family," Kennedy said.

An uncomfortable silence followed.

"Tell us more about you, Kennedy," Mrs. Marino

said. "What do you do?"

She told them about her job and how she and
Luke met over a game of golf with Bentley and Candy.

Lily piped up. "Nico told me you guys were
pretending to be engaged at Bentley's cottage while
you competed for Bentley's account."

Kennedy's face flamed.

"Oh my!" Mrs. Marino exclaimed. She held the
plate of cookies out to Kennedy. "Cookie?"

Kennedy took another one and stuffed it in her
mouth so she wouldn't have to comment further on
the fake engagement.

"Interesting," Sophia said.

"Wow!" Zoe said.

"I like Bentley," Lily said. "But most people,
including his family, don't take him very seriously."

"So you're still in competition with Luke?" Sophia
asked.

Kennedy nodded, finished chewing her cookie and
swallowed. "But I think Luke's going to get the
business. He is more experienced. He offered to bring
me on as his assistant, though. So I could learn from
him."

"Don't do it," Lily warned. "Then he'll be your
boss."

Her cheeks flushed, remembering when they'd
played boss and assistant in the shower. Luke did

know how to get her going.

"I don't know," Sophia said slowly, "Vince and I work together, and it's been going really well. It could work if you're more of a team."

"But you're not Vince's assistant," Zoe pointed out. "You're equal partners."

Sophia inclined her head. "One thing about these guys. Any of the brothers. You can't let them take over. You have to stick up for yourself and what you want, or they'll walk all over you." She walked her fingers across the table.

Lily smiled dreamily. "Nico's not like that."

"Neither is Angel," Mrs. Marino said. "But I'm afraid Luke is. He can't help it. He's got this innate leadership quality, which is great, but you don't want to work for him. Not if you want to stay his girlfriend."

"Believe me, I know," Kennedy said. "I don't even know why he said that."

"Have another cookie," Mrs. Marino urged, holding the plate out to Kennedy.

Kennedy took another one.

All of the women burst out laughing. Kennedy startled. "What?" she asked around a mouthful of cookie.

"Nothing!" Lily exclaimed before collapsing into another bout of laughter.

"What's wrong with these cookies?" Kennedy asked. "Are you playing a prank on me?"

"Not at all," Mrs. Marino said, wiping her eyes with a napkin. "We're trying to bring you into the family. Those are wedding cookies."

Kennedy spit the cookie into a napkin.

"Oh, it's too late for that," Sophia said with a laugh. "It only takes one. I ate it and married Vince."

"I ate one," Lily added, "and I'm marrying Nico in two weeks."

"I feel left out," Zoe said. "I never ate a cookie before I married Gabe."

"That's because you were overseas in Europe, honey," Mrs. Marino said. "Gabe did you one better. He got you pregnant."

Everyone laughed except Kennedy, who considered the three cookies she'd eaten in something close to horror. She would *not* be getting pregnant. She would *not* be marrying Luke.

"I'm sure Gabe'll get you pregnant again soon," Sophia said.

"He can't keep his hands off her," Lily confided to Kennedy.

"Miles is only nine months old," Zoe said. "Gimme a break!"

Everyone laughed except Kennedy, who felt sick. This was…this was insanity. She had to get out of here before the cookies took effect. Maybe you had to see the person while you ate the cookies. Maybe she was still safe.

"You guys have the wrong idea!" Kennedy squeaked, standing up so fast her chair knocked over. She quickly picked it up. "Luke said..." She swallowed. He'd said she was too young. But he'd also said she had to marry him. Was that why she was here?

"What?" Lily asked.

"Nothing," Kennedy replied. Her eyes darted to the kitchen and the way out. She drove here tonight in her own car. If she could just track down Alex, she could make a quick exit. But then she'd have to see Luke. Would the effect of the wedding cookies still work several minutes later?

"You wouldn't be here if Luke didn't feel something for you," Zoe said. "Trust me, these guys don't bring a woman home unless they're serious."

Kennedy smoothed her hair behind her ears and took a deep breath. "I-I—"

"Relax, sweetheart," Mrs. Marino said. "Have a seat. The guys won't be done their game for at least another hour."

"Bum, bum-dee-bum!" Zoe sang the wedding march.

Everyone laughed, except Kennedy, who was mortified. "I need to use the bathroom."

She bolted from the room. Why did Luke bring her here tonight? Why did he hide this wonderful thing he did as a Big Brother?

Why did she have to eat so many cookies?

~ ~ ~

Luke walked back home with Alex and his brothers, everyone in high spirits after the game. Angel hit a grand slam against one of Vince's pitches, which went a long way toward the tension between his two brothers. Alex was really good. It wasn't baseball season yet, but he had an idea to put Alex's skills to good use.

"You should do your community service with the Police Athletic League," Luke said, falling in step next to Alex. "You could coach the younger kids in baseball. They play year-round."

"I'm already supposed to clean up trash around town every weekend. Chief O'Hare called and told me to dress accordingly."

"So add this in. Maybe he'll let this count toward it too. You get to play ball and maybe set an example for kids that are worse off than you."

"Maybe," Alex replied.

"Maybe." Luke socked him in the arm. "Maybe is for wusses. Yes or no, big guy?"

Alex grinned. "Alright, yes. I'll ask him. Sure beats

picking up trash."

He walked in to find Kennedy sitting with his mom and sister-in-laws at the dining room table. A platter of Italian wedding cookies caught his eye. He should've known his mom would be up to her matchmaking shenanigans.

His mom smiled with a devilish look in her eye when she spotted him. "Kennedy really liked the cookies."

His brothers and dad trailed in behind him, everyone snagging a cookie.

"I didn't know they were wedding cookies," Kennedy said with a pained expression. "I spit the last one out as soon as I heard." Like cookies could really make someone head to the altar. Ridiculous superstition.

"Ewww," Luke teased. "Really? The thought of being married to me made you toss your cookies?"

His brothers laughed.

Luke picked up a cookie and took a bite. "Mmm, mmm. Very good, Mom." He winked at Kennedy. Her cheeks flushed pink.

Everyone laughed.

After they said their goodbyes, Luke sent Alex to the kitchen, where his mom gave him a tray of lasagna for their family. He snagged a bag full of picture books for Alex to give the kid he'd been stealing for. They were the Huddle-Cuddle series his mom wrote and illustrated based on him and his brothers. She had several copies of the series at home. The Huddles were hedgehogs (him, Gabe, and Jared) and the Cuddles were porcupines (Vince, Nico, and Angel). He loved that series.

He headed outside with Alex and Kennedy. Alex had his hands full with books and food.

"Alex, you go ahead to the car," Kennedy said. As soon as her brother got inside the car, she turned to him. "Why did you give him food?"

He heard the edge to her voice. "He said he liked the stuffed shells. We always have extra. There's a whole 'nother fridge of food in the garage." He left out that he'd specifically asked his stepdad to make lasagna, knowing Kennedy liked it.

She crossed her arms. "I told you my family's not charity."

He scoffed. "Italians like to feed people. No big. Just like my mom stuffed you full of Italian wedding cookies."

She groaned.

He laughed. "The wedding cookies are just a little family joke. You don't really get married if you eat the cookie. You know that, right?"

"That's not true," Kennedy said. "Sophia and Lily ate the cookies and now they're both Marinos."

"Aha!" he exclaimed, one finger in the air. "I'm a Reynolds. Doesn't work on the Reynolds side." She still looked worried. "You really didn't have to spit it out. That's gross."

"Your mom asked me if I was going to Nico and Lily's wedding with you," Kennedy said softly.

"Did you want to go to the wedding?" Luke asked carefully. Weddings were serious business, and he'd thought Kennedy wasn't ready to go there.

Her eyes got shiny, which made his heart clutch. "You never told me you're a Big Brother. Why did you keep that a secret?"

He shifted back and forth on his feet. "It's not a secret. I just don't talk about it. It's just something I do."

She blinked rapidly, her eyes shiny with unshed tears. "I'm sorry I called you an arrogant know-it-all. I was so wrong about you. That's why you brought me here tonight, isn't it? To show me how wonderful you are." A single tear dropped.

"No!" he said harsher than he meant to because that single tear pained him. "I brought you here to show *them* how wonderful *you* are!" Her face crumpled and the tears fell in earnest. He pulled her close and wrapped his arms around her. "Don't cry. I am an arrogant know-it-all. You were right all along."

"No," she blubbered into his shirt. "I was so

wrong."

Kennedy was strong. How could this be what set her off? Why did his family have to blab about his Big Brother gig? Geez.

"Come on, Kennedy. Please stop crying. You're killing me here."

She sniffled and wiped her nose with the back of her hand, her blue eyes red-rimmed and watery. "I'm sorry. I just realized I love you so much and I can't wait to go to the ball with you."

"But that's good!"

"I know!" Her eyes welled up again. He moved quickly to stall another crying jag, sliding his hand into her hair and brushing his mouth over hers.

She threw her arms around his neck and kissed him back passionately.

"Uh, guys?" Alex called.

"She'll be there in a few minutes," Luke hollered back.

"I've been warned not to work for you," Kennedy said, wiping her eyes.

"I never wanted you to work for me anyway." He stroked a hand down her back. "I just wanted to play boss and assistant."

"Luke!" She smacked his chest. "I just told your mom and sister-in-laws you wanted me to work for you. They were all giving me advice. You have to be honest with me. No more secrets or half-truths. Swear it!"

He swallowed, remembering the one thing he hadn't told her. That he'd asked Bentley to choose her as his financial manager. But how likely was Bentley to mention it? He'd just choose her, thinking they were both on board with the arrangement.

Guilt stabbed at him. He didn't want to lie. He couldn't tell her the truth. She'd think he was treating her like a charity case. Just handing over the biggest client either of them was likely to see in their careers.

"Luke?"

He cupped her delicate jaw and kissed her gently. "I love you." He released her and gazed into her blue eyes that were shiny again.

"I love you too," she whispered.

He pulled her close and hugged her, hoping his long game really would work out. Or Kennedy might never forgive him.

CHAPTER FIFTEEN

Kennedy wore a borrowed Chanel gown worth a fortune, thanks to Candy. Her sister, Frank, had grown increasingly worried about their parents paying her tuition bill, so Kennedy had put the tuition on her credit card, maxing it out. (Frank had a scholarship and a part-time job, so the tuition bill was a fraction of the full amount, but added on to the other bills, impossible for her parents to cover.) She'd called Candy and explained she'd have to skip the gown-shopping trip because of some family expenses. Candy had promptly arranged a night out in the city last Monday, first meeting up with her stylist friend, who lent Kennedy the couture gown worn only once by a famous actress, and then taking her out for dinner and drinks. Tonight wouldn't be the last time she and Luke had to pretend to be engaged, unfortunately. Candy had invited them both to a cocktail cruise on their yacht in two weeks. That would be the absolute last time they pretended, she promised herself.

She did a small twirl in the bedroom her siblings shared, admiring the dress. Luckily, her sister Jamie was at the kitchen table, working on a school project, or she'd probably want to try it on too. The top was black sequins with spaghetti straps, the white skirt began at an empire waist, flowing to the floor with a short train. Open at the back. It didn't overwhelm her frame. She felt light and red carpet worthy. If only she had the kind of quiet confidence to work a party the way Luke could. She smiled thinking of him. It was all so new to her, being in love. It almost felt like a fairy tale. Except, at some point, one of them would win Bentley's business and one of them would lose. She hoped that didn't mean the end of them together.

She headed to the bathroom to check her makeup. She liked Candy and hated lying to her. She'd discovered they had a lot in common. Both of them had worked hard as kids; both of them aspired to a better life. Candy wasn't one of those women who married for money. She truly loved Bentley. She had money of her own as the owner of a luxury spa to the upper elite of Manhattan. She had a brilliant, shrewd mind under that bubbly blond exterior, and they'd had a serious talk about what it would take to scale up her small luxury spa business into a national chain.

She finished her makeup, checked her hair in its

simple twist, and stared at herself in the mirror. *You can do this. Fake it 'til you make it.* All the big spenders from the city and locally would be at the charity ball tonight. This was the kind of night that led to connections that could set the path of her future career.

She took a deep breath, then another, and nearly succeeded in composing herself when the doorbell rang. Her sister Jamie's voice came out in a near shriek. "Luke's here!"

Her calm vanished. She stepped out to the living room to find Luke looking stunning in a black tux, all smiles, chatting with her family. He was still clean shaven, and she had to admit she liked him that way. He'd looked so much older with the beard.

He flashed a charming smile. "Ready for the ball, Cinderella?" He made a grand bow.

"Oooh!" Jamie squealed. Her whole family looked to her. Her parents, Quinn, Jamie, and even Alex were smiling encouragingly.

"Yes," she said softly.

He crossed to her and kissed her cheek. "You look beautiful, Kennedy." Her name on his lips sounded so elegant. She'd always thought it plain.

"Thank you. You look nice too."

Luke turned to her parents. "Did you like the lasagna?"

Her family tripped all over each other to sing the praises. She'd found the meal hard to swallow. She still suspected the food was charity. If anyone was going to take care of her family, it was her.

Luke grinned. "I'll tell my dad. His recipe. You like Italian? I can bring more next Sunday."

"We love it!" Jamie exclaimed.

Luke tapped the end of her nose and she blushed. "I'll stop by then."

"Bye!" Kennedy called. "Don't wait up."

"Have fun, honey!" her mom said wistfully.

They headed outside, Luke's hand heating her bare back. His scent, that musky cologne and pure sexy Luke, made her head swim with memories of all the nights she'd slept naked on top of him, breathing him in, her own warm bed.

"Luke, you shouldn't have told them you'd be back next Sunday with more food."

"Why not? They liked the food."

She ground her teeth together. "It's not necessary."

"I know it's not necessary. I want to."

"I know what you're doing."

"And what is that?"

"You're treating my family like a charity case."

He stopped and stared at her, then took her by the elbow and walked her to his car. "I just like a reason to stop by. My girlfriend's pretty hot."

"Oh." Now she felt silly. Maybe he really did just want to see her.

He opened the door to his Porsche and ushered her in. She studied him for a long moment. His gorgeous face with the beautiful cheekbones, the dark blue eyes framed with thick lashes, often dancing with mischief, but now just gazing back at her very seriously. Was he being honest with her? Was that what the food really was about? She couldn't bear for him to pity them. They were fine. She made sure of it.

"What?" he asked.

"Nothing." She gathered up her gown and slid into the passenger seat. She took a deep breath, reminding herself that Luke loved her. He wouldn't lie to her. He'd said there wouldn't be any secrets between them. Well, actually, he hadn't said that, but he'd said he'd loved her, which implied the same thing. At least she hoped so.

He got into the car and turned to her. "Before we go." He opened his hand, revealing a round diamond ring. She gasped and clapped a hand over her mouth. The round diamond was set off by smaller diamonds on either side, all set in platinum.

He took her left hand and slid it onto her ring finger, where it fit perfectly. "It's your engagement ring."

She immediately went to pull it off, but he stilled

her hand, cupping it between his two warm hands. "Luke! Omigod! I can't wear this. It must've cost a fortune!"

"You're supposed to be my fiancée. Don't you remember you told Bentley your ring was being sized? That was three weeks ago." He released her hand and she stared down at it, mouth agape.

He put a finger under her chin and shut her mouth. "You can give it back to me when we're done pretending."

She met his eyes, still in shock. He gazed back at her, seeming to be searching for an answer to a question that neither one of them dared to ask. Was a real engagement in their future?

"I guess we should go," he muttered and started the car.

She took a deep breath. Just because she was wearing his ring didn't mean this engagement was real. Only it was starting to feel real. She glanced at him; his jaw was clenched tight. He seemed mad, though she hadn't a clue why.

"Thank you," she finally said. "That was very thoughtful of you to remember the ring."

"Don't worry about it."

They drove in silence for several minutes.

She tried to smooth things over. "I'm looking forward to seeing Nico and Lily again. I hadn't realized she was the Spencer heiress." She'd heard Lily would be there tonight, one of the major sponsors of the event. She supported all local environmental causes.

He glanced at her. "Don't even think about trying to get your hands on her money. Nico won't have it. Even I don't go there, and if they can't trust me, they can't trust anyone."

That was interesting. "Who manages her money?"

"She does. And a lawyer that's been with her family since before she was born."

"What kind of investments does she have?"

"None of your damn business."

"Why are you so mad?"

"I'm not."

"You're a big liar."

"You're—" He clamped his mouth shut.

"I'm what?"

He was silent for a long moment. "You're my temporary fiancée."

"Do you feel as guilty as I do?" she asked. "Maybe we should tell Bentley we called the engagement off."

"Oh no. We've come this far. No backing down now."

"But you seem so mad about it."

He sliced a hand in the air. "We're seeing this through to the end."

She sighed and looked out the window. By the

time they stepped into the reserved ballroom at the Luxor Hotel, Luke was back to being polite and solicitous. He fetched her drinks and piled appetizers on her plate regularly. She had no idea why he seemed so pissed in the car, but he seemed to have put it behind him. He worked the room like a pro, and she followed in his wake as he introduced her to people.

They succeeded in only a brief hello to Bentley and Candy before they had to take their assigned seats for the sit-down dinner. Bentley and Candy were half a ballroom away. She really needed to move things forward with Bentley. The doctors recommended her dad get a second surgery because the first one hadn't gone like they'd hoped. The expense of that on top of what they already owed, with a collection agency breathing down their necks, made tonight even more urgent.

"Enjoying yourself?" Luke asked her as their entrees arrived. Steak or chicken for everyone. She and Luke both got steak medium well.

"Of course," she returned. "It's a beautiful event."

He eyed her and leaned close to her ear. "You don't seem like you're having fun."

She speared a piece of meat. "The food is delicious. The people are delightful."

He leaned in close and said in a low voice near her ear, "There's no sparkle in your eye."

She bit back a smile. Something about the way he said "sparkle" so seriously made her want to laugh. "No sparkle?"

"Yeah."

She considered him quite seriously, surprised at how in tune to her moods he was. He'd said she was an open book, but she'd never had anyone read her the way he did. "There's no sparkle in your eye either."

"Guess the sparkle died," he said, shaking his head sadly.

Which made her laugh. He grinned.

They ate and made small talk with the other couples at the table. Luke poured on the charm, and she relaxed into his easy smiles once more, many of them directed to her. Soon, the music started, a peppy swing beat, and one by one people left the tables to take to the dance floor. She and Luke stayed at the table. He massaged the back of her neck with his strong fingers, relaxing her even more. Three dances in, the music changed to a slow ballad. Candy gestured wildly for them to get on the dance floor.

Luke stood. "We're being summoned."

She stood too and put her hand in his. He led her onto the dance floor next to Bentley and Candy, who danced with their arms wrapped around each other. Bentley's face nestled into her cleavage because of their height difference. Candy didn't seem to mind.

Luke took the lead, one hand on her lower back, the other holding her hand. He was an excellent dancer, moving in a smooth box step.

"I love that dress," Candy called. "Fabulous!"

Kennedy found herself smiling. Candy had said the same thing when she'd first tried it on. "You too!" Candy wore a form-fitting sheath covered in tiny silver sequins.

"Having fun?" Bentley asked.

"Great event," Luke said.

"Stick around," Bentley said. "This thing could go all night."

"So could you," Candy purred.

Bentley's hands moved to her ass. They started kissing. She met Luke's eyes, thinking they might have a laugh, but his gaze was heated. He moved them a distance away, his hand spread wide on her bare lower back.

He leaned down to her ear, his breath hot on her skin. "It's time to play the game."

A hot shiver ran through her at the words she'd heard from him before...naked. He couldn't possibly mean...not here. No, he must mean play the fiancée game and meeting more people. He took her hand and guided her off the dance floor, but then he kept going, out of the ballroom and down the hall.

He picked up speed, and she had to lift her gown

to keep from tripping. "Where are we going?" she asked before he yanked her into an empty dark ballroom and quietly shut the door behind them.

Her breath came harsh. "Luke, I thought—"

The breath whooshed from her lungs as his mouth claimed hers, his body pinning her against the door. His mouth slipped to her jaw and then her neck, his teeth sinking in, his hands gripping her hips firmly. It was a shorthand that her body understood, already throbbing with need.

"Is there a lock for the door?" she asked breathlessly.

He pinned her wrists back against the door. "You're my lock."

"We can't!" she protested, suddenly remembering the fortune she was wearing. "My gown!"

He carefully hiked up her gown and held the bottom of it up to her. "Hold this."

She didn't. "If we get caught," she whispered urgently. His mouth covered hers as his hand slipped between her legs. Her knees buckled, and she clutched his shoulders as he slipped her silk panties to one side and slid his fingers inside her. She moaned softly. He nipped her bottom lip and sucked it into his mouth.

"That's more like it," he said, his voice rough and gravelly. "Now hold this." He placed the end of her gown in her hands and wrapped his hands around hers, keeping them in place.

"Luke," she protested weakly. She was standing across the hall from a room full of potential clients with her gown up in the air, exposing her silk panties and thigh highs. She let out a shaky breath as he went to his knees, yanked her panties down and off, and settled his mouth firmly against her. Within seconds she was bucking wildly. His hands cupped her ass, holding her in place, trapped between his mouth and the door at her back. He brought her to the sharp edge of release with his lips and tongue and teeth, again and again, until she was begging, literally begging for what she so desperately needed. And he finally gave it to her in a shattering climax that stole her voice, made her throw back her head and rock helplessly against him.

He released his hold, and she slid like a ragdoll to the floor. She couldn't move, couldn't speak. He pulled her back up and kissed her tenderly. Then he turned on the light, dimming it, and took her in.

"Sparkle's back in your eyes." He grinned, all cocky. "You look like you've been worked over good."

She checked her hair, it was half out of its twist. She frantically pulled the remaining pins out. He held his palm out. She handed them over, and he tucked them in the inside pocket of his tux jacket.

She smoothed her hair. "Okay, how do I look now?"

He stroked her hair and settled his hands on her shoulders, turning her to check her out from all sides. "Sorry," he said, not sounding sorry at all, "you still look like you got fucked in the coatroom."

She put her hands to her heated cheeks and looked frantically around. "Where's my panties?"

"I'm keeping them as a souvenir." He pulled them out of his pants pocket and held them up by one finger.

She grabbed for them, and he shoved them down the front of his pants.

"You look like you have a giant boner," she pointed out. She shoved her hand down his pants, where he already had a huge boner, making him grunt and groan, and took them back.

"Baby, you are such a tease," he said, snatching them out of her hand and holding them up high where she couldn't reach.

She eyed him as he held her panties. "You're the tease, holding my panties hostage."

He tucked them into his pocket again. "I'm not a tease. I gave you exactly what you needed."

She gave up. "Let me go back first; then you follow."

"Why? We're supposed to be together anyway. You think engaged couples don't screw around wherever and whenever they feel like it?"

She considered that. "Aren't you embarrassed?"

"I'm a god for pulling it off. Besides you look beautiful when you're ravished."

He was entirely too arrogant. "That was the last time we do anything like that in public."

His hand slid to the nape of her neck and squeezed. "We'll see."

She grasped for her already diminishing willpower. "I mean it, Luke," she said, but it came out all breathy.

He kissed her again, hard and demanding, and she melted against him.

He grinned down at her. "I would've done more, but I don't have a condom on me. Next time I'll be prepared."

"There isn't going to be a next time."

Then he was lifting her, cradling her in his strong arms. "We're going home, sweetheart."

"I need to talk to Bentley. I need an answer from him."

"Okay, we'll talk to him first; then I'll have you all to myself."

"Wait!" she said before he could open the door. "Are you going to dump me if he chooses me?" She was almost afraid to hear the answer.

"Nope. Are you going to dump me?"

"No."

"Then we're all good here."

"Really?"

He gave her a small smile. "Yeah."

"Why did you get pissed off in the car?"

His smile dropped. "Maybe I'm tired of our fake engagement."

She closed her eyes, knowing he was right. This had been her stupid idea from the beginning and it wasn't right to keep the charade going. She had to fix this without losing Bentley's faith in her or Luke. She just had to figure out how.

~ ~ ~

"There you are!" Bentley exclaimed, spotting them in the hallway. "My favorite couple!"

Kennedy flushed and wriggled in Luke's arms. He set her down.

"Hi!" she squeaked.

"Where've you been?" Bentley asked.

"Kennedy wanted to start the honeymoon early," Luke said with a huge grin.

She elbowed him. "We were just getting a breath of fresh air."

"Well, come on back," Bentley said. "Candy's about to make a speech about the Sound and all the wonderful donations pouring in."

"Sounds good," Luke said smoothly, ushering her back into the ballroom.

She settled at a table with Luke while they listened to Candy thanking the donors profusely. Lily took the mike next and launched into an impassioned speech on the importance of the Long Island Sound for the local wildlife, fishing, and habitat preservation.

"That's my sister-in-law," Luke said proudly.

"Where's your brother?"

Luke looked around. "He's right up front, staring adoringly at her."

After Lily's speech, people started mingling again while an auction was set up. They met up with Nico and Lily.

"Great speech, Lily," Kennedy said.

"Thanks," Lily said with a smile. "Every word of it is true. The Sound is critical to the local ecosystem. I hope you'll bid on some items at the auction."

"We will," Luke said, answering for her. She couldn't bid on any of the luxury items, and nobody knew that better than Luke.

"Look at that ring!" Lily squealed, holding up Kennedy's hand.

Nico shot Luke a questioning look. Luke shook his head.

"It's just for show," Kennedy whispered.

Lily looked from Kennedy to Luke. "Seriously? It looks like—ah!"

Nico had dipped her over his arm and laid a big

kiss on her. He brought her back upright and she was breathless. "We gotta go," Nico said.

"Like right now?" Lily breathed.

"Like right now," Nico confirmed.

They grinned at each other. "Bye!" Lily called.

"See ya!" Nico called with a hand in the air.

"That was so romantic," Kennedy murmured after they left.

"Want me to dip you?" Luke asked.

"It's not really spontaneous if you have to ask," she said.

"Forget I asked," Luke huffed.

"You're mad at me again?" she asked in complete exasperation.

He swooped in, dipped her over his arm, and kissed her. Some people started clapping nearby. He let her up and grinned. "We have an audience."

She looked around, embarrassed. Bentley gave them the thumbs-up.

Luke entwined his fingers with hers. "Admit it, that was still romantic."

"I guess."

"You guess? What's a guy got to do to impress you?"

"You've impressed me plenty. Please." She looked around, a few people still looked at them curiously. "Don't do anything else."

He barked out a laugh. "Since we're here, let's mingle."

They went through the entire room of people, some just with introductions, some with longer conversations. They did best, she thought, with couples. Luke would get the conversation rolling, and she'd get the women talking. Most of the big spenders here tonight were men, but it helped to have their wives on board. By the time the night ended, she felt really good about the connections she'd made, but there was still one thing she needed to do.

She found Candy and Bentley chatting in a small group of people and made her way over to them, Luke in tow. She waited for a break in the conversation and asked if they could have a moment to talk.

"Of course!" Candy exclaimed with a bright smile. "Come with me."

She pulled Kennedy to an empty table while Luke and Bentley talked. It was just as well. Candy was the one who made the decisions.

"So, Candy, I just want to thank you again for the gown and dinner," she said, easing into her topic. "I had so much fun on our girls' night out."

"No problem!" Candy said. "I had fun too."

"Good. Have you had a chance to review my proposal?"

"Not yet. I've just been so busy, what with setting

up the foundation with Luke and Bennie."

She was momentarily dazed and hoped it didn't show in her expression. Foundation? Luke was meeting with Bentley and Candy behind her back? She swallowed back her anger, remembering that Candy assumed she and Luke talked about everything as an engaged couple.

"How's that going?" Kennedy asked.

Candy smiled and squeezed her arm. "Wonderful! Our mission is so important, helping families with serious medical bills like yours. Luke suggested it, and after hearing how difficult things were for your parents and all those brothers and sisters to feed, I got one hundred percent behind it."

Kennedy sucked in air. Luke was taking care of her family behind her back even after she told him not to. He was treating them like a charity case. He pitied them. Pitied her.

Candy went on. "And Luke put his money where his mouth is, making a big donation to our foundation, so we know he's serious. Of course you know all that. Sorry if I'm repeating old news. I'm just so excited!"

"Has anyone applied for it yet?"

"We'll be up and running in thirty days. Luke said he's going to get the word out. He knows a few families that could benefit."

Or one in particular.

Candy squeezed her hand. "Now I know you're anxious to hear our decision for a financial manager, and Luke explained how important it was for your career, but we still like to take our time about these things. You know, especially with a baby on the way, we have to really think about the future. Whoever we choose, we plan on working with long term. You're both in our thoughts, though." She smiled. "We promise to make a decision by the cocktail cruise. Okay?"

She nodded numbly. Two more weeks until the cruise. Two more weeks of pretending to be engaged to a man who saw her as an incompetent, weak woman who needed to be taken care of.

Kennedy stood, practically vibrating with rage. What the hell was Luke doing? He felt so sorry for her that he told Bentley and Candy about her private family troubles and set up an entire foundation for it? Told them to choose her to take care of her? She'd told him she could handle her problems on her own. He had zero faith in her abilities. None. He'd lied and gone behind her back.

Candy stood. "Are you okay, honey?"

Kennedy nodded. "Yes, I'm fine."

"Let's do lunch soon, okay?"

"Sure, yes," she said numbly. "Okay, bye."

She turned to see Luke in serious conversation with Bentley and marched over to him.

~ ~ ~

Luke took one look at Kennedy's furious expression and quickly said his goodbye to Bentley and steered her straight out to the parking lot. "What's wrong?"

She glared at him. "What do you think you're doing throwing your money around in a foundation created just to take care of my family?"

Candy must've spilled the beans.

"Well?" she hollered.

"Let's talk in the car."

He guided her to the far end of the parking lot and into his car.

"How could you!" she yelled as soon as they were in the car.

He held up a hand. "I was going to tell you about the foundation."

"When?"

"When it was done."

"You went behind my back!" she hollered. "You told Bentley and Candy to hire me. Why would you do that?"

"I wanted you to have it."

"You just handed it over."

"Yes."

Her lips formed a flat line. "You're going to lose your job. You *forfeited*. That's not business. You handed it to me because you felt sorry for me. You don't believe I can handle myself, my family, or my career. You think I'm just like those troubled kids you mentor. Someone you just quietly help on the side so you can feel good about yourself."

"Kennedy, that is not true."

"Then why? Why did you want me to have it?"

He blew out a breath, knowing he had to be one hundred percent honest. "Because I wanted you to eat. I didn't want to worry about you."

"I told you I can take care of myself!" she hollered, her voice hitting high volume. "I'm fine! I don't want you to take care of me!"

"Too bad." He wouldn't apologize for doing what he felt was right.

"Too bad? No! I refuse to accept that. Don't you see? This means nothing if I don't earn it! You said you'd treat me like any business competitor!"

He was really getting sick of her yelling at him. He hadn't done anything that horrible. "That was before I fucked you."

Her blue eyes widened. "Before you fucked me?" she yelled.

"Yes!" he yelled right back. "And you liked every *fucking* minute of it. And I love you and this is what I do for the people I love. Okay? I make sure they're taken care of. I'm sorry if your ego is too big to accept even one tiny bit of help."

"It's not help!" she shouted. "It's charity! You don't get it because you've never been poor! I can't believe you did all this behind my back!"

"Calm down!" he barked. "I was going to tell you."

"When?"

"After Bentley finally got off his ass and chose you. I even offered to act as your consultant so he'd finally sign something. I knew how badly you needed it."

She huffed. "Like he didn't want me without knowing I had you to back me up? Do you realize how insulting that is?"

"What do you want me to say, Kennedy? I was trying to do something good here. I have the experience. You don't. Everyone knows it. But I still wanted you to have it because I care what happens to you."

She got quiet. Finally. "You don't respect me. You have no confidence in my abilities." She crossed her arms and faced front. "Just take me home."

He pulled out of the lot and onto the road back toward Clover Park. "So what? You want me to take the job from you now?"

"I don't want you to do anything else. Just…leave me alone."

A beat passed in silence. He couldn't believe how unreasonable she was being about what was basically something good.

"I don't think we should see each other anymore," she said quietly.

"You're dumping me because I tried to help you?" he roared.

"I'm dumping you because you lied! I'm dumping you because you went behind my back! And most importantly because you have zero respect for me!"

"I have respect!"

"You don't. You treated me like a child, and you treated my family like a charity case."

"It's not charity to help out a little!"

"It is when you've been told not to. That's why you kept bringing food to them." She lifted her stubborn, defiant little chin. "I am *not* charity."

"Get over yourself."

"You get over yourself! And find someone else to quietly do your good deeds for."

"Maybe I will! Someone who actually appreciates it. Ungrateful witch."

"Fuck you!"

He was so furious he didn't know what he'd do, but it wasn't good. "Don't speak one more word. I mean it. *Not one.*"

She enunciated each word clearly, "Go to hell."

He slammed on the brakes and pulled the car over. His breath came harder as he glared at her. She turned her head away and looked out into the darkness.

He got out of the car and slammed the door, pacing the shoulder of the road, trying to get himself under control. Several minutes later, he returned to the car and drove her home in stone-cold silence.

CHAPTER SIXTEEN

Two whole excruciating weeks later, Luke drove to Kennedy's apartment with grim determination. He could admit it, he was happier with her than without her. But he was still so mad at her. Acting as if his love meant nothing but a threat to her independence. Today was the yacht party with Bentley, Candy, and friends. Bentley had promised to make a decision one way or another.

Dammit. He wasn't a threat to Kennedy at all. She was a threat to him. She threatened to end his long-enjoyed bachelor existence and make him a family man. It was like *he* was the one poring through bridal magazines, imagining some rosy future all this time. Life wasn't all wine and roses, and no one knew that better than he did. His parents' divorce had been nasty. His dad, who'd always been cold and withholding, became even more of an asshole after his wife left him. He brushed off his three sons like their visits were an annoyance forced on him. Only Luke had tried to remain loyal. He hadn't liked his mom letting a strange man and his three sons move in to their home, go to their schools, sharing everything with them. It had changed him. First for the worst because, like Alex, he'd acted out. But ultimately for the better, as his stepdad showed him by example and sometimes with heart-to heart talks what it meant to be a man—to stand by your family, to provide, to care for, to love.

That was all he'd done. Acted like a man for the woman he loved.

He parked and headed to the door of her apartment. If anyone deserved an apology after their fight, it was him.

He stood at the door in his usual business casual outfit, button-down shirt and tailored pants, and hesitated. Maybe he should be the bigger person and apologize first. *No.* This was on her.

He knocked and the door opened a minute later to Kennedy wearing a bright yellow sundress with a white cardigan. Her sour expression didn't match her cheerful outfit. He felt uncharacteristically nervous. Like it was the first time they were going out or something. He glanced down at her hand to see she still wore the diamond engagement ring he'd given her. For some stupid reason, he felt relieved. It wasn't like they were really engaged. He just liked her wearing his ring.

"Hello," Kennedy said stiffly, stepping outside her family's apartment quickly so he couldn't do more than wave to them looking at him curiously.

"Hi."

He got into his car and didn't bother to escort her in the other side.

"Luke, you're going to have to try better than that if we're going to be a believable couple."

He started the car and pulled out of the lot. "I'm sorry I called you a witch," he blurted.

"But not sorry you called me ungrateful?"

He shut up because he wasn't sorry for that. She *was* acting ungrateful.

"You still don't get it," she said.

He let out a long-suffering sigh that he hoped spoke volumes.

"I met with Bentley for golf yesterday and ran my ideas by him," she said. "And he liked them."

"What the hell! Why didn't you call me?"

"We weren't exactly on speaking terms. Besides, you met with Bentley and Candy plenty behind my back."

"Only to help you," he snapped.

"I don't need help," she fired back.

"You know what? Let's just not talk. I don't want

to have the same damned fight with you again."

"Fine."

"Fine."

He blasted the radio with a sinking feeling that no matter how things went with Bentley's final decision today, Luke was the one who stood to lose the most.

He was the one who was going to lose his heart.

~ ~ ~

Kennedy worried how she was going to keep pretending to be engaged to Luke when he was treating her so coldly, but by the time they got on the sleek white yacht, Luke was back to putting on a good show. He acted so warm and affectionate, even she started to feel like everything was okay again. Bentley and Candy were over-the-moon happy to see them, which almost made her suspicious. Was something going on? But what?

They had cocktails and hobnobbed with more of Bentley's friends—an oil sheik, four major league ball players, a rock 'n roll band. An eclectic group of people he just liked to hang with and his two potential advisors. It was kinda hard to fit in with this crowd, who wore their wealth so easily. After an hour of small talk and a glass of wine, Luke told her he had someone he wanted her to meet. She followed him below deck, where he stopped and boxed her in against the wall, his hands on either side of her waist.

He leaned close, and her breath caught. She put her hands on his chest to stop him. "Luke—"

"Shh, kiss me. Please."

She dropped her hands at the surprising plea in his voice.

"You want me to beg?" He dropped to his knees and looked up at her.

She went damp, remembering the last time he'd knelt in front of her. "Get up," she hissed.

"Not until you agree to forgive me. I didn't do anything wrong."

"You did!"

"We should apologize at the same time and move on," he said. "That's more than fair." His hands slid up the outside of her legs, under her dress.

"Luke!"

"Kennedy!"

"I'm still mad at you! Get up!"

"Shh!"

A voice reached them from the end of the small hallway. "Oh no. Are you two fighting?"

They both turned to see Bentley standing there. He crossed to them. She grabbed Luke's arm and tried to pull him up, but he wasn't budging. Her cheeks burned.

"We're fine," Kennedy assured Bentley. "Luke's

just joking around." She pulled at his shirt, but he still kept kneeling in front of her.

Luke turned to Bentley. "I'm begging her forgiveness, but she's being stubborn."

Bentley pulled a key out of his pocket. "This is no good." He unlocked a room next to them. "I need you made up and happy by the time we dock in one hour. Get in there." He gestured to what appeared to be a guest cabin dominated by a queen-sized bed.

Luke finally stood and grabbed her hand.

Kennedy gulped. "That's not necessary," she told Bentley. She turned to Luke. "You're forgiven."

Luke smirked. "Bentley's right. We need to work this out. Thank you." He yanked her inside. "Lock the door, Bentley."

The key turned in the lock.

"Hey!" Kennedy hollered through the door. "You can't lock us in here! I want to talk to Candy!" She rattled the doorknob. She pressed an ear to the door and heard him walking away.

"Give it up," Luke said.

She whirled. "Did you put him up to this?"

He raised his palms. "Nope. But I'm on board."

She threw her hands up. "Augh!"

He advanced on her, a very determined look in his eye. She took a step sideways, realized the futility of that in such a small space, and stood her ground. He flashed a smile before scooping her up and tossing her over his shoulder.

"Luke! This is not how people work things out!"

He carried her over to the queen-size bed nearby and set her down gently. "There. Wasn't that romantic? I think I'll do that on our honeymoon."

"There won't be a honeymoon," she said through her teeth.

"Let's pretend." He flopped down next to her and stretched out on his side. "Hello, wife. How are you?"

"I'm irritable."

"You look ravished."

"I do not."

He pinned her wrists and had her on her back in one swift move. "Give me a little time." He sank his teeth into the cord of her neck and an electric jolt ran through her. He loosened his hold and rained hot, open-mouthed kisses down to her collarbone. She melted into the mattress.

"You're so easy." He released her wrists. "I love that about you."

She rolled out from under him. "I am not easy."

He snagged her by the hips and dragged her back, settling on top of her but taking his weight on his forearms. "Don't take offense." He gazed down at her warmly. "It's a compliment."

"That is not a compliment." She gritted her teeth.

"And I'm still mad at you."

"Okay, but here's the thing. I didn't do anything that isn't fixable. First, if you don't want me to bring any more food to your family, I won't. Even though it's what us Italians do. We feed people."

"You're not even Italian!"

"I am by marriage. Second, yes, your family inspired the foundation, but you don't have to apply for funding if you don't want it. There's plenty more families in similar circumstances that could benefit."

She couldn't deny that. It was scary how quickly medical bills could pile up with one injury or serious illness.

Luke went on. "And, finally, yes, I did recommend Bentley pick you, but here we are, both still in the running, so that wasn't a forfeit at all. He would've picked you already if he wanted you. Maybe he's torn because they know I'm the better candidate."

"I can do the job just as well," she grumbled, but she had to admit he was right. They were both still in the running. Nothing he'd done she had to go along with.

"I sense forgiveness," he said with a grin.

"But how do I know you're not going to keep on doing this? Going behind my back, fixing my problems for me in whatever way you think is best with no regard—"

"I won't go behind your back again. I can't promise not to fix things. I told you I take care of those I love, but I'll try to remember to keep you in the loop."

She thought about that. "No more secrets. I need one hundred percent honesty."

"I honestly love you." He kissed her tenderly. "You have my heart." His dark blue eyes gazing at her spoke of the depth of his emotion, which made her tear up. "Don't break it."

The words she'd said to him came back to her, making it hard to speak. "I won't."

He dipped his head and kissed her for a long time, long enough to draw out a sigh and a total relaxation of her body. He lifted his head and smiled. "I love when you surrender."

"All right. Get up."

"Get up?" he echoed.

She waved him on. "We can tell Bentley we made up."

"We're not completely made up until we have the makeup sex."

"I can't have sex with you here! Everyone will know."

"What do you think they think we're doing here in a locked room with a bed?"

"Arguing, working things out."

"We've still got time. You owe me makeup sex for the excruciating two weeks I had to endure away from you." He gave her a long look. "I missed you."

She threw her arms around him. "I missed you too. So much."

He kissed her long and deep. Then he reached over to the nightstand drawer and produced a strip of condoms. "Clearly Bentley expects his guests to enjoy themselves. You owe me at least this much."

She eyed the strip of six condoms. "Luke, please."

"Good, good, I like when you beg." He rolled out of bed, stood, and stripped down. Despite all their fighting, he had a massive erection. Maybe because of it. She couldn't tell with Luke. She swallowed as he rolled a condom on.

"Your turn, sweetheart." He peeled off her cardigan and dress. Flicked off her bra by the front clasp in one smooth move. She wiggled out of her panties on her own, which earned her a grunt of approval.

She waited for him to pounce. Instead he sat next to her, gathered her up in his arms and snuggled into her neck, placing a soft kiss there. She maneuvered herself to wrap her arms and legs around him, rose up and took him inside.

He hissed out a breath. "No foreplay, huh? Still in a hurry?"

"We have to get back to Bentley and Candy," she said, digging her nails into his shoulders.

But, Luke, as always, took things his own way, which in this case, meant slow. Unbearably slow and sweet, his touch still firm, but his movements unhurried, his kisses tender. She tried to move him along, bucking wildly, but he rolled them, pinning her under him and continuing his slow rhythm.

"Luke!" she cried. "I need—"

"I know," he said, yet he kept going slow and deep until she felt like screaming in frustration, used to a fast release or at least a speedy acceleration with him.

"Then give it to me!"

A small smile played over his lips. "I am giving it to you." He gave her another long, slow thrust.

She threw her arms and legs to the sides, giving up on moving him along.

"Come with me," he urged.

"I can't, I need—" Her breath caught as he gripped her chin, his dark blue eyes boring into hers. The intensity skyrocketed. More slow, deep thrusts. He hovered over her mouth; they shared a breath and then another as their gazes locked. Her insides coiled and tensed. His mouth drifted to her neck and she exploded, rocking helplessly against him. He followed, shuddering against her before he stilled and lifted his head.

She pushed at his shoulder. "We have to get dressed. Bentley could be back any minute."

He rolled off her and they dressed quickly.

She finger combed her hair. "How do I look?" she asked anxiously.

One corner of his mouth lifted. "Your fiancée made his mark on you for sure. You've got a bite mark right here." He indicated the side of his own neck.

She looked around for a mirror. There wasn't one. "Oh God. When did you do that?"

"You don't remember? When you were having the biggest orgasm of your life."

"I was so…lost in that. I didn't even know what you were doing."

"I could pretty much do anything to you, couldn't I?" He smiled lecherously. "Good to know."

The boat bumped.

"I think we're docking," Luke said, shoving his feet into his shoes.

"Omigod, how long have we been down here?"

"I don't know. I didn't check my watch when I was giving you the biggest orgasm of your life." He grinned and crossed to her. His hand cupped the back of her neck and squeezed. Her knees went weak. "It was, wasn't it?"

"Luke," she said weakly, "you're not helping." She clung to his shirt, her body in heated overdrive.

He released his hold and grabbed her hand. "Get ready. It's showtime."

~ ~ ~

Luke couldn't help but smile as Bentley unlocked the door with a grin and led him and Kennedy back up the stairs to the main deck. They were at the end of the line of disembarking passengers. Bentley kept stopping and chatting with them about the foundation until he finally got off the boat in a hurry. He and Kennedy were the last two off the boat.

"Surprise!" everyone on shore hollered.

Kennedy grabbed his hand and swayed. He wrapped an arm around her, keeping her upright.

It was a surprise engagement party. For them. A huge banner strung in front of a white tent proclaimed Congratulations Luke and Kennedy!

"Shit," Kennedy said under her breath.

Luke pasted on a smile and took the last few steps to shore with Kennedy in tow. "Wow! You guys! What a surprise."

Bentley gestured for them to follow him across the grassy lawn to where a white tent had been set up. Candy stood under it, smiling and waving. Bentley rushed to her side. Then both of them turned and hugged him and Kennedy.

"Isn't this a great surprise?" Candy asked. "We

were trying to figure out how to keep you from seeing it, and then when you were arguing, Bentley had the brilliant idea to put you in the guest bunk. We didn't want you mad at each other at your engagement party! We knew it was just a lovers' quarrel." She smiled at them both. "And look how happy you are! It all worked out!"

Luke glanced at Kennedy, a bright pink flush to her cheeks and neck, which only drew more attention to his bite mark. The Neanderthal part of him really dug that.

"Come see your gift," Bentley said, bouncing on the balls of his feet in excitement. He led the way further into the tent. Luke took a quick glance around. Jared and Angel waved. Bentley got a hold of his family? Where the hell were the rest of them? Wait, this wasn't a real engagement.

Kennedy stiffened and stopped dead in her tracks. "My boss is here," she whispered.

"Here it is!" Bentley exclaimed. He pointed to the gift with both hands in a ta-da gesture. It was an oil painting of him and Kennedy.

Kennedy gasped. Luke bit his tongue and took it in. It looked like it was created from a picture from the party back in Greenport at Bentley's summer cottage. They were looking at each other adoringly, sexual chemistry zinging between them. Was that how they looked to everyone? He knew exactly why Kennedy had gasped. Not only was the painting huge, but the artist had added crowns and jewels, as well as a golf ball on the table to the side of the painting. Like they were golfing royalty.

"Do you like it?" Bentley asked. "It's your engagement present."

Luke recovered first. "It's amazing. What a generous gift. Thank you, Bentley and Candy. For the party too. This is such a surprise to us, but really...nice." He squeezed Kennedy's hand because she was still staring at the painting in open-mouthed horror.

Kennedy nodded and quickly agreed.

Bentley and Candy took turns hugging them and congratulating them. And it finally clicked for Luke that for Bentley the line between business and friendship was nonexistent. He would only work with friends. That could work well or terribly, depending on who your friends were.

"We looked up your families to invite them too," Candy said. "Hope you don't mind."

"Not at all," Luke said. He was frankly shocked that Jared and Angel hadn't immediately called to warn him about the party.

"My family?" Kennedy whispered.

"It took some persistence with them," Candy said.

"No one replied to the first email, but I finally got through today with an alternate to your mom."

Kennedy looked around wildly for her mom.

Candy went on. "And, Ken, when Bentley called your work to see if anyone wanted to come, your boss was very enthusiastic about attending." She smiled and nodded. "Now that's a nice firm." She waved a hand in the air. "Luke, your boss was too busy."

Luke inclined his head. "Well, I typically run things on my own. They give me enough rope to hang myself."

"Hahahaha!" Candy tittered.

"Excuse me," Luke said. "I'm going to say hi to my brothers." Kennedy followed, grabbing his elbow and hanging onto his arm. Jared and Angel had dressed for the occasion in button-down shirts, dress pants, and dress shoes. They were currently snarfing down expensive hors d'oeuvres like they were a meal.

"Hey, guys, thanks for coming to my engagement party," Luke said wryly. A waiter stopped by their side with glasses of champagne. He took one and handed one to Kennedy. She took a big gulp.

His brothers each took a glass and the waiter moved on.

"Hi, guys," Kennedy said, a pained look in her eyes.

Jared grinned. "I had to come and see for myself.

What a sham you got going."

"I sure as hell hope you'll come clean," Angel said, popping a lobster springroll in his mouth.

"Where's everyone else?" Luke asked.

"They said they'd wait for the real deal," Jared said. "We're mostly here for the food and the rich ladies looking to get laid." He looked around, taking in all the well-dressed guests.

Angel rolled his eyes. "I'm here for you. Whose idea was this whole engagement thing?"

Luke jerked his chin toward Kennedy, who looked like she wanted to slink away.

Ding, ding, ding. Bentley tapped on a glass to get the crowd's attention. He picked up a mike. "A toast to the happy couple. May your marriage be as happy as mine and Candy's."

"Hear, hear!" Jared boomed, lifting his glass in a toast.

Luke clinked his champagne glass against Kennedy's and wrapped their wrists around each other so he could tip his glass into her mouth. She followed along, letting him sip from hers. Everyone cheered, but he barely heard them as his gaze had locked with Kennedy's and the look in her eyes was not her usual fire, but worry. He wanted nothing more than to take that worry away. He slowly set his glass down, along with hers, grabbed her head, and kissed her. She melted against him. He wanted her again so badly he ached. Someone wolf whistled and he broke the kiss, still holding her in his arms. Kennedy was satisfyingly flushed and breathing hard.

"Damn," Jared said under his breath.

Angel stared.

He pulled away. "Alright, guys," he said to his brothers. "Show's over."

Kennedy's boss appeared at their side. He knew Simon Barrett from the Barrett Group by reputation. He was a hard-ass that micromanaged his employees to death. "Congratulations, Ken. Luke." He shook both their hands.

Kennedy stood straighter. "Thank you."

"I appreciate all the legwork your fiancée has done," Simon said to Luke. "Couldn't have gotten that 'in' without her impressive work on the golf course." He turned to Kennedy. "I'll take it from here. Thanks."

He walked off, heading toward Bentley. Kennedy rushed after him, probably pleading her case. Simon smiled and nodded and continued walking.

"What'd he say?" Luke asked when she returned to his side.

Kennedy spoke in a monotone, her eyes glazed over. "He says I'm not ready to handle this amount of money."

"That's bullshit. He said you'd get a promotion if you brought in Bentley."

"It's over," she whispered.

~ ~ ~

Kennedy had never felt so low. All this effort, all this time and deception, and, yes, heartbreak, only to have it taken away from her at the last minute. Now what was her family going to do? They'd have to declare bankruptcy soon. Her dad couldn't afford the surgery he needed. He'd never fully recover, never get his job back. Unless they applied for that funding. Dammit. She hated asking for a handout.

Her mom suddenly spoke right in front of her. She hadn't even noticed her approach. Her mom beamed. "Ken, why didn't you and Luke tell us this big news?" She hugged them both and then turned to Kennedy. "I wasn't happy to hear the news secondhand, but the important thing is that you're happy."

Her mom beamed at them both, looking happier than she had in months. Kennedy couldn't take it. Her mom was only going to be disappointed when she found out it wasn't real.

"Mom, I have to tell you something."

"Don't," Luke said.

"What is it, sweetheart?"

Kennedy's gut twisted. She leaned close and

whispered the truth. That it was a fake engagement designed to get an "in" with a potential client. She was ashamed of herself.

Her mom's jaw dropped.

Kennedy turned to Luke. "I'm so sorry I dragged you through all this." She took off the diamond engagement ring and held it out to him.

"No," Luke said, pushing it back to her.

"A fake engagement!" her mom exclaimed.

Kennedy took a step back, startled at the outburst. Her mom rarely raised her voice. "Mom, please lower your—"

"Your dad was actually happy about something for the first time in months!" her mom exclaimed.

The group of people near them quieted and then started whispering. Luke took her hand and slid the ring back on her finger.

He held up a hand. "Just a misunderstanding!" he called.

But it was too late. The news traveled fast all the way to Bentley and Candy.

Candy came barreling toward them, already yelling on her way. "I trusted you!" Her words were directed at both of them. "I let you into our life. I thought we were friends. Friends don't lie to each other!"

Kennedy's guilt and shame multiplied. Candy had been good to her. So had Bentley, for that matter.

Bentley appeared at Candy's side.

"I'm sorry," Kennedy said sincerely. "This was all my idea. Not Luke's."

"But he went along with it," Bentley accused.

"I wanted to be with her," Luke said. "But that's no excuse. I apologize for my part in the deception."

"I don't see how you can trust either of them," Candy said. "Come on, Bennie."

"No! Wait!" Kennedy said. "Luke's innocent. You should choose him."

Luke ran after them, talking and gesturing. Bentley and Candy kept walking.

She could only hope Luke could salvage the situation. Her boss stormed over to her. "Thanks for losing our chance at Bentley. I never should've trusted you when you went behind my back to secure the meeting. You're fired."

"What?"

"You heard me." He stormed off.

Kennedy stood there in shock at how quickly everything crashed down around her. Her life was never going to get better. The bills would just keep piling up. There was no way the foundation would help them now. Her family would be torn apart. She looked around the crowd of people, most of them that she didn't know. She'd failed. Fallen flat on her face. There was nothing left to do but retreat.

Her mom headed toward her, cell phone in hand. "The police picked up Alex."

"Let's go," Kennedy said and headed home to help with whatever trouble Alex had gotten into this time. There was nothing more she could do to make things better here anyway. She'd ruined everything.

CHAPTER SEVENTEEN

Kennedy returned home after they picked up a sorry-looking, hungover Alex.

"I'm never drinking again," he mumbled before stumbling down the hallway to the bedroom.

They'd thought he was spending the night at a friend's house, but the police had found him passed out in the woods behind the high school with an empty bottle of whiskey and the remains of a campfire. The slew of charges against him—an illegal fire, underage drinking, and loitering—were mitigated by the fact that he broke down and told Chief O'Hare his story in between gulping sobs. Even she and her mom got teary-eyed. Alex had finally told Carla he loved her, and she'd told him she only liked him as a friend. Worse, he said he'd take care of her and her daughter and assured her he'd be a good dad. She told him he was just a kid with no clue about the real world. He was, understandably, devastated.

And though Kennedy thought it was for the best, she still thought Carla was too harsh. Couldn't she at least have said they could be friends?

"What's the damage?" her dad asked her mom.

"They added to his community service," her mom said, sinking to the sofa. "He told Chief O'Hare a sob story. Even I was teary-eyed. So he's got trash duty and coaching duty, along with a stern warning." She told him the whole story.

"Damn," her dad said. "Maybe it's for the best."

Her mom went on. "You know what was kinda nice? He said he'd be a good dad because he learned from the best."

Her dad sucked in air. Her mom put a gentle hand on his shoulder. "I'm going to check on him." Her mom left.

Kennedy sat on the sofa and leaned her head back.

"I've let him down," her dad said quietly. Then he broke down in tears, shocking the hell out of her. She'd never seen him cry. "It's my fault. If I hadn't gotten in this damn accident, he'd still be an honor student. Instead he's a delinquent."

She put a gentle hand on his arm, careful of his back. "No, Dad, it's not your fault."

"It is. If I could afford it, I'd ship him off to military school."

"He's fine. He's just going through a hard time."

"He needs a real dad."

"He has a real dad."

He grabbed a tissue from the nearby TV tray and wiped his face dry. "I'm not the same dad to him I was to you."

She met his dark brown eyes so full of pain. "You've been great to both of us."

He blinked back tears, and she got choked up too. This man, in so much pain that he was a fraction of his old self, had stepped up and taken responsibility for her when he damned well didn't have to. She'd always secretly wished she was one of his biological kids.

"Dad, Alex has issues, yes, but they're not all on your shoulders. He's in love with Carla. It's just one of those fluke things." She should know. Falling for Luke was not something she'd ever expected to happen when she'd first met him. He'd been arrogant, full of himself, a regular know-it-all, teasing and challenging her at every turn, until he'd finally shown her the man he was underneath. A good, kind man who put those he loved ahead of himself. She'd never forgive herself if he lost Bentley and his job because of her.

Her dad scrubbed a hand over his face. "This is all news to me."

"You haven't been easy to talk to lately."

"I know. Maybe the next surgery will go better."

"Can we afford it?"

"What's the alternative?"

They looked at each other, both knowing how much worse things could get before they got better.

Her dad broke the heavy silence. "Tell me what's going on with you. Your mom said you faked an engagement to win a big client."

She cringed. "I'm sorry. I should've told you. I never should've done that."

"I liked Luke. I was disappointed, but not too surprised at what you pulled."

"What?"

"That has Kennedy written all over it. That's the kind of go-big-or-go-home attitude you've always had."

Her shoulders slumped. "I guess."

"Not saying it was the right thing to do."

"It wasn't." She gripped her hands together in her lap, the shame and embarrassment of the day's events swamping her. "I fell flat on my face. Lost my job. Lost the client."

"And what about Luke?"

She considered her words carefully. "I basically ruined any chance he had at the client and his promotion, so I…" Her throat closed. "I don't know."

They sat in silence for a minute, both thinking hard about their respective troubles.

Would Luke ever forgive her for what she'd put

him through? All the deception, the lost client, the loss of his job. He'd said he needed to pull in Bentley as a client to keep his job. She swallowed hard and stepped outside for a much-needed breath of fresh air. That night she called Luke multiple times only to get voicemail. Was he avoiding her calls?

She vowed to try again tomorrow. She didn't give up that easily, and he was worth fighting for.

~ ~ ~

Kennedy sat on her parents' sofa the following morning in shock. "But I'm going to land something soon and then I'll help you guys get back on your feet."

"We don't want you to," her mom said in her quiet way. "Though we thank you. It's time you found your own place, time you branched out and had your own life."

"But the kids need me," Kennedy said. She'd always done her part, more than her part, to take care of the siblings that were rightfully the kids of her parents. She was the one adopted into the family and never wanted her dad to regret that move.

"It's time," her dad said.

"I don't understand," Kennedy said. "Mom?"

"This fake engagement thing went too far, Ken," her mom said gently. "People got hurt. We think your heart's in the right place, but we don't want you to do anything else crazy on our behalf. Understand?"

Kennedy stood there in shock for a full minute. Her parents began a quiet conversation. And then she packed a suitcase, along with her laptop, and walked out the door.

She stood on the sidewalk, considering her options, and then called her friend Hailey, needing a place to crash and get started with a job search. Hailey was out, but told her to make herself at home in her small basement apartment, so Kennedy retrieved the key from under a ceramic turtle and set up base on Hailey's sofa. The first thing she did was a massive resume email blast to every firm related to finance she could think of in the city. Then she finally got up the nerve to call Candy and apologize profusely for the fake engagement.

"It's okay, honey," Candy replied. "Luke explained it to us last night."

"What did he say?"

"That it was inevitable. The engagement would be in the works sooner or later and you just moved things along. I'd do the same thing with a hottie like that."

She sank back into the sofa. *Inevitable.* That was exactly what she said about them hooking up in the first place. Did he really mean that?

"Inevitable?" Kennedy echoed weakly.

"Yes. Say, I'm glad I got you on the phone. My friend Christina was asking about you. Give her a call. She wants to talk to you about Griffin's finances."

She shot straight off the sofa. "Griffin Huntley?" she squeaked.

"Yes! Remember him from the party?" Only the biggest rock star in the entire world.

"Of course I remember!" she exclaimed.

"Good. Here's the number." She rattled it off. "Call Christina right away. She's really been bugging me about it, but I've been so busy, what with the foundation and planning a stealth engagement party, I didn't have a chance to tell you."

"So you went with Luke?"

"We did. We like him, like his experience and his moral character. He really went to bat for you back at the cottage. He has the kind of altruistic nature that we trust."

Kennedy sagged to the sofa. She should've trusted that from the beginning too. She was so relieved she hadn't ruined his career after all she almost forgot about calling Christina, until Candy reminded her before hanging up.

She stood, took a deep breath, and called Christina.

She hung up in shock.

Christina wanted her to manage Griffin's fortune.

At first under Christina's supervision and then on her own. Christina was tired of doing it and felt she didn't know enough to really make it multiply to last for Griffin's lifetime. She wanted someone young and trustworthy. Someone with a fire in her belly, which Candy had assured her she had. Again Candy had come through for her. She was going to hug her like crazy next time she saw her.

Kennedy immediately went for pure honesty. "Christina, I don't know how much Candy told you, but I was only pretending to be engaged to Luke. I thought if we were an engaged couple, Bentley might want us around more and I'd have a better chance to win his business. I just want to be up front with you, and please know I'm never going to do anything like that ever again."

"Could've been worse," Christina said. "Though I appreciate your honesty. Hell, I admire you for not taking the easy way and marrying into money. Luke told us how independent you are and how you take care of yourself."

"You talked to Luke?"

"Yup. I'm on the board of the foundation. I'm an oncology nurse and I've seen plenty of families in dire financial need because of illness."

"Wow," she muttered under her breath.

Christina then launched into an accounting of all

Griffin had earned in the last three years and where she'd invested the money, mostly in mutual funds and a trust for a man with Down's Syndrome, who Griffin considered family, though they weren't technically related. Then she asked her to forego a percentage of the investments in favor of a mind-boggling salary with benefits, and finished with a request for Kennedy to house-sit their Brooklyn brownstone for a month while they went on a tour of the South.

Kennedy's knees went weak, and she sank to the sofa. "Yes to all of that."

"No negotiating?"

Kennedy quickly realized her mistake. Christina wanted aggressive confidence in her financial manager. "I need an advance on my salary."

"Ooh, you are ballsy. How much?"

She quoted the exact amount of her sister's tuition bill plus the minimum needed to satisfy the collection agency.

Christina replied, "Done."

After she hung up, she noticed she had a text from Luke. *I want to see you.*

She felt weak with relief. *I'll meet you at your place.*

Kennedy left a quick note for Hailey and headed to the city, suitcase in hand for her house-sitting job. But first she headed to Luke's apartment on the Upper West Side of Manhattan, desperate to see him and share all that had happened.

He answered the door with a big smile.

"Luke." The one word was all she could manage with all the emotion clogging her throat.

"Hello to you too. What's with the suitcase?" He grinned and grabbed it. "You moving in?" He winked. "I'm not sure I'm emotionally ready."

She followed him inside and blurted all about her new job.

"That's great!"

"And you had nothing to do with it?" She had to check because Christina had talked to him.

He gave her a look. "I told you I'd tell you stuff before I did it. That was all Candy's influence. Come see our engagement gift from Bentley. He gave it to me after you left." He went to the coffee table and picked up a photo album. He opened it to show her. In it were pictures of her and Luke—at the party at the cottage, on the way out to his car to get Alex out of jail, coming out of the spa freshly massaged, below deck on the yacht with Luke kneeling in front of her.

"It's like they were spying on us all along," she said.

"All they saw were two people madly in love." He set the album down and wrapped his arms around her. "That's what he told me when I came clean about us. I explained why it was so important to you to have him as a client, and then I thanked him for bringing us together. I would've met up with you last night, but Bentley finally wanted to talk business. The three of us went back to his yacht and spent hours hammering out the details on his financial future."

She wrapped her arms around his waist. "Candy said you said our engagement was inevitable."

"True."

So arrogant. So overly confident. So *right*.

She stared at him as she struggled for the words to tell him what was now glaringly obvious. Luke was her future. She was meant for this man as some part of her had known all along.

He stared right back, his dark blue eyes teasing and tempting at the same time. "Move in with me."

So…irresistible.

She lifted her chin. "I thought you weren't emotionally ready."

He held her chin firmly, a smile curving his lips. "I was using my devilish charm to get under that prickly defense of yours. I love you, Kennedy. Always."

Her eyes stung, but she couldn't look away with his hold on her. His dark blue eyes gazed back at her, so full of love that she burst into tears. He scooped her up in his arms, cradling her.

"I-I love you too," she sputtered, burying her head in his chest and soaking his shirt with her teary declaration. "For always too."

"Forever," he said gruffly before carrying her to the bed. Then he joined her, kissing her in the tender way that did her in, his hands stroking firmly but unhurried. After a lot of kissing and not much else, she became concerned. Well, he had managed to get them naked, but he was going so slow.

"Luke, are we always going to make love now, like, really slow and gentle?"

He cocked a brow. "Is there a problem?"

"No, it's fine, but—"

He pinned her wrists above her head and kissed her hard. "You want to be bossed?"

Her breath caught. "Only in bed."

"You're in luck. It comes naturally." He kissed her again, long and deep. "And so will you...when I say so."

She shivered in delicious anticipation.

He released her wrists and cradled her cheek with one hand. "I really think Bentley will be disappointed if you don't marry me for real after all the trouble he went to for our engagement party."

"Is this more of your devilish charm?"

"Is it working?"

"Yes."

He flashed a smile. "Then it is. Will you marry me? I hope you still have the ring." He lifted her hand to check. She'd stopped wearing it after the engagement party.

She sighed happily. "Some part of me already has married you."

He stared at her hand. "Where's the ring?"

She laced her fingers with his. "In a safe place."

"Well, put it on," he demanded.

"It's not with me. I'll get it later." He frowned, and she hurried to reassure him. "Luke, my heart's been yours from the minute I saw how badly you sucked at golf."

He put a hand to his ear like he couldn't hear her. "Sorry, was that a yes?"

"Yes!"

He kissed her passionately, breathlessly, and settled between her legs, resting on his forearms to gaze down at her. "I hope you know our kids are going to have beautiful names like Kennedy."

She couldn't help but smile. "I never liked my name until I heard you say it. But I need to wait on kids. I feel like I just graduated from raising my siblings."

"You get six years."

"You'd wait that long?"

"Yes. I expect you to pop out at least two starting at age thirty." He kissed his way along her jawline, leaning down further to nip the side of her neck and then soothe the stinging spot with his tongue. "I need time to explore this body."

"Six years?" she teased. "You'll be so old."

"I will not be so old. Geez." He pinched her nipple in retaliation and hot tingles raced through her. "You'd better get that *old* thing out of your head."

She grinned cheekily. "Or you'll be forced to prove your virility," she teased like she had the very first night they'd gotten together at Garner's.

"Your new name is *mine*." he said, picking up right on cue. "What's my new name?"

"Husband," she said softly.

"Very good," he crooned and rewarded her in her favorite shuddering way.

~ ~ ~

Kennedy and her whole family were invited to a Sunday family dinner/engagement party the following week at Luke's older brother Gabe's house. It was a casual dinner celebration, which was just fine with them. They'd already done the fancy yacht engagement party and much preferred the family get-together. More and more family get-togethers were at Gabe's house in Clover Park, Luke told her, because his family was getting too big to fit into his parents' small ranch home. Gabe's house was the house Luke had grown up in, and she loved seeing it. As a kid, she'd ridden her bike up and down this dead-end street never knowing her future husband lived there. Everyone was happy for them and admired her ring, which she wore proudly. Even her dad's spirits were lifted. He'd decided to join Alex in coaching the Little League team from a chair on the sidelines. He was still in a lot of pain, but the strain of letting his family down financially had lifted thanks to Kennedy getting the collection agency off their back.

Nico and Lily were on their way home from a two-week honeymoon in New England, where they took in all sorts of odd sights like a landlocked ship and a giant trebuchet that hurled pumpkins. Luke's family was really growing on her, especially the women in the family. Everyone was hanging out in the kitchen, snacking on a veggie tray and chips that Gabe's wife, Zoe, had put out. Of course, Mrs. Marino brought a platter of wedding cookies to celebrate their engagement. She was puffed up about her influence on current events.

Vince's voice suddenly boomed out above the buzz of conversation. "What's the matter with you?"

"I'm fine!" Sophia hollered before making a dramatic exit out the back door.

"The female fine," Jared said, shaking his head. "That's never good."

She and Luke grinned at each other, remembering

how Luke had said the same thing to her "fine."

"Get back here!" Vince hollered.

He started after her and Mr. Marino stopped him. "Son, letting loose in the short term on your anger isn't going to give you any satisfaction long term. You don't ever hear me yelling at Allie."

Vince scowled. "She's yelled at you."

"But I don't fire back. It's not worth it."

Mrs. Marino wrapped her arms around Mr. Marino's waist and smiled.

The tips of Vince's ears turned red. "I don't know what's wrong with her. She's been snapping at me all week."

"PMS?" Jared offered.

Vince sliced a hand in the air. "That's what I thought. But the tampon box has the same amount in it."

The men groaned. The women exchanged amused looks.

"You seriously keep track of that?" Luke asked.

"It's self-defense," Vince explained.

"Vin-cent," Zoe sang.

Everyone turned to Zoe. She was a jazz singer with a beautiful voice.

She turned baby Miles upside down from her waist, so they were both smiling at Vince. She continued her song, looking right at Vince, "Maybe

Sophia's going through a thing...or two."

Vince stared at Miles, smiling his tiny-baby-teeth smile. Realization dawned, and he staggered back comically. "You mean..." He shoved both hands in his hair and pulled. "You think..." He bolted out the back door.

They heard Sophia squeal, the low rumble of Vince's voice, and then silence.

"Are you saying what I think you're saying?" Angel asked with a big smile.

"Why all the hinting around?" Jared asked. "Why don't you just say it?"

"I only know because she had a question," Zoe said. "It's up to—"

The back door slammed open and Vince burst into the room, arms flung in a V of victory. "I'm gonna be a daddy!"

Sophia slipped in behind him. "I thought we were going to tell them together," she said wryly.

Vince hauled her against his side. They both grinned like fools.

Everyone congratulated the happy couple. Mr. Marino gave Vince some advice on TLC for pregnant women, which Gabe heartily agreed with. Zoe warned him that Sophia might get even more emotional and it totally wasn't her fault.

"You think Nico will come back from the

honeymoon a daddy too?" Luke asked.

"He'll sure as hell try," Jared quipped.

Everyone laughed.

Luke wrapped his arms around Kennedy from behind and leaned down to her ear. "We'll have to try a lot too."

"Just practice," she said, peeking at him over her shoulder.

He kissed her. "I'll never get enough of you."

She sighed dreamily, knowing it was true. "I love you."

"I love you too," he said gruffly.

"When's the happy day?" Mr. Marino asked, looking over to Luke and Kennedy.

"Every day," Luke pronounced.

"Awww…" everyone chorused, making Kennedy blush.

"I told you those wedding cookies were powerful," Mrs. Marino said. "Jared, Angel, eat up."

Jared backed away, making an X with his fingers. "Get those things away from me, you voodoo woman!"

Angel laughed and took two.

EPILOGUE

Four months later...

Luke felt satisfied. Married and so deeply in love he knew it was the real deal. The forever kind that he'd glimpsed through his brothers—Gabe, Vince, and Nico—and hadn't ever thought would happen for him. Lightning had struck in the form of one Miss Kennedy Ward, now Mrs. Kennedy Reynolds. They'd had a small wedding the weekend before Valentine's Day and were now on their honeymoon in Hawaii.

Kennedy was determined to improve his golf game while they hit the best golf courses the islands had to offer. She gave him pointers the entire game. He readily complied, though he wasn't as quick a study as she was a patient teacher.

"I have a feeling this is going to be a boost for my career," he told her as he lined up his shot. "I may even play the PGA Tour."

She smiled and adjusted his wrist. "Let's not get

ahead of ourselves."

He grinned. "If I hadn't sucked at golf, we never would've been fake engaged."

She leaned up on tiptoe and kissed him. "We never would've been real engaged if you didn't turn out to be so wonderful."

He snagged her with one arm around her waist and pulled her flush against him. "Kennedy, Kennedy, Kennedy." She rubbed herself against him. "How can I focus on golf when you're talking dirty to me?" He sighed and shook his head. "Take off your clothes."

She peeked around the golf course. They were not alone. It was broad daylight.

"I will not," she said quietly, though he could tell she was hoping he'd insist on it. Her quiet voice was a seductive invitation. She lifted her chin. "Besides, I wasn't talking dirty."

He kissed her, and she kissed him back with passion and a whole lotta love. He broke the kiss and held her tight for a minute the way she liked. He couldn't feel her ribs anymore because he kept their apartment stocked with all her favorite foods, though he told her they were all his favorites. They were now anyway. He pulled back and gazed into her beautiful face. "I love you."

She smiled big time. "Love you more."

"God, we sound like Candy and Bentley."

"Aren't we lucky?"

A golf cart appeared from around the bend, driving excruciatingly slow. "Wait up, guys!" Bentley called. He was the most overprotective husband now that Candy was showing. She was six months pregnant.

"Yoo-hoo!" Candy called with a big wave.

"Get over here, you crazy kids!" Luke hollered.

Kennedy laughed. Their two closest friends joined them for a friendly game of golf. Bentley and Candy were enjoying a Valentine's Day vacation before the newest heir to the Williams Oil fortune was born.

Kennedy won. Again.

But Luke knew he was the real winner because Kennedy was all his forever. He smiled to himself. He'd gone for the long game and it paid off. He'd never felt richer, never been richer, honestly, thanks to Bentley putting his faith in him and letting him double down on some really lucrative investments. But all that mattered to him was Kennedy.

She worked as the financial manager for Griffin's fortune and had picked up three more clients through him. She was becoming the go-to financial manager for the rock 'n roll crowd. Kennedy worked from their home and traveled to her clients as needed. Luckily, his office was a short commute from their apartment, so they could still play one of their favorite games where he was the boss and she was the assistant. Only after hours, of course.

Only when he demanded it.

Only when she craved it.

Only for love.

~THE END~

Thanks for reading *An Ambitious Engagement*. I hope you enjoyed it! Look for the other books in The Clover Park Series too!

Turn the page to read an excerpt from *Clutch Player*, Jared and Emily's story.

CLUTCH PLAYER

KYLIE GILMORE

He's the guy you turn to in a clutch…
Surgeon Jared Reynolds has always been an adrenaline junkie, which makes him the go-to guy in emergencies. He just never expected an emergency that made him wear a…porcupine costume.

Nurse Emily Maguire works the pediatric oncology ward, a challenging, but rewarding job that suddenly becomes unbearable when the full-of-himself Jared steps in for his sweet brother during the Saturday morning Captain Cuddle visit. She knows his rep for hooking up with nurses and refuses to fall for his obvious charms.

Until an emergency brings them together that has Jared falling into the deep end of love, and Emily wondering if a clutch player is just what she needs.

CLUTCH PLAYER EXCERPT

Jared slapped together a couple of ham and cheese sandwiches and poured Fritos on the plates. Emily had already settled at the round table in his eat-in kitchen, sitting ramrod straight. He figured she was tense after being front page news again. He set a plate in front of her and took the seat next to her. He dove into lunch and gave her a sideways glance to make sure she was eating too. After a few moments, he asked, "You want to tell me your side of the scandal story?" She'd never spoken about it publicly. He was really curious to know her take on it. And now that she was sitting in his kitchen, so close, so beautiful, he also really needed to know if she was married.

Emily froze, sandwich halfway to her mouth. "Can I get a drink?"

"Sure, what do you want? Water? Milk? Gatorade?"

"Any alcohol?"

"Oh, ho, ho. Hitting the hard stuff this early are we?"

She blew out a breath. "I've had a rough couple of days."

"I hear ya." He stood. "How you like scotch?"

"Never had it."

"Well, you are in for a treat. This is the good stuff." He poured them both a small amount in a couple of glass tumblers and set them on the table. "Bottoms up." He took a healthy swallow, felt the burn down his throat to his stomach. "Ahh."

She did the same, swallowing the whole thing down, and then started a coughing fit that made him laugh. Newbie.

"You like it?" he asked.

She wiped her eyes. "Yes," she croaked. She took another bite of sandwich.

He took pity on her and got up to fetch her a glass of milk.

"I'll take another," she said.

He froze. "Really?"

"Hit me." She slammed the glass on the table.

He shook his head. "All right, but I expect some juicy secrets after two drinks."

She tried to glare at him but just ended up looking adorable with her pink pursed lips. He poured her a glass of milk, and then with his back to her, he watered down her next serving of scotch. He set them both in front of her, grabbed a glass of water for himself, and took his seat again.

She drank the whole glass of scotch in one long swallow, wiped her mouth with the back of her hand and coughed. "Thanks," she croaked.

They ate their lunch in silence for a few minutes. He'd discovered that a well-timed silence could get women talking. Emily didn't disappoint.

"You know the problem with men?" she asked.

He leaned in. "Tell me."

"Big cheaters," she pronounced with a nod. She pointed a Frito at him, looked at it, and took a bite.

"That's hardly fair to paint us all with the same brush. I never cheated. I just don't stick around. So your ex was a cheater. Fuck him. He didn't deserve you."

"I'm never gonna fuck him again!"

He raised his fist for a fist bump, and she gave him one. He took a bite of sandwich and then a drink of water. "So, tell me your version of the scandal. We've all heard his side but you refused to speak about it."

She sighed and took a bite of sandwich.

"I'll tell you one of my secrets."

That got her attention. She pushed her long dark brown hair behind her ears and regarded him curiously. "Really?"

"Really. Only if you promise to share one of your scandal secrets."

"You first."

"Okay. I, uh, gosh this is hard for me." He looked at the table, fighting back a grin.

She took his hand and held it. "It's okay. This won't leave this room."

"Sometimes I have impure thoughts."

She scowled and shoved his hand back on the table.

"Ouch. Be careful." He lifted his hand and wiggled his fingers. "These hands are precision instruments."

"Are you ever serious?" she asked.

"Not if I can help it."

She stared at a Frito then licked it. His jeans got tight.

"Are you still married?" he asked.

"Nope." She put the Frito in her mouth and chewed. "I'm never getting married again. Men are pigs."

"Is that why you turned me down?"

"I told you why I turned you down." She fed him a Frito. "Your reputation precedes you."

He wanted her, there was no question. He couldn't resist trying one more time. "My rep is overrated," he informed her.

She raised a brow. "Yeah? They say you're one and done but it's worth it."

He chuckled. "Maybe it's not overrated then. That doesn't make me a pig. Everyone knows going in it's just for fun."

"Yeah, yeah. That's what they all say." She went back to her sandwich. "Tell me a real secret," she said around a mouthful of sandwich. "I really want to know about you."

No one ever asked what was in his head. Most women just liked the package, his body and what it could make them feel. He double checked if she really wanted to know. She set her sandwich down and stared at him, her body stockstill. "Go on," she said softly.

He put his sandwich down, took a deep breath, and blurted, "I never commit because then they might figure out I'm not so great and leave me." A weight lifted from his shoulders just saying that out loud. He'd had that fear in the back of his mind ever since Jen left him.

Her brown eyes widened. "Jared, wow. That was so deep." She propped her head on her hand and stared at him. "Has that ever happened to you?"

"Once. Right after med school." He ate some more sandwich and when she just sat there, head propped on her hand, listening, he added, "We lived together for six months. She left because I wasn't exciting enough. As much as I'm an adrenaline junkie, I also love working on the house. You know. Fixing things, making stuff. Sometimes I'll work on the truck. I always find something to do."

She stared at him with those sympathetic brown eyes for so long he feared he would blurt out more deep shit so he stood and poured himself some more scotch. Finally, she spoke, "This doesn't leave this room."

He returned to the table, eager to hear her side of the sex scandal story. "No, m'am."

"My ex wanted things he couldn't get from me, so he hired prostitutes to do them."

He hissed. "Bastard."

She seemed to warm to her topic, leaning toward him to confide even more. "He called them all Emily and made them wear brown-haired wigs and dress in nurse's outfits so they looked like me."

"That's sick. Was he kinky or something?"

"He wanted a threesome." She pounded a fist on the table. "Like one me wasn't enough."

"It's more than enough."

She pointed at him so close her finger grazed his cheek. "Thank you!" She licked another Frito, her pink little tongue driving him crazy. She met his eyes over the Frito. "He wanted to spank me and…"

He was almost afraid to speak. "And?"

"And screw me in the ass when I have a perfectly serviceable vagina for just that purpose!"

He forced a straight face. "I'm sure it's perfectly serviceable."

"Damn straight!" She beamed at him. "You're so easy to talk to. He screwed my neighbor and former best friend at the same time a week before the wedding." She jabbed a thumb at herself. "I'm the idiot that went through with it. I believed him that it was a drunken fluke and would never happen again."

He took her hand. "You're not an idiot. You just didn't want to lose the deposit on the wedding reception."

She laughed, which made him smile. She shouldn't have had to go through all that.

He went on. "The caterer, the DJ. That ball was rolling."

She gave him a watery smile that made his chest ache.

"C'mere," he said gently.

She didn't move.

He squeezed her hand. "I'm not kinky. I'm a real old-fashioned guy that likes good old missionary position. A few other positions too since we're being so honest. I'm perfectly content with a serviceable vagina."

"I'm not sleeping with you." She leaned a little closer, gave him a soft kiss, and smiled.

"Of course not."

Get *Clutch Player* now!

Also by Kylie Gilmore

The Clover Park Series

THE OPPOSITE OF WILD (Book 1)
DAISY DOES IT ALL (Book 2)
BAD TASTE IN MEN (Book 3)
KISSING SANTA (Book 4)
RESTLESS HARMONY (Book 5)
NOT MY ROMEO (Book 6)
REV ME UP (Book 7)
AN AMBITIOUS ENGAGEMENT (Book 8)

The Clover Park STUDS Series

ALMOST IN LOVE (Book 1)
ALMOST MARRIED (Book 2)
ALMOST OVER IT (Book 3)
ALMOST ROMANCE (Book 4)

Acknowledgments

A huge thank you to Mimi who saw the forest for the trees with this one. Mwah! Thank you to my family for cheering me on. Thanks, as always, to Tessa, Pauline, Mimi, Shannon, Kim, Maura, and Jenn for all you do. And big hugs and thanks to my readers, I couldn't do this without you!

About the Author

Kylie Gilmore is the *USA Today* bestselling author of the Clover Park series and the Clover Park STUDS series. She writes quirky, tender romance with a solid dose of humor.

Kylie lives in New York with her family, two cats, and a nutso dog. When she's not writing, wrangling kids, or dutifully taking notes at writing conferences, you can find her flexing her muscles all the way to the high cabinet for her secret chocolate stash.

Praise for Kylie Gilmore

THE OPPOSITE OF WILD

"This book is everything a reader hopes for. Funny. Hot. Sweet."
—New York Times Bestselling Author, Mimi Jean Pamfiloff

"It's intriguing and complex while still being light hearted and truly romantic. To see a male so twisted and turned is unusual but honestly made the book all the more enjoyable."
—Harlequin Junkie

"Ms. Gilmore's writing style draws the reader in and does not let go until the very end of the story and leaves you wanting more."
—Romance Bookworm

"Every aspect of this novel touched me and left me unable to put it down. I pulled an all-nighter, staying up until after 3 am to get to the last page."
—Luv Books Galore

DAISY DOES IT ALL

"The characters in this book are downright hilarious sometimes. I mean, when you start a book off with a fake life and immediately follow it by a rejected proposal, you know that you are in for a fun ride."
—The Little Black Book Blog

"Daisy Does It All is a sweet book with a hint of sizzle. The characters are all very real and I found myself laughing along with them and also having my heart ripped in two for them."
—A is for Alpha, B is for Book

BAD TASTE IN MEN

"I gotta dig a friends to lovers story, and Ms. Gilmore's 3rd book in the Clover Park Series hits the spot. A great dash of humor, a few pinches of steam, and a whole lotta love…Gilmore has won me over with everything I've read and she's on my auto buy list…she's on my top list of new authors for 2014."
—Storm Goddess Book Reviews

"The chemistry between the two characters is so real and so intense, it will have you turning the pages into the midnight hour. Throw in a bit of comedy – a dancing cow, a sprained ankle, and a bit of jealousy and Gilmore has a recipe for great success."
—Underneath the Covers blog

KISSING SANTA

"I love that Samantha and Rico are set up by none other than their mothers. And the journey they go on is really hilarious!! I laughed out loud so many times, my kids asked me what was wrong with me."
—Amazeballs Book Addicts

"I absolutely adored this read. It was quick, funny, sexy and got me in the Christmas spirit. Samantha and Rico are a great couple that keep one another all riled up in more ways than one, and their sexual tension is super hot."
—Read, Tweet, Repeat

RESTLESS HARMONY

"Kylie's writing as usual is full of laugh out loud humor, touching moments, and heat that will make you fan yourself... If you are looking for a book that will having you laughing out loud and feeling good when you are done, this book is for you."
—Smut and Bonbons blog

"My heart broke for Gabe's past, but it soared for the understanding and love in which he got through from a family born of true love and commitment. Kylie brought the real with this one. Heartache, love, support, sexiness, and beliefs."
—Reading by the Book blog

NOT MY ROMEO

"Their sexual tension and continuous banter had me smiling. I couldn't get enough and stayed up late just to finish their story, because I had to know where it went."
—Book Junky Girls blog

"They may not have been Romeo and Juliet, but they sure made one hell of a story that kept me laughing and reading on."
—Smut and Bonbons blog

REV ME UP

"The way Lily and Nico met cracked me up. Let's just say it was a wild case of mistaken identity! It pulled me in and I couldn't put the book down!"
—Romance Novel Giveaways blog

"It was Clover Park series perfection. Love. Italian wedding cookies. Unity. Forever."
—Reading by the Book blog

ALMOST IN LOVE

Thanks!

Thanks for reading *An Ambitious Engagement*. I hope you enjoyed it. Would you like to know about new releases? You can sign up for my new release email list at Eepurl.com/KLQSX. I promise not to clog your inbox! Only new release info and some fun giveaways. You can also sign up by scanning this QR code:

I love to hear from readers! You can find me at:
kyliegilmore.com
Facebook.com/KylieGilmoreToo
Twitter @KylieGilmoreToo

If you liked Luke and Kennedy's story, please leave a review on your favorite retailer's website or Goodreads. Thank you!